T0030863

THE BURDEN OF POWER

JOE CARGILE

Severn River Publishing
www.SevernRiverBooks.com

ISBN: 978-1-64875-594-1 (Paperback)

ALSO BY JOE CARGILE

Blake County Legal Thrillers

Legacy on Trial

In Defense of Charlotte

The Wiregrass Witness

The Burden of Power

To find out more about Joe Cargile and his books, visit

severnriverbooks.com

For Brittany,
who believed in this path.

PART I

THE ARRAIGNMENT

1

The crowd waited at the edge of the barricades lining the north end of the courthouse square. Donning ponchos and sharing umbrellas, collections of serious faces stood huddled together in small packs. Their cardboard signs bore scrawled attacks on the judiciary, verses from the New and Old, and slogans from the movement. Prepared to exercise rights—namely those guaranteed by the First Amendment—the people on the square showed resilience as they suffered under sheets of heavy rain. Unwilling to break ranks, even as the weather worsened across much of the region, the mob appeared ready for a storm in Blake County.

From a large window on the second floor of the Blake County Courthouse, the Honorable John J. Balk stood alone. He considered the faces in the crowd that waited below, listening as their muffled chants entered into the safety of his chambers. They were into hour four of the protest, and the tension brought on by the agitators had begun to unnerve all who waited inside the walls of the old building, including the judge.

"They just keep on coming," he murmured as he performed another rough headcount of those on the square. His third of the day. When he lost count, somewhere after two hundred, he cursed under his breath. "Where in the hell are all these people even coming—"

A knock sounded from the door to the judge's chambers, but he made no move to answer it. Instead, he kept his eyes on the scene below, still considering the unfamiliar faces in the crowd. Twenty-five years on the bench. Another fourteen before that spent practicing in courtrooms throughout South Georgia. John Balk knew his circuit well—especially those who hailed from Blake County.

These weren't them.

Another knock at the door, this time louder, before it opened. The judge's attention stayed on the square and out-of-towners below.

"Your Honor," began a voice from the doorway. Sheila Lambert, his secretary, got straight to it. "Two men from the senator's security detail are waiting at the back door to the courthouse. They've asked to speak with you before—"

"That'll be fine," Balk said, without glancing in her direction. "Go ahead and send them up."

A pause. "Yes, sir."

As he heard the door begin to close, another chant began stirring in the crowd outside. This one directed a crude attack at the special prosecutor who'd been assigned to handle the controversial case. John Balk sensed his secretary still stood at the doorway. Together, they listened as the words intruded on his chambers. In unison, louder and louder: *The ho must go! The ho must go! The ho must go!*

Balk turned from the window and found Sheila standing where he expected. She wore a conservative dress, dark purple, along with an expression that matched his own.

Almost gleefully, the crowd continued: *The ho must go! The ho must go!*

Balk waited another moment for her to turn and leave. Sheila stayed put, though, as she seemed to consider him from where she stood. The two communicated easily without words. He knew her moods, and she his. Their sense for the other helped avoid conflict, except when the judge decided to poke the bear for his amusement.

"Quite the welcome party outside," Balk said, once it became apparent that she planned to stay for conversation. Sheila hadn't talked to him all morning, a sign that she'd been stewing over the situation at hand. "How long would you say they've been out there waiting on our man to arrive?"

"*Our* man?"

The judge noted the cool response. He tiptoed on, aiming only to loosen the mood. "I'd say it's been at least four hours, right?"

She nodded. "At least."

"That wind out there reminds me of the last time I cancelled court." Balk grinned. "We had that hurricane party out at the lake..."

She didn't bite. "We remember it differently, then."

He nodded. "That's my mistake."

"It's okay," she replied, pausing as rain began again against the window. "We all make mistakes, John."

The rain outside looked to be the tail end to the storm, one that had conveniently—*maybe providentially*—prevented all aircraft from landing that morning at the county's small airport. The weather had also delayed all court proceedings, including an arraignment calendar set to be called in Blake County Superior Court. Cases set for arraignment usually ran as efficient little hearings that offered zero appeal for courtroom spectators. *Usually* didn't apply to *State of Georgia v. William H. Collins*, a case that was the first of its kind.

Nor would it.

2

The *ping! ping!* of a notification sounded from a nearby cell phone.

"I have a message here from one of the agents, Judge." Sheila Lambert paraphrased what she read from the screen of her iPhone. "Says his last name is *O'Conner—*"

Balk kept his attention on the secretary, waiting to hear more.

"—the senator's plane is on the ground, apparently, and they'll be keeping him at a secure location for now. They also still want to meet."

"Anything else?"

Sheila looked up from the phone. Shook her head.

"Secure location," Balk grunted. "We have one of those here at the county jail, too."

"You've locked people up for less, Judge." She didn't hesitate in her advice. "They should be required to give you his whereabouts, right? The man is charged with a serious—"

"I know what the man is charged with," Balk said, waving her off. "I'll tell his security boys to drop the secrecy with this office. Besides that, there isn't much else I can do until he's here."

"Why not a bench warrant?" she asked, pushing back.

Another round of protesting began from the crowd outside. The interruption gave the judge a moment to consider his secretary's words. She watched him closely, waiting for him to respond. He listened as the cries from the square seemed to grow louder. The mob's current one-two combination pounded the walls of the old court building, like fists warming to a heavy bag. The hundreds on the square shouted: *Free Bill! Free Bill! Free Bill!*

Two more high-pitched notifications—*ping! ping!*—as more messages arrived. Sheila glanced at her phone, then said, "It's O'Conner again. He says he needs to know something." Her voice seemed to have taken on the impatience of the agent. "Should I tell him you need to know where Collins is first? Or, that you're considering a bench warrant?"

The crowd outside seemed to have plenty left in the tank. *Free Bill! Free Bill!*

Balk couldn't willingly add fuel to the crowd's ridiculous demand, certainly not the narrative they followed. They proclaimed support for the senator, without any understanding whatsoever as to who it was that waited beyond the politician's veneer. The people only saw his story—the folk hero's lore—as it slowly built on itself. A few nights in jail served no one other than the accused. If anything, a bench warrant signed by the judge only moved the man one step closer to his ultimate goal. Balk hoped to avoid that.

Sheila's frustrated voice pulled him back. "Waiting on you to respond."

"I'm not signing a bench warrant at this stage," Balk said, finally dismissing the idea. "It's not appropriate."

"Should I make some demand or *something* about his whereabouts?" she asked, obviously confused. "Anything?"

"That agent won't be authorized to disclose anything about where they've placed him." Balk tried to sound confident in his blank assumption. "Now look, there are going to be some security interests here, and it'll seem like secrecy with—"

Her hand went up to stop him. "I understand the need for secrecy, John. That won't be a problem."

The judge considered the layers in his secretary's words. She knew him well. She overheard conversations intended to be private and picked up easily on the unspoken. He knew this to be the inevitable by-product of the occasional blending of their two lives: personal and professional.

"I'm talking about the secrecy involved in protecting a US senator." Balk tried to talk as if he really believed such things were necessary on that day. Bill Collins—a hometown boy, right in the midst of another term in Washington—had a reputation for paying anyone who gave him an added measure of control. Security personnel. Lawmen. Commissioners. Even judges. "His safety is still going to be the priority in this—"

Sheila snorted. "Our fine senator isn't in any danger today."

The judge conceded a nod. *The man was untouchable.*

"In fact," she plowed on, "those agents should be thinking about some of the other people who might need protecting around here!"

"This courthouse is secure."

"Have you thought about Maggie?" Sheila asked this while she pointed a finger toward the large window facing the square. "What's being done to keep one of those crazies at the pep rally from following her home tonight?"

The judge's secretary kept her eyes on his while he considered the question. In Blake County—a rural, southwest Georgia enclave set against the waters of the Chattahoochee River—the local legal community was on a first-name basis with one of the best attorneys in the South. Maggie Reynolds was without equal in her class of trial lawyers, and the relentless courtroom advocate had a brand that was all her own. She took the toughest cases, while providing tougher advocacy—even with a target on her back.

"Maggie doesn't have anything to worry about," Balk replied, although that wasn't entirely true. There'd been threats. Plenty of them. "The sheriff has his best people watching her around the clock. He knows better than anyone the kind of attention this case has brought to town."

Sheila didn't look convinced, but she didn't offer another opinion.

"Now," Balk said, clapping his hands together, "I think we've kept our friends from the federal government waiting long enough. Let's get this show on the road."

Sheila nodded to him. They'd worked together long enough for her to voice her honest opinion about the cases that came through the office. It was obvious she didn't agree with his decision to preside over the senator's trial, but she didn't have the power to make that call. Only he did.

"I'll bring them up myself," she said, starting to pull the door closed. "I'm sure they'll have more good news for us."

He smiled. "That's all for now, Sheila."

"*Yes*, Judge."

He watched her leave.

3

The judge started toward the leather chair at his desk. He felt the fatigue beginning to set in. Having spent the entire day waiting in his chambers—held hostage inside the eye of the storm—he mostly just wanted the day to end. He knew that wasn't an option, though. Not with the uncertainty swirling outside.

Balk dropped into the chair, then leaned back with its familiar tilt. Hanging on the wood-paneled walls, he saw pieces of his life. Diplomas. Certificates. Photographs of his family and friends. Sketches of his favorite hunting dog. They were the foundation for his reputation, one built on sound judgment, some luck, and his own merit. But it all formed a life he felt proud of—all except the piece that had been bought and paid for.

The calm ended as another chant stirred outside. Balk smiled at the newest of the mob's demands. As a trained lawyer, of course he respected the citizens' long-standing right to protest. He just preferred it be done elsewhere.

Balk must go! Balk must go! Balk must go!

He listened as the mob heckled and shouted, directing its ire toward the historic courthouse. The voices all wanted justice, accountability, and some manner of redress. Most of all, though, the judge knew that the people outside wanted to be heard by the accused—their innocent man.

Again, the same demand. *Balk must go! Balk must go!*

The judge stood from his chair and started toward the window. He wanted to remind the protestors on *his* square—along with the senator, wherever he was—that the Honorable John J. Balk wasn't going anywhere. The crowd could scream and holler and shout, but Balk stood right where he was supposed to be.

Balk must go! Balk must go!

The chants quieted for a long moment when the judge made it to the large window. Then—*smash!*—shards of glass peppered the jurist's face. A moment of shock enveloped him and sent a chill down his spine that matched the cool air rushing in through the broken window. Rain drops soon followed and snapped the big man back to the moment. He quickly scanned the floor and found a brick at the center of the room. He stared down at it, more surprised than anything.

Anger rose in him. *Protesting. Ridiculing. Complaining. That was all fine,* he thought. *Now, people would go to jail. As many as it took.*

The judge started for the phone on his desk. He could hear the deputies outside already shouting at the mob to back up. Balk knew the protocol, as did they. All courthouse personnel had to remain in the building, with all doors locked. *No exceptions.*

Balk placed the receiver to his ear, ready to give the order to lock down the building. He didn't hear the phone's dial tone, though. He only heard the shots—*crack! crack! crack!*—before he hit the ground.

4

Splinters flew from the doorframe as two men forced their way into the judge's chambers. In a matter of seconds, the pair pulled the honorable judge to his feet—all two-hundred-fifty pounds—and had the big man moving, fast. They angled toward the door, away from the screams and excitement pouring in through the office's smashed window, then directed the judge toward the rear hallway.

Balk's mind started working through a worst-case scenario. He imagined the scene in his head. Mayhem in the streets below. People scattering as they tripped over one another, trying to clear the packed courthouse square. Bullets spraying in all directions. Bodies bleeding out onto the historic brick streets. A massacre right here in downtown Blakeston—his town.

"Keep your head down, sir!" shouted one of the men. He held tight to the underside of the judge's arm. His partner gripped the other. They hustled along, ping-ponging the judge back and forth as the trio made its way down the hallway. It was a secure corridor that ran the length of the courthouse, ending in a private stairwell that allowed authorized personnel to exit at the back of the building. "We're taking you with us, Judge."

"I can walk, dammit!" Balk shouted as he started a protest of his own.

He pulled back with one arm, an attempt to break free from his handlers. The men only gripped tighter, though, each digging into the soft tissue near the judge's armpits. "I said, I can—"

"The vehicle isn't far, sir. We'll get you to safety."

"I have my own deputies who handle my security. You'll leave me here with them and I'll make sure—"

"Negative," the same voice replied, interrupting the judge for the second time, "we need to get you to a secure location. That's on the senator's orders."

Balk recognized that the adrenaline from the moment had confused his senses. Unlike the men who flanked him, the judge didn't have any training that prepared him for a moment such as this. "Tell your boss that he and his secure location can kiss my—"

"You can tell him yourself, sir. Let's keep moving."

There wasn't anything else to be said as the younger, stronger agents shoved through the rear door of the courthouse and maneuvered the judge to a waiting SUV. The black-on-black, government-issued getaway vehicle offered no clues as to who waited inside. The tinted windows provided zero visibility, especially under the dark clouds that covered the sky above.

"I told you I'm not going anywhere," the judge growled. "I'm responsible for everyone inside that building."

Three more shots clapped off—*crack! crack! crack!* The back-to-back-to-back bursts sounded close by, probably somewhere just around the corner of the building.

"I'm sorry, Judge, but we've been given our orders," yelled one of the men. He opened the rear door, revealing an empty back seat. "Now, get in the vehicle, please."

More excitement could be heard as people ran by on the streets. The judge watched them for a short moment—committing the fearful scene to memory—before ducking low to enter the SUV. Water splashed up from the gutter as he stepped between the vehicle and the sidewalk, drenching his dress shoes. He felt the chill of the rainwater as it soaked into his socks, then the first twinges of shame as he accepted their retreat.

Two more doors slammed on the vehicle. "Let's go!"

The judge leaned back in his seat and exhaled. He wouldn't admit it—never out loud, at least—but they needed him safe. Their boss needed him to live.

The SUV jerked left, then accelerated away from the curb. Off they went.

5

No one spoke as the SUV sped down several narrow side streets, snaking its way out of Blakeston's historic downtown. Small groups of people, most appearing wet and frazzled, hustled along the brick-cobbled roads on foot. The driver honked at any stragglers that stepped near the roadway, and he did so with a firm touch, the kind that one acquired through driving on the big-city streets of urban America.

Calm and quiet, like his two comrades who hustled the judge from the courthouse, the driver wore the same standard-issue dark suit. Same navy-blue tie. Black watch around the left wrist. His only accessory, if one even called it that, looked to be the toothpick he flipped back and forth between his teeth. Otherwise, the man behind the wheel appeared to be a carbon copy of the other two nameless faces seated nearby.

"Tell me which one of you is in charge," Balk demanded. "I deserve to know who's running this little extraction."

While Balk waited for his response, he again considered the appearances of each agent. He remembered the name O'Conner from earlier discussions, but it gave him little for a profile. All were white, with close-cropped haircuts. No visible shamrock tattoos. No discernible Irish features. No politically incorrect stereotypes to latch onto whatsoever. This left the judge with his gut, and it told him O'Conner rode shotgun.

"Tell me where we're going, O'Conner." Balk shook the headrest on the passenger seat in front of him. "If you can't at least do that, then turn this truck around. You can all get prosecuted for—"

"We're going to the airport," offered the man at the wheel. His toothpick clicked as if to punctuate his reply to Balk's empty threat. "We're eight minutes out, sir."

The judge noted the driver's precise response. The provision of only the information that was necessary. These were no-nonsense men—whoever they were—and they clearly operated in an environment that dispensed with the usual concerns that surrounded the legalities of carrying a private citizen against his will.

"You boys aren't giving me any options here," Balk said, speaking to the driver. "I don't like that."

"We understand, sir." Nothing else.

Balk decided he needed to send a message to Sheila, and probably his wife, too. Feeling his pockets for his cell phone, the judge realized he'd left it behind in the scramble from his chambers. A mistake that he guessed might add another layer of panic to an already chaotic situation at the courthouse.

"Look." Balk still spoke to the wheelman. "I need to get a call over to my office, but it seems I've left my phone behind." He paused to keep himself from laying blame. "I'm sure you know how these things can be—certainly better than me, of course—and I don't need anyone worried, you understand?"

The driver didn't offer a response. He just casually moved the SUV into the opposite lane of travel and mashed the pedal. They passed two cars back-to-back, traveling at close to triple-digits on the speedometer. The driver's hands, steady at ten-and-two, never allowed the SUV to fishtail. In fact, Balk never felt the vehicle wiggle—not once—as they continued their getaway over the wet, country roads.

Balk turned his attention again to the man who rode shotgun. "Hey O'Conner, I said I need to borrow a cell phone."

No response.

Another jiggle of the headrest in front of him. "I know you hear me."

"Turn is ahead," the man said, obviously ignoring the judge's antics while he directed the driver. "On your left."

"Copy."

The judge gave the headrest one more slap, then settled back into his seat to smolder. He soon felt the SUV slow for a left-hand turn. The Blake County Airport—a small, uncontrolled airfield—began to appear from behind a stand of tall pine trees.

The agent in the front passenger seat turned as best he could. Suddenly willing to interact with the judge, he began speaking over his shoulder. "We're pulling up to the local airport, sir. We'll be heading to the large hangar, it's—"

"Save the commentary," Balk replied. "I know where we are."

Quick and polite, he responded: "Of course, sir. I see now that I should've pegged you as a fellow aviator."

Balk nearly corrected the agent, but for his ego and all. No, he wasn't a pilot, nor did his judicial salary afford him enough to charter private flights. *Not even close.* He flew several times each year out of the small airport, though. Another local lawyer invited him up on occasion to curry favor, usually a simple up-and-back to Atlanta for a ballgame. And a Bahamas trip happened annually, usually to chase fish with old friends—all doctors, of course—who'd partnered together on an ageing jet. Glamorous trips, at least by local standards.

Balk stared out the window of the SUV. He remembered visiting the airport as a boy, soon after it opened. It'd been nothing more than a piece of converted farmland, with parking under the shade of a few oak trees and a single-wide that served as an office. The pilots were few, but Balk remembered them as real, larger-than life characters. The kind of men who learned to fly when the country called on them to hunt down fighters with bullet-ridden swastikas, or to down Zeros emblazoned with the flag of the Rising Sun. Over the years, though, as the airport continued to grow, the pilot community moved beyond just crop-dusters and the legends he'd admired. The more affluent took to flying lessons, and the Joneses began adding Cessnas to their ever-growing list of assets. In a sense, the well-to-do took that old airfield—like anything that served them—then shaped it for their own purpose.

Balk looked back to the front of the vehicle. "Y'all aren't going to put me on a flight, are you?" One never knew with the senator. "Because that'd better not be the plan."

No one responded to the question. All three suits just kept their eyes on the path ahead as the SUV maneuvered through a small parking lot, slowing only to wait for the automatic gate to open at the edge of the airfield. As they waited, the driver's eyes moved to the rearview mirror and found the judge. Another flip of the toothpick.

"I asked a question." Balk held eye contact with the driver as he spoke. The judge had a reputation for being able to easily intimidate those who entered his courtroom. He wasn't used to people not answering him when he spoke. "Are you planning to put me on a flight somewhere?"

Gritted teeth. "Sir, that—"

Balk stopped him. "Goodness, son, lose that damn toothpick when you speak to me."

A pause, then he pulled the stick out with his index-finger and thumb. "That's not the plan for today."

"And where's that cell phone I asked for?" Balk pressed.

"I'm told your office is aware of the situation."

"What's that supposed to mean?"

He paused for a moment, then spoke slowly. "That your office is aware of the situation, sir."

It was obvious to the judge that these men weren't authorized to give him anything more. Irritated, he leaned back and returned his attention to the surrounding airport, an operation that had expanded greatly over recent years. The now less rural airfield included a handsome terminal, three sizeable hangars, and a pair of wide runways perfectly suited to accommodate larger aircraft. Everything had been *modernized*, thanks in large part to a chunk of federal money that conveniently found its way down from Washington, DC. The luxury and expansion primarily benefitted the well-to-do, but most voters in the area still viewed the updates as a win for the People and praised the man responsible—Senator Bill Collins.

All Hail Collins!

6

The SUV rolled to a stop inside the large hangar. On one side of the building, a row of single-engine aircraft waited patiently for the skies to clear. Balk recognized a few of the manufacturers in the line-up—Piper, Cessna, Beechcraft. The small planes had nowhere to be, unlike the sleek jet that mocked them from the other side of the hangar.

The gold-striped Bombardier—newly-waxed, ready for the prom—looked out of place among its smaller brethren. Like the conceited jock at the wrong high school party, the high-end machine had been parked off to the side. The beautiful plane seemed to be beckoning its admirers—Balk included—enticing them to come check it out. Climb the shiny stairs. Step through the plane's open door. Explore the lavish interior. No one on the outside even needed to know.

Inside the SUV, still admiring the jet, Balk knew who it belonged to.

"I'm Special Agent Collier O'Conner," began the man seated in the back seat. His accent fit the name. "I'm assigned to Senator Collins's protective detail, and I'll be accompanying you onto the aircraft for the meeting."

"I appreciate the introduction, *O'Conner*." Balk didn't skimp on sarcasm as he looked the thirty-something agent over. As the youngest of the three, he'd offered zero words during their short ride over. Balk mistakenly pegged him low man on the totem pole. "We've got a little problem, though, because your wheelman told me I wasn't getting on a plane."

O'Conner seemed to absorb the judge's stare, then responded calmly. "I believe my transportation specialist only confirmed that we had no scheduled flight—"

"Don't argue semantics with me, *Collier.* Enough of that goes on in my courtroom. And quit playing all these games."

Although Balk possessed the tools to act as a perfect gentleman, he couldn't deny the fact that he liked to resort to interruptions and bully tactics when reprimanding others. He often dropped titles and formalities in an attempt to bait his targets into reacting poorly. He believed that the first to get angry in any argument often lost. A good strategy, unless the one attempting to implement it was already furious.

"We don't play games, sir." O'Conner sounded calmer than before. "Our practices limit information because the whereabouts of Senator Collins is a national security matter. I'm sure you can appreciate—"

"It doesn't matter at this point, just give me a cell phone." Balk extended a hand, then held it there, palm up. "Right now, I don't much care if my office is already *aware of the situation.* I intend to call them myself."

"You'll need to talk to the senator about that."

"I don't think you heard me correctly."

An edge finally entered O'Conner's tone. "I heard you just fine, *sir.*"

The judge glared a moment more at the younger man, then turned to pull the handle on the door. He cursed as he swung it open and stepped out onto the hangar floor. A cold front had followed the day's stormy weather. He felt its bite as the wind whipped icy air through the open door to the hangar.

"Judge Balk," called the agent, still seated inside the vehicle, "It's important you know that—"

The judge slammed the door behind him with as much force as he could muster and started toward the private jet. "Bill!" Balk yelled. "Where the hell are you?" The judge's deep voice carried inside the large building, even with the noise from the rain still pounding on its steel roof. "I swear to God, Bill, if you don't come out here now, I'll make sure you never get out of jail while your case is on my docket."

The judge reached the bottom of the stairs leading up to the plane. He stopped, stood tall, and pulled both arms across his chest. As the doors opened and slammed shut on the SUV at his back, Balk hoped they didn't plan to force him onto the plane.

"Sir, you can go on up to speak with him." O'Conner's voice moved with the sound of footsteps. "He's expecting you."

"No, that won't happen." Balk turned to look at the agent as he said this. He stared at him a long moment, then asked, "Where're you from, O'Conner?"

The agent waited a moment to answer. "I'm from Worchester, sir." Definite pride in the response. "Grew up in South Main."

"They teach you to keep your word up there?"

He nodded.

"Good." Balk pointed the agent's eyes back toward the plane. "Then you go inside and explain to your boss what it means when a man gives you his word. He appears to have forgotten."

O'Conner seemed to understand. Balk watched as he signaled to one of the other agents at the SUV, then eased by where the judge stood to make his way up the metal stairs. The young man's pristine dress shoes didn't skip a step—*pang, pang, pang*—nor did they slow when he reached the cabin door. Once the agent disappeared to somewhere inside the plane, Balk pulled his sleeve back and glanced at the time.

One-forty-eight, Christ.

Balk could only shake his head, though, as he wondered how much it was that they all really knew back at the courthouse. He hated himself for thinking that the victims involved in the shooting on the square might serve as a distraction from the truth. Yet even distractions didn't keep things buried for long. No, only concealment did—a lie.

Their lie.

Balk lifted his eyes to the cabin door, narrowing them as he saw a familiar face step from just inside.

7

Bill Collins stepped to the top of the stairs and spread his arms wide. He offered a smile, then started making his way down to the judge. He looked as comfortable as a man prepared to welcome a long-time friend into his home.

"Big John Balk!" he roared, hand already extended. "It's good to see you, old friend."

"I don't want to hear it, Bill." Balk shoved his hands into his pockets as he said this. "Let's just forget all the old buddy crap. It's not the time for that."

Collins stopped at the bottom of the stairs and dropped his arms to his sides. He stood four or five inches shorter than the judge and at least fifty pounds lighter. Trim and fit, as usual, the Senior United States Senator for Georgia exuded a healthy glow of un-tapped energy, a trait that the judge envied, as well as the full head of hair that still sat atop the politician's head.

Bill offered a wink. "What—I can't say hello to an old friend?"

Balk frowned as he took in the familiar face. Even with the years, remnants of the boy he once knew still remained. A reminder that the two —judge and accused—were more than just contemporaries. They had a shared history, one linked by the simple details which amounted to the lottery of life: family, geography, and circumstance. Details that some people—often men—returned to over the years, weaving and appropriating them into their own origin story, until they eventually informed, maybe even justified, their actions of the present.

Balk acquiesced. "Fine. Hello, Bill."

Collins chuckled. "Come on, John, don't be childish. We've known each other a long time."

Balk and Collins came from similar folks. Born in Blake County during the post-World War II boom, they were the sons of men and women who barely survived the Great Depression. Raised to live with little, they worked harder than their peers. They graduated high school a year apart from one another—'73 and '74—both valedictorians of their respective classes. Collins, then Balk, avoided the jungles of Southeast Asia, and headed on for college. Both the first to do so in their respective families.

"Today was *your* arraignment, not some optional reunion." Balk had waited hours to issue a verbal lashing. But now that he had the chance, his words lacked their usual vigor. He felt his pulse slowing, his anger subsiding. Natural responses to being near a fine statesman. "If you can't at least understand that, then I can't help you."

"Very well, John." Bill seemed to give the impression that negotiations would be ongoing. "I hope that since we were once friends, it's not a problem to call you John?"

The two—Collins and Balk—never considered the other to truly be a *friend*, at least not in the traditional sense. And although the two hometown boys attended the University of Georgia around the same time, each had kept the other at a distance during those years. One didn't necessarily dislike the other, but their frequent comparison was what fostered a sort of natural competition between the boys from Blake. As neither had excelled in sports enough to secure an athletic scholarship, they'd both survived on academic merit during their time in Athens. So, they looked for the other's name when the dean's list came out at the end of each quarter. They kept tabs on what menial job the other had to do part-time to pay expenses. And they especially watched for which co-ed the other walked arm-in-arm with on campus.

Balk finally sighed. "Fine, but that all changes in my courtroom."

"I bet you're looking forward to that."

Balk shook his head as a sly grin crept across the politician's face.

"Oh, come on, John. It feels good when people have to show you respect, right?"

"That's not what this is about."

"Yes, it is," Bill replied, still grinning. "That's why we all want the power. We want that respect to be given."

"Giving it and showing it, they're not the same."

Bill paused for a long moment. "That's not true. Power is what ensures respect. The rest is immaterial."

Balk looked away. He didn't respect much about the man in front of him. That clear, furious ambition that fueled the senator was the kind that never stopped wanting more. It'd broken the judge when the two competed in college, and it'd broken most who hadn't readily bent to its will in those years since. Political opponents. Business partners. Even his wife—Lucy.

"Let's take any one of those criminals that come into your courtroom." He sounded unable to resist adding to his argument. "If that defendant is convicted of something, then you handle the actual sentencing of that person, right?"

Balk nodded. He only half-listened as he tried to remember when he and Lucy saw each other last. *Two, maybe three years ago.*

"It doesn't matter whether that person you're about to send away to prison *shows you respect,* Judge. He's going to be forced to *give you respect,* because you have the power to lock him away. You have that power."

Balk understood his point. "That's how it is with everything for you. Just more power. More respect. More, more, more..."

"Stop oversimplifying things, John."

"No, it's *real* simple with you. Everyone has to show *you* respect. The other party. The people of Blakeston. Your son. All of them."

The senator breathed in deep through his nose.

"Hell," Balk continued, waving his hands around him, "you even had to drag me out here to the airport. All just for *me* to show you your damn respect. That's what this is all about, right?"

"I think it's you who should be thanking my men for saving your life."

"Don't change the subject."

"I'm not," Bill replied with a smile. "I'm just saying you might want to thank them."

Balk took a step closer to the senator. "You mean, you want me to thank *you*."

"That's not what I said."

Balk lifted his gaze to the ceiling for a moment. Seeing the senator reminded him exactly what it was he loathed about the man, which offered a clear problem in serving as the trial judge assigned to the case. It was a conflict, of course, but those kinds of things had to be disclosed by someone aware of the conflict. In the senator's case—judge and accused already had an understanding.

Balk lowered his eyes. "What was it really that got you about her in the end?"

Bill raised an eyebrow. "Who's changing the subject now?"

Balk held his eyes on the senator's. Neither looked away.

"Why'd you do it, Bill?" Balk asked after another moment. "I have to know."

The senator seemed to consider the question—one no judge ever asked of the accused—then shook his head as he turned toward the plane. Balk grabbed his elbow.

Bill stopped, then slowly moved his eyes to the hand grasping his arm. An offense. "We'll talk inside, John."

Balk gripped the arm a little tighter. "Tell me."

"Don't do that."

Tighter. "Tell me why you had her killed."

Before a response of any kind—other than a wince, maybe—two of the agents had their arms around the judge, moving him again. Not back to the SUV, though. This time toward the plane. And not being all that polite about it anymore.

8

At two-oh-five that afternoon, the Blake County Sheriff's Office issued the *all-clear.* The courthouse. Adjacent streets. The square. All quiet and littered only with the debris that'd been left behind after gunfire and a standing start sent hundreds of protestors scattering. Tattered signs, flags, and effects, discarded in their wake, offered the only evidence of their existence. Proof of the chaos that lasted until the ambulances and first responders and protectors rushed in.

Zero dead. Five at Blake General. One missing.

Tim Dawson stood behind the courthouse with three other deputies. *His deputies.* He took long, intentional breaths as he worked to bring his heart rate down. The task proved difficult with the adrenaline still coursing through his veins. He'd just led a team through the old court building. A tedious sweep that took them room by room, clearing each with weapons at the ready. Thankfully, the task ended without incident and revealed no injuries to those they accounted for. Only minimal property damage, a few broken windows. A relief, until Tim realized they hadn't accounted for one person who was supposed to still be in the building.

And they had a shooter on the loose.

Tim and his deputies huddled close together. Eyes fixed on a county-issued tablet. It was in the hands of the courthouse's head of security,

Marlin Buck. A greybeard at the end of his career, Buck—known to most as *Tracker*—hadn't seen a lot of excitement at the courthouse since his transfer over to manage the building's security. No shootings. No riots. No kidnappings. Just time at a computer, mostly.

Buck held the screen steady. "I'll pull up what I have from surveillance, Sheriff."

Tim nodded at the old deputy. At the mention of his title: *Sheriff.* It still didn't sound right on the ears, but that mattered little. The weighty, ill-fitting role was one that'd fallen onto his shoulders five weeks earlier. All because Blake County's elected sheriff—Charlie Clay—had himself ousted over allegations of misconduct. The removal wrecked the chain-of-command at the BCSO and left some of its more tenured grumbling about unfairness, unreadiness. *And maybe they were right*, but Tim still tried to ignore the naysayers—even the one in his head that sniped: *imposter*. He didn't expect to shut them all up, but he planned to try.

"Alright, here we are," Buck said, after a few swipes at the screen.

Tim leaned closer. Clear image. No audio. "Tell me what I'm looking at."

"This'll be him coming out the back door, passing right over where we're standing now." Tracker then pointed to a corner on the tablet. "See the timestamp there at the top of the footage?"

"I see it."

"Well, they'll come through the heavy door at one-twenty-two, on the nose."

Tim watched as a dark-colored SUV idled in the frame of the video. People hurried by on a sidewalk that ran between the building and the vehicle. No one stayed in the frame long. None gave a second glance to the vehicle with the impenetrable tint.

Tim noted 13:21:48 on the screen. Less than four minutes after the first shots. "Is this the only camera we have out back?"

Three fingers went up. "There's a few of them out here. Two are up high. This one comes from over the heavy—"

"Sheriff, you probably know it as the restricted door," interrupted a younger deputy, *possibly Johnson*. "To get in through the heavy, someone has to buzz you in."

"And to get out?"

"Anybody can open it from inside."

Tim nodded as he watched three men enter the frame. 13:22:00. Two of the three men wore matching suits. Dark. The odd man out—John Balk—wore dress pants and a white shirt. They crossed the sidewalk to the curb, where one of the suits shoved the judge toward the SUV, arguing only for a moment before the judge ducked inside the vehicle. A suit then went around to the opposite side of the SUV, while the other stepped into the front passenger seat. They were gone from the frame within seconds.

"You need to see it again, Sheriff?"

Tim's eyes went to the street, shaking his head slowly while he considered the next step. *Work the problem,* he told himself, *but don't waste time.* He looked off for another moment in the direction the SUV traveled, which didn't matter much. With more than forty-five minutes already gone, the driver had a head-start as far as Alabama or Florida by now.

"No need." Tim looked back at the tablet. "Have you pulled a plate from the video?"

"They were riding without one."

"Good." Tim glanced around the huddle and grinned. "A registration number might make it too easy for us to tag these assholes."

All mirrored his grin, adding a few grunts to welcome the challenge. They were with him.

"All right." Tim placed a hand on the old man's shoulder. "Show me what you tracked down inside the building, then."

Marlin Buck was within months of hitting his thirty-year mark with the BCSO. He was known as a man who didn't care much for climbing rank, mostly because he worked to live and not the other way around. What he did with that time out of uniform usually involved being deep in the woods. There, he'd spent much of his life crafting a reputation for bagging trophies and finding just about anything that moved. He quietly carried a secret, though. Tracker's big mounts came from his knowledge and patience—but the biggest on his walls came with the help of technology.

"I have it for you, Sheriff." Tracker said this as he moved things around on the screen easily. He seemed to defy the stereotype that his generation didn't handle modern electronics well. "This'll be the three of them coming through the secure corridor. You'll get a good look at each."

Another video was up. Paused at 13:20:25. The camera angle covered the length of the courthouse's second-floor corridor. Another restricted access area. The door to the judicial suite sat at the top of the screen. A door to the rear stairwell waited just outside the bottom of the frame. A distance of three hundred feet, maybe less.

"At the thirty-second mark, they come through the door up top," Tracker added. "You'll see resistance from our judge, but he gives up easy."

The video played.

"That's him fighting back right there," Tim said, pointing at the image of the same three men from the footage outside. A better angle on each gave them solid IDs. The brief, pitiful attempt by the judge to halt his escort down the hall gave them aggravated circumstances. Another nod to the old deputy. "Damn fine work, Tracker."

He shrugged. "I can have the screenshots ready to—uh, well—" his words trailed off.

Tim noted the man's hesitation to offer the next step. "Finish your thought."

"Well, you tell me where to send the images." Deferring, still. "I'm just here to help you hunt these boys down."

Tim realized all eyes were on him now. His membership in the fraternity of lawmen was founded on his work as an investigator who collaborated well with his peers. Now, as the *Sheriff*, that group expected him to do more than just contribute talent. They needed Tim to act as the decision-maker—their leader.

"This needs to be out there." Tim leaned in as he said this, thinking out loud. "Once I release this news to the public, it'll be a shitstorm."

More grunts from the men. Nothing more.

He glanced up at the sky, feeling the eyes on him still. No one had heard a word from the judge since the protest broke. *Almost an hour gone. It didn't make sense.* And the men on the video, they didn't come from the same school as those radicals who occupied the square earlier in the day. Suited up and efficient in the way they worked, the kidnappers walked into the courthouse without masks or any concern for their identities. They were confident professionals, not second-rate militia. They had to have something planned to ensure their protection, *but what?* Tim weighed the unknown a moment longer, eyes on the widening strips of blue sky that ran above.

"Sun's shining now," Tim lowered his eyes to the men, "and these guys don't strike me as the kind that're too worried about what this looks like in the light of day. They have to know we've seen their faces by now."

More nods from the huddle. No opinions.

"So, let's give them something to worry about." He pointed in the direction of the old deputy. "Tracker will get photos out to all of our people on the road. We share them with all agencies, and we get them to our local media contact. Somebody out there knows these guys."

Tracker already had a hand swiping, working to get the images where they needed to be. High-priority emails fired off to inboxes within seconds, with photos that'd be on the news within the half-hour, maybe sooner. The judge's kidnapping wasn't something Tim could afford to keep under wraps for long. He'd seen what he'd seen on the surveillance footage, and he wasn't worried about being wrong.

"When you're done with that," Tim stepped back from the huddle, "pull up the footage from in front of the building. I need you to find our shooter."

"On it, Sheriff."

Tim turned and headed in the direction of the courthouse square. He knew finding their mystery shooter might not happen by nightfall. He could handle having to continue that piece of the hunt with Tracker and their team. *Not the judge, though.* Tim needed that resolved before they closed up shop for the day.

And it was on him to make it happen.

9

The shiny Bombardier still hadn't moved an inch from its space inside the hanger, and this was the topic of conversation for the two voices in the forward compartment. John Balk listened to their exchange from his *assigned* seat, gathering what he could from the pilot-speak. They reviewed the status of their departure—an amended flight plan, their fuel levels, the improving weather conditions, and so on—then punched through a short checklist with precision. It all sounded routine, with no cause for alarm whatsoever. They were *ready to push* once the senator dealt with the hold-up: *Him.*

Balk couldn't do anything about the delay—at least not while restrained in his seat. He thought about this as he glanced down again at what held him in place. Zip-ties for the wrists, each secured tightly to an armrest, and a taut shoulder belt that connected with the one across his lap. The FAA-compliant equipment ensured Balk's torso remained pinned to the seat, while allowing freedom of movement for his lower body. An *accommodation* —on account of his bad knees, apparently—one the agents made as they strapped him in. *Absurd*, he mused, closing his eyes, *all of it.*

A heavy *thud thud* sounded from under the judge's feet. It jostled the plane. Again—*thud thud.* Eyes closed. Unconcerned. Calm, all things considered. A newfound peace numbed Balk like a strong sedative, one that'd hit him as the agents put their hands on him. It'd filled him as they moved up the stairs to the aircraft. And now, he felt nothing.

"I do apologize, John."

The familiar voice came from the front of the plane, and the padding of footsteps brought it closer.

"I've gone and kept you waiting long enough."

Balk's seat faced the rear of the airplane. He'd tried turning around once already and found he couldn't see the front of the cabin without straining. He didn't need to look to see who it was, though. He opened his eyes and chose a nearby window, instead.

"I'm being pelted with a bunch of pesky little problems back in Washington." The collegial tone sounded careful. "And, on top of that, I'm trying to deal with the plantation while I'm down here, salvaging what I can from the mess that fire left behind."

Balk didn't respond. Didn't turn from the window to look at the man. A pause, then leather creaked from a nearby seat.

"Given the way this day has been," the senator continued, "I mean, the last thing—"

Balk interrupted without a glance. "It's fine."

Quiet filled the cabin. Balk didn't care about business in DC. He cared less about plans to reclaim the charred remains of Kelley Hill Plantation—a massive hunting preserve, opportunely left to the senator upon the passing of his late wife. Balk cared least of all, though, about any kind of apology from the man.

"It needs saying, uh—" a rare stumble from the statesman "—well, I regret that we needed all of this..."

Balk lifted the palm of a hand. Plastic dug into his wrist. "I don't accept."

Another pause. "All right."

The window above the judge's right arm faced the front of the hangar. Its two large doors sat open. Afternoon sky showed blue in the distance. "When are you planning to leave?" Balk asked.

"That depends."

Balk smiled. It was a lawyer's response. *I'm the one who gets to tell you that,* he wanted to say, turning from the window to face the politician. The judge tried to muster up that same vitriol from earlier. Nothing, though.

"Are we negotiating?" Balk asked.

Bill seemed to consider this. His seat faced the judge's, consistent with the layout that'd been designed for that area of the cabin. They were big, leather, reclinable seats. Much nicer than any Balk had flown in before. And perfect for horse-trading. He couldn't think of a much better place to discuss the ruin of his own career.

"You look uncomfortable." Bill said this as he pulled a pair of pliers from his suit jacket. "I'll go ahead and cut those ties on you."

A low table separated their seats from one another. The theatrics Bill planned for the moment fell flat as he awkwardly kept the table between them, leaning over to clip the restraints on Balk's wrists. Balk did his best to appear comfortable, stretching his legs out under the table, while Bill carefully snipped the last plastic bracelet.

Bill sat. "There, that should be better."

"Don't expect me to thank you." Balk flexed both hands to loosen them, then slowly undid the metal buckle at his midsection. He felt better already. "I'll tell you this, Bill, I can't even imagine what all these people around here think about—"

"I don't care what they think."

"You should," Balk smiled, "because most of them are witnesses to my kidnapping and false imprisonment."

Bill chuckled at this.

"I'm glad you think it's funny," Balk said, turning his wristwatch over, "but I see it's getting on towards three, so I say you get me back to the courthouse and we'll deal with your current charges. We can handle these new ones on another day."

"We'll get to that."

Balk was the one to laugh now. Big, belly laughs that kept on coming.

"Take a moment to gather yourself." Bill reached under his seat as he said this, then placed a large tablet on the table between them. "When you do, there's something I need to show you."

Still smiling, Balk asked, "What's this?"

"Take a look for yourself."

Balk leaned forward in his seat. The website for one of the big news networks already took up the screen. He could make out part of the main headline.

"Everyone already knows where you are, John."

Balk leaned closer. "Press play on that video there."

10

Maggie Reynolds stood in a crowded, windowless room below the ground floor of the Blake County Courthouse. It was her first time inside the massive, somewhat hidden space. From a back section of concrete wall, she took in her surroundings. Aging boxes, stacked three-high, took up nearly half of the floor, while a mishmash of dated office furniture sat over much of what was left. Stuffed in a far corner, stacks of old pews rose to the ceiling like Tetris pieces. And in another, the one closest to her, a collection of plaques, certificates, and waxy portraits gathered dust. She recognized several names from the old frames. All were lawyers who'd once donned the robe. Judges, *all of them men,* gone and waiting to be forgotten.

Maggie pulled her phone out to check for a signal. *Still no bars.* Under the dim lighting, the iPhone glowed bright against her face. Its status bar at the top of the screen remained unchanged, like the photo of her and Tim set to the background. She looked down at their smiling faces, trying to remember when they last looked that way together. They were strangers, now, unless their paths crossed at work. *Ironic*, given the fact that *her work* was what brought on their final argument, the kind with packed bags at the door. He'd called her *deceitful* and *selfish*, even accused her of breaking the law. *I know the law,* she'd countered, unrepentant, *and I understand its exceptions better than you.* Her poor reply ensured that the bags left, along with

Tim. *You're probably right, Mags, but the way you used it—the way you used me, like a pawn in your plan—that was a bridge too far.* She stared at the photo on her phone's screen, considering those words a moment longer. *Maybe it was.*

Maggie returned the phone to a pocket on her blazer. She knew that the thick walls and lack of cell service only left time for her to second-guess herself, which was the last thing she needed. She'd survived the last decade-plus as a criminal defense lawyer, a courtroom brawler who wasn't afraid to put herself at odds with anyone. *Yes,* it pained her that her husband didn't agree with the strategy of her most recent assignment. The strategy worked, though, and Tim needed to at least respect the results. As *Special Prosecutor,* Maggie now stood for the State in one of the country's most important criminal matters—*State of Georgia v. William H. Collins.* The once-in-a-lifetime opportunity gave Maggie the chance to prosecute a historic case. Winning on this stage guaranteed an enduring legacy, one that didn't end with her accomplishments stashed away in some courthouse basement, gathering dust, waiting to be forgotten.

"Here we go!" exclaimed someone at the other end of the room. "Look at this old Zenith."

The excited voice pulled Maggie from her thoughts. She lifted her eyes and saw a man happily wedging himself inside a tall cabinet. Once halfway in, he grunted and strained, fooling with a boxy looking TV on a high shelf. Cords could be heard slapping the cabinet's wood backing, and soon the interested in the room moved to the area around the television. The rustling stopped. The TV flipped on.

Pride swelled in the man's voice as he shouted, "I think it's got a signal, too!"

A few people murmured, watching the man as he wiped sweat from his brow with one hand, and adjusted the channels with the other. He passed several snowy frames until he found a decent picture. A flip of the knob for the volume and cranked-up audio cut through the air.

People clapped and the weight of uncertainty seemed to lighten, slightly.

A newscaster announced the name of the local station, a CBS affiliate, before jumping straight into updates on the day's developing story.

Maggie's heart rate picked up as she took several steps closer. She could see most of the screen. A middle-aged woman seated at a generic news desk. *Breaking News* at the bottom of the frame.

"It looks like they're—" began the man.

A collective *Shhhhhh!* stopped him, though. His moment was over. All were glued to the news coming in from the outside world.

"Good news everybody!" came another voice—different than their man-of-the-minute's. This one shouted from the direction of the only stairs in the basement. "Y'all are welcome to come on upstairs. Sheriff Dawson issued the *all-clear* about—

Shhhhhh! hissed several in the group, again.

Maggie turned and noticed a uniformed deputy at the bottom of the stairs. Their rebuke seemed to confuse him. Scanning the courthouse personnel, he finally came around to her standing at the back of the group. Maggie knew the deputy, an older guy, known to most as *Tracker.* She offered him a shrug, then turned her attention back to the news.

The on-screen talent went full-nasal from the top of the story: *And welcome back, this is Audrey Kelter with WBAX—your most trusted, local news provider. We're staying with you live and commercial free while we bring you today's developing story in Blakeston. Protesting in front of the Blake County Courthouse turned ugly this afternoon when gunfire started on the north end of the courthouse square. At least five were taken to the hospital for medical attention, with reports that others may still be receiving care elsewhere. The shooter is still at-large, and unknown to law enforcement. Our on-scene correspondent, Ben Moss, is standing by on the square, ready with an update on this scary situation.*

Standing tall in the frame, Ben Moss looked sharp with the courthouse looming behind him. Maggie knew the handsome, twenty-something journalist. They'd worked together—*or she'd worked him, at least initially*—on an article that intersected with her work for a client. It was a story that proved instrumental in helping execute Maggie's plan to get the senator indicted. Ben recognized this after the fact, of course, but never revealed her as a source in his follow-up stories. He was a professional who wasn't long for small-town media, but today he had another shot at national exposure.

What do you have for us out of Blakeston, Ben?

I'm told from a source in the courthouse that the building is secure, Ben started, smooth in his delivery, *and that the all-clear has been issued. This is good news for the men and women who've been locked down inside the building since the shootings, especially given recent findings.*

Voices murmured to one another as an image appeared on the screen. Maggie recognized the central figure in the photo immediately. It was Judge Balk—his familiar scowl more prominent than usual—with two men in suits alongside him. Both gripped the trial judge by an arm.

Ben, we have an image up on the screen for our viewers, added the newscaster. *It shows the two unknown individuals escorting the Honorable John Balk from the building.*

A few in the room gasped. Maggie knew these people offered the most genuine feedback because they, like her, at least knew the man. Some liked him. Most didn't.

And we've confirmed that this photo, the one our viewers are seeing on their screens right now, is an image from the courthouse's surveillance system. We're told that it was captured only moments after the gunfire and confusion began in the square.

Maggie felt a tap on her shoulder. She turned slightly and noticed the deputy standing beside her. Closer than she liked.

"Ma'am, I've been asked to bring you upstairs for a meeting."

"Okay," Maggie said, easing a step over as she turned her eyes back to the TV. "Who's asking?"

"Sheriff Dawson wants to talk to you about today's situation."

Maggie paused, considering her response while still half-listening to the updates from the news report. It sounded to her like the acting sheriff wanted her advice on something more than just the case against Collins.

"If it's a meeting on the *alleged* shooter, then it doesn't involve me. He can talk with the DA's office. I'm only here to prosecute the case against Bill—"

"It's not about the shooter."

Maggie turned back to the deputy. She raised an eyebrow, waiting for more.

"It's about the judge, ma'am."

Maggie heard Ben's voice from the television slow as he delivered the words *kidnapping* and *missing* to his audience.

"Judge Balk was kidnapped?" Maggie blurted, louder than intended. "That's what Tim wants to talk—"

"That's not exactly the case." He motioned for her to keep it down. "Although that's what it looked like at first."

Maggie turned and took in the group of at least twenty in front of her. Listening with rapt attention, their eyes were still fixed to the newscaster, along with a panel of serious faces, who now discussed the implications of kidnapping an elected public official in Georgia. The group in this room was only a small fraction of the regional station's viewership. The numbers here didn't even compare with those of the behemoths running the national media. If the story had been picked up, then it had to already be in front of millions.

"How's it not exactly a kidnapping?" she asked, turning back to the deputy. "And why would Tim—I mean, the sheriff—release that it was?"

"Like I said, it looked like that at first—"

"Where is the judge?" Maggie's mind started running. "He needs to be in on the meeting."

"He's supposed to be back here at the building at four. The sheriff wanted you to come up and talk to him about that."

Maggie shook her head at the evasive answer. She could feel a problem coming on, one well beyond her husband's clumsy misstep with the media. They needed to get in front of it. Now.

She placed a hand on the deputy's shoulder. "It's Tracker, right?"

He nodded.

"Where's the judge now?"

The wrinkles deepened on his forehead, thinking.

"I need to know," she pressed, "so I can help out."

He cleared his throat as he looked over at the group of courthouse employees. The television still clipped along with discussions about the protest and subsequent chaos. When he spoke, he didn't look at her, but she sure as shit heard every word.

"He's with the senator, ma'am. Has been for at least the last hour."

"Seriously?"

Tracker didn't respond. He just turned and started toward the stairs. Maggie didn't move from her spot, though, as she took a moment more to absorb the information. She knew that she needed to keep herself from assuming things, like a scenario that involved judge and accused spending the hour cavorting with one other. And while something wasn't right, Maggie didn't need to look much further than the reporting that continued on the nearby television for a reminder as to the dangers of drawing conclusions from bad information. They were still running kidnapping scenarios—an exercise that only stood to take their viewership deeper into the rabbit hole.

She needed to climb out of it.

Maggie decided to hold off on assumptions, then turned and started after the deputy.

Out of the dark.

11

John Balk paced up and down the cabin aisle. A live news broadcast played from the tablet he held in one hand. The other, he balled into a fist, holding it at his side as he listened to the words of the journalist heading up the news segment. She provided a pointed summary of the day's events, while footage from the protest in Blakeston ran in the background. Ominous, well-crafted scenes portrayed an enhanced version of the mob he'd witnessed that day. It felt surreal, watching it all being replayed on the screen, like some kind of reenactment produced in his small town. He knew it was real, though. He'd been there. And the reporter reminded her viewers of this fact while teasing the network's top story—*his* rescue.

"This is unbelievable," Balk groaned. "How do these people not know this is a hoax?"

No reply to his question, of course. Since giving the tablet to the judge earlier, the senator hadn't moved from his seat. In fact, he hadn't said a word about anything. *And why would he?* The man had the media machine doing all the talking for him.

"Come on, Bill, say something." The judge loosened a finger from his fist, pointing it at the senator. "This has your signature all over it, and they'll see right through it soon enough."

"That's quite a lot of credit to be handing out, John."

"Have you seen this?" Balk shot back, turning the tablet around. "This is manufactured chaos."

"How is that my doing?" His palms out wide. "Show me where there's evidence of that."

Balk flipped the tablet back around. The big network led the segment with production-quality images, the kind that showed the several hundred agitators from an angle that made them appear larger, rowdier. But the images playing on the screen now came off of social media. These looked more authentic, and made the mob feel closer to what it was, dangerous. Mostly taken from cell phone cameras on the square, the content had view counts in the hundreds of thousands because it'd already spread like wildfire across the major platforms. One startling clip—credited to *@Freebird-Rob1789*—captured the deafening *crack! crack! crack!* of gunfire as it erupted outside the courthouse. It even preserved the chilling screams from the crowd in the ensuing panic. It was the kind of video that couldn't be ignored.

And millions more would see it.

Admittedly, Balk's understanding of social media was pretty limited. What he knew came primarily from dealing with it in his courtroom. Any interest that extended beyond those walls was more that of a curious observer. He'd gone from watching its steady proliferation from one side of the technology divide, to grappling with issues as to its admissibility in nearly every trial. And because of this, the judge had developed a familiarity with its basic terminology, as well as concerns over the sheer reach of its influence. Balk understood that the disturbing content from the courthouse square had already gone *viral*—a highly coveted award—but he just didn't understand why he seemed to be the only one who recognized the true *influencer* of those events.

"I'm not talking about this," Balk said with a sigh, although he initially was. He lifted his eyes back to the politician and threw his arms up. "I'm talking about all of this, Bill. Hijacking this process, having your agents kidnap me from my courthouse, taking me—"

Bill pointed at the tablet. "They're calling it a rescue effort."

"Because someone fed that to them."

"Not true, John."

"Yes," Balk growled, "and they lapped that crap up, like you knew they would."

"Careful with that," Bill said, pausing to readjust his sanguine color tie, "it sounds like you're trying to discredit the work of some good men."

The coverage on the thin screen finally arrived at the main story. Balk looked down and saw an image of himself outside the courthouse, stepping into a waiting SUV. The reporter explained that agents from Senator Collins's protective detail arrived at the courthouse earlier that afternoon to coordinate the US senator's safe passage to the courtroom. That instead of having their meeting, those brave members of the United States Secret Service were called on to rescue the local superior court judge in his time of need. Balk shook his head as another video appeared on the screen, an interview with Agent Collier O'Conner.

We'd just been permitted entrance into the courthouse when the first shots were fired outside the building. We continued toward Judge Balk's chambers on the second floor in an effort to still contact him. We found his office covered in glass and debris from an apparent attack. O'Conner's professional tone and trustworthy appearance glossed over the stilted, scripted account. *At that moment, I had the senator on the line, ready to join in on any discussions about logistics. I relayed the information to him about the situation at the courthouse, and he explicitly told me to protect the judge, even evacuate him if necessary. So, my team did what it had to. We took Judge Balk outside and got him to safety.*

Balk stayed silent as he watched the segment all the way to the end.

"Thank goodness they were there," Bill began again, parroting the reporter's last words from the interview, "because who knows what might've happened, right?"

Balk unclenched his fist. Heartwarming posts from commentors and followers of the network's *socials* started filling the screen. They hailed the rescue as a miracle ending to the day's madness. Prayed for the judge's safety. Thanked the senator for his leadership. Applauded the agents for their bravery. Thousands and thousands of comments, pouring in from all over the world.

Balk looked up. "They're calling O'Conner and the others heroes."

"American heroes." Bill clarified. "And we should drink to that."

12

Balk eyed the politician for a long moment. He recognized the conspirator's grin. Remembered it still from the day they'd made their pact.

"I do need that drink."

"Good." Bill slapped his knees as he stood. "There's a nice rye here onboard. I'll grab it for us."

"Bring a revolver with it."

The senator chuckled as he made his way to the rear of the cabin. Balk returned to his seat. From there, he could see the politician rummaging through the hospitality station, clearly unaccustomed to serving the drinks on his own plane. He eventually rustled up what he needed from inside a cabinet.

"Ice?" Bill called over, holding up a pair of square glasses. "I have some in the galley."

Balk shook his head.

"I shouldn't have asked." Bill said this as he made his way back. "Plenty of rocks between us, right?"

Balk watched the senator settle into his seat, then pointed to one of the empty glasses on the table between them. Two fingers of small-batch bourbon went into each.

"Now," the senator began, lifting a glass, "I told you I needed to talk about—"

The judge picked up his own from the table and drained it in one, smooth motion. Stored at the perfect temperature, the corn-based spirit toed the line between Kentucky honey and something spicier. He returned the glass to the low table, before the liquid finished its burning descent behind his sternum, and pointed to it again.

"Okay." Bill paused only a moment, then drained his own in a similar motion. He added a heavier pour between them. "One more, Your Honor, before we take you back."

Balk absorbed the thought in silence. *I can't go back.*

"Look, I'm not here to ruminate with you, John." His intuition was remarkable. "What I am here to do is—"

"I can't just have your charges dismissed, Bill." It felt good to say it out loud. "It doesn't work that way."

Another pause. "I'm not asking you to."

"Not that I expect to be in this much longer," Balk added, hoping he was right. "Knowing Maggie Reynolds, she already has a motion ready that'll ask me to recuse myself because of this stunt you pulled today."

"It's possible." A swirl of the glass. "But I don't really think she wants that."

"You'll have to excuse me, Senator, but I'm pretty sure I have a much better feel for what's possible. And I sure as hell know Maggie better than you do."

"You're certainly more familiar with her." A casualness to his tone. "That doesn't mean you understand her."

"And you do?"

He smiled. Nothing more.

"Care to enlighten me?"

"What you need to understand, John, is that she wants to keep you as her judge. To remove you would take time, and the last thing she wants is for my case to be delayed. She's going to push and push and push this thing along quickly, hoping to avoid any setbacks whatsoever."

Balk snorted. "That's because she knows she can nail you to the wall."

“Maybe so.” Bill paused, sipped. “But you know Maggie isn’t prosecuting my case with that as her ultimate goal.”

“I’m not sure I agree. She seems to take a lot of pride in nailing people—”

“That’s because she’s a mercenary, John, a sell-sword who strikes to win.” Bill leaned forward. “But she’s a government prosecutor now, and the rules of the game are different.”

“In some ways.”

“That’s right. So, if she wants her big interviews and glory and fame, I’ll have to give her a trial, right?”

Balk leaned back in his seat, no longer interested in his glass. It sounded to him like the senator just wanted her to come after him. *Stupid.*

“Do you understand, John?”

“To be clear,” the judge said, slowly, “this whole sit-down isn’t about you asking me to hinder the prosecution in this case?”

“Of course not.” An incredulous look. “I think this is the kind of thing where nothing should be held back. Not a shred of evidence should be kept from the courtroom.”

The judge often heard exhausting arguments from criminal defense lawyers who wanted him to exclude evidence—usually the incriminating kind. He typically leaned toward giving the State an opportunity to present its full case, but there’d been plenty of matters involving prosecutors over the years who’d tried to overstep. He knew Maggie liked to push the envelope, so the judge was already prepared for her transformation into one of those tricky, arguably overzealous advocates for the Government.

“If ever in doubt,” Bill added, standing to move toward the aisle, “just sic ’em on me.”

“I see.” Balk was at a loss. “And that’s it? You’re asking me to use my discretion in a way that allows the special prosecutor to call a full-on blitz?”

“That’s it, John.”

Leaving the rest of his drink on the table, Balk began to stand as well. He hadn’t expected the senator to take this approach, but the judge knew there was a reason for this brazen strategy. It just hadn’t been uncovered, yet.

"It's time we get going," Bill said, moving now toward the front of the plane. "I believe we're due back at the courthouse by four."

"What about Lucy?" Balk asked. "I'm not leaving until you tell me."

The senator had his back to the judge. He stopped moving toward the exit but didn't turn around.

"What is it about my wife that you can't let go?"

"That you had her killed."

"Not that."

Balk noticed the long, despicable pause that followed, one that should've included a denial. He waited on it.

"It's difficult to explain things—" Bill sighed as he turned back around "—to a man who only knows the things that're safe."

"Don't change the subject."

"You wouldn't understand what happened because you don't understand the hard decisions that inevitably come with the gamble, the risk. That's just who you are, John. You stayed here, married plain, and started your little law practice—only to hate all of it."

"This doesn't have—"

"So, instead of doing something about it, you decided just to settle for being the local judge who screwed whatever he could on the side."

Balk finally felt his anger returning.

"It's pathetic, really," Bill continued, "that I'm even having to remind you that things wouldn't have been different if Lucy had stayed here. Not for you at least."

Balk shook his head, trying to restrain himself.

"You would've just done the same thing, John. You'd still have represented E.B., in that same lawsuit, and I'd have found out about the money."

"Leave the Acker case out of this."

"Why?" Bill scoffed. "E.B. Acker is why you're standing here, remember? Have you forgotten already?"

"Stop."

"It was just a few extra hundred thousand in the account. Money that could've gone to his boys—Lee and Cliff—but then you offered to split it with me, remember?"

Balk didn't say anything else. It didn't matter. He'd done what he'd done to his client—E.B. Acker—right after the man died all those years ago.

"I remember, Bill."

"As do I, old friend."

Balk thought about that time in his life. It was March of 1998 when E.B. Acker walked into the small, three-man shop that John Balk kept two blocks from the courthouse square. E.B. asked lawyer Balk to file a lawsuit for him because he needed someone he could trust. His target was a rising politician, Bill Collins, that'd gathered some clout, and E.B. thought Balk didn't care too much about all that. A deposit of $425,000 went into Balk's trust account, and a lawsuit was filed against Collins over their land deal that'd gone south. E.B.'s lawsuit sought *specific performance*—which simply meant he wanted the court to order the politician to make good on the deal he'd reneged on. Balk's client died a week after the filing of that lawsuit. Suicide, apparently.

"Be angry at that," Bill added. "Be angry at me for helping you cover it up. Let the rest go."

"What if I don't want to?"

The senator shook his head and turned to start back down the aisle. He looked back only for a moment before he walked off the plane, leaving behind the last of his irreverent words for the judge to remember.

"You didn't then. So, what makes you think you'll do the right thing now?"

Balk watched him turn and go.

13

With the old deputy already several steps ahead, Maggie Reynolds started up the basement stairs, picking up her pace a bit to get the blood pumping in her chest. As the last few planks creaked, she could feel the slight uptick in her heart rate. The steady drumbeat urged her other senses—those dulled by the gloomy basement, the lack of control—to ready themselves to perform again.

She took a deep breath in and stepped into the first-floor hallway, the courthouse's main throughfare. It seemed brighter, much quieter than she could recall ever seeing it. As the central artery for all who passed through the building, the often-bustling hallway stretched front-to-back across the entire first level. Transom windows topped the doors on both sides. They sat propped open above the entrances to the clerk of court, county tax assessor, local magistrate, probate court, and office of elections supervisor. Each of the government offices looked identical to one another from the outside, aside from the gold stenciling on their glass paned doors. The main entryway waited at one end of the hall, while at its other, a divided, heart pine staircase led upstairs to the building's beating heart—the courtroom.

"He should be upstairs, ma'am." The deputy said this as he broke off toward the heavy doors at the entrance to the courthouse. "I'll be in my office, if he needs me."

"Okay," she managed, watching him hustle off, "I'll let him know."

With service restored to the cell phone in Maggie's pocket, it soon started buzzing and pinging as notifications rolled in. It'd take time to sort through the emails, text messages, and voicemails she'd missed while on lock-down. Still, as she started toward the large staircase, Maggie pulled the iPhone out and checked the screen for anything that struck her as urgent. Nothing from personal friends or family. All work-related.

No surprise.

Maggie looked up from her phone as she reached the bottom of the stairs. Her gaze first went to the impressive window that framed the landing on the staircase. It surprised her to see a blue sky and sunlight pouring in through it. She stopped a moment before the first amber-colored step, and let her eyes adjust a bit more. When she opened them, she saw a man waiting on the landing. She recognized the familiar way he leaned against the railing—and his unsmiling face.

He nodded to her. "Hey, Maggie."

"Hey yourself."

Maggie took the twelve or so steps up to the landing and stopped. In uniform, Tim didn't look much different from the other deputies with the Blake County Sheriff's Office. *He was different, though.* She knew it.

"You doing okay?" he asked.

"Yeah, good." Maggie noted the gun on Tim's hip. The folio under his arm. The surprising calm on his face, given the stress of the day. "You?"

"Good." Nothing more.

They hadn't been together alone since their separation more than a month ago. Tim seemed to acknowledge this as he cleared his throat and glanced around for anyone else.

"It's good to see you're okay," Maggie added. "I was worried."

His face remained serious as he pulled the folio out from under his arm. Their conversations over the past month dealt with business only. Meetings with current members of law enforcement. Calls with a few retired investigators. Nothing personal beyond basic pleasantries. Tim stuck with the program.

"I assume you know there's a situation with the judge." He kept his eyes down, reading something from a page in his notepad. "One that happened this afternoon at—"

"I don't know enough about it." Maggie paused, waiting for him to look up and acknowledge the interruption. He didn't. He kept with the stoic, monotone version of himself. This bothered her for some reason and a pettiness inside of her wanted to elicit more of a reaction. "Your deputy—Tracker, I think that's what they call him—he told me there'd been some kind of misunderstanding when he came to fetch me. A blunder about a kidnapping that wasn't."

"Judge Balk went missing for a time." He scribbled something on the pad. "I mistook it for a kidnapping."

"Walking that back will be fun for everyone." Another provocation. "How'd you manage to go and put your name on that mistake?"

Tim finally looked up at her. "That's a problem I'll have to own, but I'll deal with giving an answer on it later. It doesn't matter much right now. My focus is on the decisions that need to be made going forward."

His even response showed no interest in engaging with her whatsoever. She was about to say something more—*maybe even apologize?*—when the phone in her pocket began vibrating again. Through her blazer, she pressed a button on the side of the device to silence it.

"What matters is that every news station outside the building right now—which, to be honest, Maggie, is more than I've ever had to deal with—is calling Judge Balk's disappearing act some kind of *rescue*."

The phone began buzzing again in her pocket. "Was he attacked or something?"

"We're still trying to get to the bottom of that. A few bricks through the window in his office is the only evidence we've found of any danger he may have been in."

Maggie thought a moment about this. She felt her husband watching her, waiting to see what she had to offer as far as insight. She didn't have all the facts, though.

"Well," she paused to silence the phone again, "couldn't the gunfire have been directed at him?"

Tim didn't answer. Instead, he pointed to her pocket. "Get that if you need to."

"I'll get it in a minute, Tim." Her words had more of an edge to them than she'd intended. "Sorry, talk to me more about the gunshots."

He paused. "This isn't official, okay?"

She nodded.

"I had a team scour the square and the streets around it. They found seven blank cartridges on the north end. Courthouse surveillance confirmed that the shots originated from that area. Only one shooter on the camera. Same number of blanks."

"Blanks?"

"That's right."

"Shit."

He smiled.

"Okay," Maggie continued, slowly, "so, someone might be playing games—"

"*Might* be?"

"Someone *is* playing games."

He nodded.

"I assume you have a theory."

"I do, but I want yours first."

She grinned at this. It felt good to be on the same team.

"You have a name for your shooter?"

"Not yet."

"What about the injured? I heard something on the news about people at the hospital."

"No gunshot wounds, of course. Those are people who were trampled in the rush to get away from—"

"From the diversion."

"That's how I see it."

As Maggie absorbed this, the sound of chattering voices began from farther down the first-floor hallway. She guessed that the others from the basement had finally decided to make their way back upstairs. Doors opened to the varying government offices, while heels clicked along the quiet corridor.

"Where's the judge?" Maggie asked.

"Collins's protective detail claimed responsibility for pulling Balk out of the building. He's with them now."

"With Collins, too?"

"I've not confirmed that. All I know is what his secretary told me."

Again, her phone—*buzz, buzz, buzz.*

"Sheila?" Maggie asked, although she knew the judge only had one secretary. "When was this?"

"Sheila Lambert spoke to him about an hour ago, apparently. He's supposed to be here at the courthouse by four."

Maggie thought about this as she finally pulled her phone out. The time read *3:50. Unidentified Caller* flashed on the screen.

"You need to get that?" Tim asked.

It stopped ringing. Maggie noticed it was the sixth missed call from an unknown number.

"Strange," she murmured. Her phone started ringing, yet again. "I guess I need to."

Maggie pressed the phone to her ear—but only listened.

"Maggie?" a deep voice asked on the other end of the line. "Are you there?"

"This is she." Maggie knew the voice. It was one she couldn't forget. She'd presented her first case in his courtroom, and countless others after that. Still, she had to ask: "Who's this?"

"Don't play dumb, counselor. It's beneath you."

Maggie bit back a retort, then snapped her fingers to get Tim's attention. She mouthed: *Balk's on the phone.*

"Look, Maggie, I'm on my way back to the courthouse." He sounded harried, anxious. Very much unlike the tyrant she'd known throughout her career. "Are you there now?"

"I am." Maggie paused. "Been here all day."

"Good." The sounds of other voices, the drone of a vehicle, occupied the background. “Have you heard much about this confusion from the last two hours?”

“To be honest, Judge, I’m still playing catch-up.”

“Okay,” he replied, “well, listen closely, because this is all you need to know.”

Maggie motioned for Tim to lean down close to her. He did, and she sandwiched the phone between their ears. Touching for the first time in over a month, the two listened in silence as the judge explained the situation.

14

When John Balk ended the phone call—he felt the weight. *Another brick*, he liked to call it, when he lectured from his perch at the front of the courtroom. Now, alone in the back seat of a federally owned SUV, he wondered how many times he'd given his spiel about the weight of a person's decisions. Grim faced, looking down from the bench on some sorry defendant, he'd explain that the time had come for that person to take responsibility for their choices. *For the bricks on their cart.* He'd said those patronizing words hundreds of times, while not once taking stock of his own poor choices. *Embezzlement. Lies. Conspiracy. More lies.* The judge felt those bricks stacked high on his cart, growing heavier in his return to the courthouse.

"We're almost there, Judge." The driver of the SUV met Balk's eyes in the rearview mirror. He seemed to recognize his intrusion on the moment of reflection.

"Good. Drop me out back."

"I doubt you'll be able to sneak inside the building unnoticed, sir."

Balk smiled. "Who said anything about sneaking?"

The roadway under the SUV changed, signaling the last half-mile of their return trip. Leaving behind the paved roads that made up much of Blakeston, a steady rumbling from tires on hundred-year-old bricks started below the chassis. The *thud thud thud* reminded the judge again of his courtroom lectures. *To get to my courthouse*, he'd say, prompting eyerolls from attorneys who recognized the old saw, *everyone crosses those brick streets outside. Me. You. Your lawyer. Your momma. We all come here the same way, understand?* Some defendants listened like good students, vying for last-minute points. *But, if a day comes when one of us must trudge into town for judgment, then we bring with us the choices from our past. We load them up—stacked like bricks—then cart them down the street for all to see.* Using his most regrettable tone, he'd then say: *Unfortunately, Mr. Defendant, your day has arrived, so let's have a look at the bricks on your cart.*

"Slow it down." It was O'Conner who spoke this time. He sat shotgun. "We're doing okay on time."

The awkward bump in the street jarred the vehicle and took the judge from his thoughts. The driver bit down on the toothpick in his mouth, but still did as he was told.

"I have to tell you, Judge," O'Conner said this as he turned in his seat, "these downtown roads are almost as bad as the cobblestone up East."

"You trying to make small talk, O'Conner?"

"The thought just came to mind, sir. I guess I just haven't spent much time in the South. It's surprising to see a city this old, this far inland."

"It's been here a good while. You'll see plenty more of it if you stick with the senator."

"That's not really my call," O'Conner replied, somewhat hesitant. "See, we go where—"

"You always have a choice," Balk said, meaning to step on the young agent's rationale. His words stung with hypocrisy on his own ears, though. "We all do, really."

O'Conner seemed to consider the words a moment, then eased back to the topic of Blakeston. "I bet there's some good history around here."

"That depends on who you ask, but the town itself goes back to 1833, officially."

"Officially?"

Balk smiled. "It's a long story."

"Give me the beginning, then."

"All right," Balk said, noting the curiosity in the man's face. "There'd been trappers, and bushwhackers, and scallywags here long before there was a Blakeston. The land near the western river attracted the Natives first, then the people who came later to take it from them."

"Settlers?"

"Does it matter?"

O'Conner paused a moment. "I guess not."

"Whether bandits settled here, or folks from across the Atlantic, those people took what they took just the same, right?"

The agent seemed to sense that he was being cross-examined now. "I wouldn't know, sir."

"It's okay to have an opinion based on limited facts, O'Conner. You just need to be able to change that opinion if you get newer, better information."

"That land is all divided up across the city, though. There's no one left to blame."

"Not all the land." Balk paused. "In fact, the largest swath of privately held land in this state runs right through western Blake County, a hunting preserve. Some still call them plantations down here."

"And this is all along that same river?"

Another nod. "The Chattahoochee."

"And you want my opinion on what?"

"On whatever you'd like," Balk said, hoping to learn something from the agent's frustration. "It's okay if you can't manage one."

O'Conner came back quick. "I say whoever built this town—settlers, bandits, or whatever you want to call them—they probably did what they had to do. The land was different. The times were, too."

"People are still killing for land."

The agent turned back around, leaving Balk's comment unanswered. The SUV slowed as it entered the oldest portion of downtown Blakeston, a quadrant of uneven streets that surrounded the courthouse and square. An orange-and-white sawhorse sat in the vehicle's path, and four BCSO deputies stood guard.

"Pull up there." O'Conner pointed to one side of the barricade. His tone sounded agitated. "Let's see what these Barneys want."

15

With an ear to his cell phone, Tim Dawson listened to his lieutenant's description and make-up of the SUV.

"It's pulling up now, Sheriff. Black SUV that looks good to go. Dark tint, maybe reinforced glass, and probably some kind of heavy protection package. Looks almost identical to what we have on courthouse surveillance."

"Is the judge in there?"

"I see two white males seated in the front. Neither of them—"

Tim waited as it sounded like his deputy was straining to get a better look.

"—wait, I do see a third man. He's leaning forward in the back seat. Yep, it's definitely him."

"Is Collins one of the other two men?"

His man on the other end of the line paused, probably taking a hard look at the faces. Tim didn't expect the senator to be in the vehicle. At least, that's what he'd gathered from Maggie's phone conversation with the judge.

"He's not with them, Sheriff."

"Before you let them through, call down to whoever it is that we have watching the exit at the airport. Find out whether Collins has already left."

"I'll be happy to tell these guys to wait—especially the passenger up front. I can hear his accent from here. Sounds like a real asshole."

"Call me back."

"Yes, sir."

Tim pocketed the phone, then stepped to the edge of the courthouse's rear portico. From where he stood, no more than ten feet from one of the back doors, Tim could see the full length of the one-way street that ran behind the building. A pair of deputies stood at one end, with a BCSO Charger pulled across the road. At the other end, four more uniforms stood along the sidewalk. Sawhorses had been erected at their end to cordon off the members of the media. Tim noticed that several of the cameras were directed at him. He acknowledged this with a nod as his cell phone started to ring.

"This is Tim."

"I'm back with you, Sheriff." The lieutenant on the other end of the call sounded frustrated. "I'm going to need to do something with this SUV. The chowder head in the front seat keeps mouthing off and—"

"Keep everyone calm," Tim said, cutting in. He could hear what sounded like people yelling in the background. "Tell me what you heard from the airport?"

"A second SUV left a few minutes ago. Hawkins is behind it now. He and Cardenas picked them up together, so they're all coming into town as we speak."

"ETA?"

"Hawkins was making the turn onto Pine when we hung up, so I'd say —um, I don't know—maybe another six or seven minutes."

"Okay, good." Tim thought a moment about how he wanted to space the arrival, security wise. "When we hang up, hold the judge's SUV for two more minutes, then bring it through."

"Yes, sir—" His voice turned muffled as he seemed to cover the phone. A few profanities were all that made it through. "—two minutes, and they're coming to you. How about the senator?"

"Wave him straight through," Tim said.

"You've got it."

Tim looked down at the screen as the call ended. He texted Maggie: *Judge is about to pull up. Collins won't be far behind.* He almost added something more to the message, hesitating only a moment before he nixed the idea. They'd split off from one another after her call with Balk, but not immediately. They'd decided it was best to take a few more minutes together to exchange notes. In that short window of time, they spoke more to one another than they had throughout their entire separation. Married couples usually shared their own intimate language, which allowed them to move a discussion quickly when necessary. He and Maggie possessed this, of course. They shared another kind of shorthand, though, one that came to them effortlessly. Having worked nearly six years as the primary investigator for Maggie's law firm, they flowed best together when they talked case strategy.

Maggie replied: *Heading to the courtroom. The lawyer for Collins is supposed to be here soon. Let me know if you see him. Keep me posted, Sheriff.*

Tim's fingers hovered over his phone's keypad. Their earlier reunion and impromptu strategy session hadn't resulted in any kind of joint action. They were on the same team, though. Maggie had several follow-up questions that she wanted answers on from the judge, and Tim's gut told him that Balk's timeline needed to be checked out. His wife, always the smooth tactician, wanted to give things time to play out. Her advice to him was to tread with caution—which he planned to. Sort of.

Tim typed back: *Play nice.*

Her response: *Only if you do.* A smiley-face emoji capped the end of her message.

Tim couldn't help but grin.

While pocketing the phone, Tim heard the sounds of activity beginning in the corner that'd been blocked off for the media. A black SUV crept down the brick one-way. Tim pushed off the top step, leaving the portico behind and starting toward the street. He took a deep breath, then directed the feds to come to him.

16

Heading toward the courtroom, Maggie Reynolds started down the Blake County Courthouse's second-floor hallway. She carried a red binder under one arm with *Discovery I* plastered along the spine. Taped to the front was a single sheet of paper with the caption: *Entry of Appearance.* It'd been faxed to the Blake County District Attorney's Office some five minutes earlier. The routine filing consisted of contact information and was used to notify the court and other parties of a lawyer's official entrance into a case. The new counsel of record—Ryan Park, Esquire—wasn't a name that Maggie was familiar with, but the tactical decision to enter the last-minute filing certainly was. She'd done it herself to prosecutors in the past, as it kept them from scouting the competition before their first face-to-face. A small thing, really, because Maggie wasn't expecting the senator's choice in lawyer to be anything less than capable.

He'd better be.

Maggie stopped at a plain door near the end of the hallway. It served as one of two side entrances to the courtroom—this one designated for courthouse personnel only. Tapping her new ID badge on the card reader, she reached for the handle on the door. She recognized the moment as another *first,* one in a long list of more to come. She'd entered the courtroom that waited on the other side of that door hundreds and hundreds of times.

Never from this side, though. It was a special entrance reserved only for those who could be trusted, like lawyers who worked for the State. Criminal defense lawyers didn't get this privilege. Instead, they came to the courtroom through the main doors, with the people they defended—the public.

"You're the prosecutor, *right*?"

The door behind Maggie hadn't even closed yet when the unfamiliar voice called to her. She cut her eyes in its direction and found a woman standing alone at the front of the courtroom. Maggie didn't offer her an immediate response. Instead, she took a few steps toward one of the tables reserved for the lawyers, while also giving the courtroom a quick once-over. No other faces.

"Are you not Maggie Reynolds?" the woman asked, assembling the words in a way that sounded less like a question, and more like an accusation. "You're prosecuting the case against Senator Bill—"

"That's right," Maggie said, placing the red binder at the table reserved for the prosecution, "just putting my things down is all. How can I help?"

"How about you start with telling me what's going on."

Maggie kept her eyes on the woman. They both stood in the well of the courtroom, an area that was *across the bar.* In any other room, the short mahogany wall that ran the width of the space might be called a divider of sorts. But in a courtroom, the bar was the official barrier between the public's seating in the gallery, and the space reserved for the work of lawyers.

"I don't follow," Maggie said, slowly. "In fact, I don't really appreciate what it is that you're trying to insinuate here."

"And I don't appreciate being jerked around," the woman shot back, before pointing to a nearby window. "Take a look at this. Tell me one more time that you don't know what's going on down there."

Situated at the front wall—the judge's bench between them—two floor-to-ceiling windows cast their light over the silence in the room. The window closest to Maggie offered a view for those in the jury box, while the other provided glimpses of freedom to anyone seated at the table for the defense. Maggie had accumulated countless hours at that table, defending clients some ten feet from where the surprisingly fired-up woman now stood.

"Okay," Maggie said, slowly starting toward the window that the woman pointed to. She scanned the courtroom one more time. The stylish briefcase, she noticed it now, tucked against one of the chairs at the defense table. Looking back at the woman, she considered her anew. Skirt suit. Dark blue. Toeing the line at the leg but complemented by a traditional white blouse. Tall, even in her conservative pumps. But young. "Are you with defense counsel?" Maggie finally asked.

"I *am* defense counsel, ma'am."

Before Maggie could remove her foot, the woman calling her *ma'am* pointed again toward the window.

"Go ahead," she added, "you can't see from where you're at."

Maggie stopped short of the window. She knew exactly what was out there. The front of the courtroom was really the back side of the courthouse. The tall windows didn't offer picturesque views of the courthouse square, nor quaint downtown streets. They provided ample light, but the view amounted to nothing more than the backs of the buildings on the next block. The only thing occupying the space between them was a narrow one-way street, the only point of access to the courthouse's rear entrance.

"I need to apologize." Maggie extended a hand to the woman. "I take it you're Ryan Park. I knew you'd arrived, but I made the mistake of assuming you were someone else."

"Forget it." The reply was brusque. She took Maggie's hand, though, and shook it. "Now, tell me about this mess outside."

Stepping to the edge of the window, Maggie felt out of her routine. The chaos from the day. The changes in energy across the aisle. The moment with Tim. And now, this.

"*This* was not something I was made aware of." Maggie knew she spoke the truth, but the words sounded unconvincing on the ears. "I'll get down there, though, so that we can get an explanation."

Park huffed at this. "*Your* county deputies," pointing again at the window, disgust in her tone, "they're arresting federal agents as we speak. For God's sake, they're arresting the people sworn to protect my client. You're going to tell me you can just saunter down there and get some kind of plausible explanation? That I'll just accept that?"

Maggie bit her tongue, ignoring the unprofessionalism of the young attorney. She'd let it slide because Park had a client to defend, maybe even a legitimate gripe. And until Maggie knew more in the war on information, she didn't plan on firing back much of anything.

Park pulled a cell phone from her pocket. "Senator, hello, if you'll please give me just one moment—" she cupped the phone, then turned to Maggie. "I'm going to step in the hall and speak with my client. I'd like to hear that explanation after." Not even waiting for a response, Park continued through a low gate at the center of the bar, heading toward the courtroom's front doors. "No, sir, I'm working on it right now—"

The young woman's voice trailed off as Maggie turned back to the window. The lights from a Dodge Charger flashed at the far end of the one-way. With BCSO emblazoned on its side, it blocked the only exit. Several uniformed deputies stood behind a pair of federal agents, searching their suits. They had them pinned up against the rear of a black SUV. It was the perfect shot for any photographer who was worth a damn.

"What a day." Maggie murmured this to herself, searching the street for Tim. She spotted him at the other end, the only entrance to the one-way. He soon started pointing as the lead pickup in a trio of vehicles started up the street. Two pickups with BCSO insignia bracketed another black SUV as they rolled to a stop. From where she stood, Maggie could see the rear window rolling down on the SUV's passenger side. The face of Bill Collins appeared. Acknowledging Tim with a handshake through the open window, he then stepped out to wave at the reporters packed nearby. Sharply dressed, smiling, Collins placed a diplomatic hand on Tim's back. "What an unbelievable cluster fu—"

"Maggie!" came the sharp interruption from behind. "Can I speak with you, please?"

This time the woman's voice sounded familiar. Maggie turned and looked in the direction of the courtroom's other side door—one that led to a secure corridor and the courthouse's judicial suite. Sheila Lambert, the judge's secretary, waited in the doorway.

"The judge is in," Sheila added. The way she said it made it seem like he'd only stepped out for coffee. "He wants to speak with you."

"Of course, Sheila. I'll grab my things."

Maggie took one last glance down at the street. Tim and the senator were already gone from view. She knew they'd soon be upstairs, as would the media and anyone else who could pack inside the room. She turned back and started toward the red binder on her table.

"He asked that you come quick," Sheila hissed. "Come on!"

"Okay," Maggie replied, turning on the spot to head toward Balk's chambers. "I'd hate to keep him waiting."

Sheila grinned back, waving her through the door. "I do it all the time."

Maggie only smiled. She didn't want to know.

17

Maggie followed the secretary through the side door, then made the turn into the adjoining corridor. Even with the exchange of pleasantries at a hurried pace, Maggie was still able to spot two of the surveillance cameras positioned along the hall. It was Ben Moss who'd first delivered the news on Judge Balk's disappearance, and the images from that same hallway were what provided the key bits of physical evidence to back up his reporting. Ben wasn't with a big network, yet, but Maggie knew what he was about. His approach to journalism was one that relied on local, credible sources. And if his people had reason to believe it *wasn't* a kidnapping—especially two hours after Balk's exit—then Ben wouldn't have continued reporting it as such.

And he'll keep asking questions until he finds out who got it wrong—and why.

As Maggie reached the end of the corridor, she couldn't help but consider all of her own questions that also needed answering. *Why didn't you call someone sooner, Judge?* Was just one of the dozen or so that'd cropped up after her last phone call with Balk. Also, *Why'd you only call Sheila?* Or *You're saying you didn't have any direct contact with the senator while under his protection?* and—the one she hoped to avoid—*Judge, how in the hell do you expect me not to ask that you recuse yourself?* But now wasn't the time to ask those questions. Not yet. No, she needed to take a step back from the events of the day, let the dust settle before making any rash assumptions. That was the kind of thing that led to damaged relationships, and Maggie couldn't afford more of that in her life—especially not with the judge.

"I'll let him know you're here," Sheila said, once they entered the small waiting area inside the judicial suite. "Have a seat if you like."

Maggie nodded, choosing instead to stay on her feet. Sheila disappeared around a corner, and Maggie soon heard the sound of knocking down the hall. Low, murmuring voices followed. *Was that a third voice?* she wondered, taking another step closer. The judicial suite occupied a front-facing corner on the second floor of the building, and Maggie knew the layout of it well. It consisted mainly of the judge's chambers, a conference room, the waiting area, and Sheila's office. There were two additional closet-sized offices that went to summer clerks each year, but it was early January. Maggie listened for another moment. Crept a step closer.

"Come on back, Maggie." Sheila's voice flowed from down the hall. The sound of her footsteps soon followed, until she appeared again from around the corner. "The judge is ready for you."

"Oh, perfect," Maggie replied. "Is it only the judge—"

Her voice trailed off when Sheila lifted an index finger. The phone on the secretary's desk had started ringing. The woman moved toward it, evidently more interested in the call than listening to Maggie's words. The secretary picked up the phone.

"Office of Superior Court Judge John Balk, this is Sheila." Smiling, nodding as she listened. "Hello Donna, yes, he's in, but in a meeting right now with—" Still lively, Sheila paused mid-sentence when she noticed that Maggie hadn't moved from where she stood. "Hold on one second, girl."

Maggie couldn't help but smile at this.

"Yes?" Sheila asked.

"Who else is with—"

"I have Mrs. Balk on the line, and I need to update her on how the judge is doing." One hand cupped the phone. The other made a sweeping, mother-goose-like gesture toward the hall. "He's waiting on you, now go on ahead."

Her tongue growing raw, Maggie bit back an ill-advised quip and started toward the meeting. Singsong in tone, Sheila resumed her call with the judge's wife as Maggie left the waiting area.

Fight back assumptions, she reminded herself, *and stay focused on the prize.*

The wooden door to Balk's chambers leaned nearby. Missing a hinge, cracked, and splintering at both ends, the heavy door occupied a space on the wall several feet down from the exposed doorway. Maggie listened to the sounds of the voices inside the next room before rapping several times on the discarded door. The voices stopped.

"Come on in." Balk's booming voice had returned to its familiar decibel. "The door's open."

Maggie stepped through the doorway. The three faces in the room turned from their meeting to acknowledge her, confirming suspicions. Judge Balk at his large desk, with two more lawyers before him. The judge actually stood and started coming around from the other side of his desk. *Another first.*

"I hope you don't mind that we've gotten started, Maggie." His eyes seemed to consider her carefully as he came across the room to meet her halfway. He extended a mitt-sized hand for her to shake. "I called this little impromptu meeting to get us steering in the right direction."

"Good idea, Judge." She took the hand, standing tall. "And welcome back."

"Shall we get to it, then?" Balk released the handshake first. "I'll pull over another chair for you to join us."

"I'd prefer a dry seat, if you have one."

"Yes, I apologize for the mess." Balk seemed to chuckle gratuitously at her joke—*that's three firsts*—then sort of motioned in the general direction of the debris and rain-soaked furniture. It'd been pushed together into a pile near the tarped-off window at the front of the room. "The maid comes on Tuesday..."

Maggie didn't reciprocate with a courtesy laugh. Michael Hart—the *real* prosecutor in the room—took care of it for her instead. "We don't mind,

Judge. It gives the room character." Hart half-stood from his own seat as he said this, reaching to Maggie for a handshake. "Afternoon, Maggie, it's good to see you."

"Come on, Mike." Maggie moved to him and shook the hand. "If you're going to go for something, don't go halfway. Go all the way."

"Damn right," Balk added, pulling a chair over. "Now, sit."

Maggie smiled as she took a seat next to *Super Mike*—a moniker she'd pegged him with recently. His presence was to be expected, sort of. Hart served as the *supervising attorney* in the prosecution of Bill Collins, which was something she'd not bargained for at the beginning of her work for the government. There'd been a deal, in fact. She'd come to the State with what they needed to build their case—the proffered testimony of Liam Hudson, a key witness against Senator Collins—and with that she'd also brought the State her conditions. It was a package deal, with clearly stated terms as to an arrangement that allowed Maggie to serve as special prosecutor in the case against Collins. Hart—under good authority, apparently—readily agreed to it all in writing. And with that, she'd made good on her assurances. Her witness, Hudson, testified magnificently before a Blake County grand jury, which paved the way for a historic moment. Then, on the morning that the indictment against the senator was set to be returned in open court, Hart pulled her aside for a "quick chat."

Balk noted the obvious tension in the room. Clearing his throat, he said: "I believe you've met Ms. Park, right Maggie?"

"That's right, Judge." The shoo-in for next year's professionalism award —Ryan Park—was who answered first. "We spoke earlier in the courtroom."

Maggie only nodded. Park had obviously hustled over to the judge's chambers after their initial encounter, but that didn't explain why the young defense lawyer knew to be there before Maggie did. *Was her client backchanneling with the judge?*

"Good." Balk clapped his hands together. "This'll be the plan, then. I'll take the bench in about—"

Park cleared her throat, then interjected, "Judge, if I may—"

Unaccustomed to interruptions, Balk continued, "Five minutes and we'll have the defendant, Mr. Collins, brought in quickly for his arraignment. There's still quite a bit of media fussing around here and—"

"Judge," Park began again, louder this time, "I actually have a waiver here that I'd like to bring to your attention."

Balk seemed to take a deep breath. He stopped.

"I've been authorized by my client—Senator Collins—to file a *Waiver of Arraignment* on his behalf."

Maggie couldn't believe her ears. The hellish day that was nearly behind them could have potentially been avoided with such a waiver. Defendants had the option—in some circuits—to file a document with the court that waived their right to a public arraignment. Constitutional safeguards guaranteed a defendant in a criminal case the right to be brought before the public, in some fashion, so that the accused could demand a reading of the charges being offered by the government. Grounded in the Founders' experiences with corrupt regimes—ones that accused citizens in private courts behind closed doors—the right to a public arraignment was a protection rooted in transparency. It was the defendant, though, who had the right to waive this right to a public reading of his charges. Not the State.

"Fucking unbelievable." The words came instinctively from Maggie's mouth. "The gall you must have to request—"

Balk interrupted. His sharp reply wasn't directed at Maggie, though. "Denied, counselor."

"But Judge."

"Denied."

"My client has a right to enter a plea of *Not Guilty,* waive his formal arraignment, and move forward—"

Maggie tried to help. "I'd stop, Ryan."

"Not another word!" Balk thundered from across the desk. "Ms. Park, I strongly recommend you take the special prosecutor's recommendation."

Park stayed quiet.

"Now, there are two things that might have happened. Either your client chose not to hire you until sometime earlier this morning, which allowed you only a few hours to file your entry of appearance with my court." Balk's voice still teetered on the edge of another outburst. "Or—your client hired you, Ms. Park, then instructed you to *not* file your entry in this case until today. All in an attempt to play games with me and the prosecutors and everyone else in this county."

"Don't answer that." Maggie quickly added.

Balk nodded. "The woman that'll be across the aisle from you may be a prosecutor, Ms. Park, but she built her reputation doing your kind of work. I'd listen to her."

Park appeared cool, even in the uneasy silence that'd filled the room. Eventually, Hart decided to play his role.

"Judge, I'm sure the State can be ready within five minutes."

Balk nodded. He shifted his eyes to Maggie.

"I'll be ready, Your Honor."

The eyes then shifted to Park. "Speak!"

Not a flinch. "As will the defense, Your Honor."

18

The judge stood at the door, listening for what waited on the other side. Voices from the packed gallery gave off a steady buzz, a current of conversation that seemed to fill the entire courtroom with energy. He could almost feel it through the door. It was the pent-up, excited kind that usually led to the downright unpredictable. Balk's plan to avoid something of the sort was to simply move things along at a breakneck pace. Barring any grandstanding from the lawyers, he could be as quick as Earnhardt in '87. He'd assume the bench, arraign the son of a gun, then be back out the door in a matter of minutes.

"We've almost got the courtroom organized, Judge."

Balk offered a nod to Marlin Buck, the old deputy who waited with him. When the calls for quiet started coming from the opposite side of the door, the judge reached down for the zipper on his robe. His fingers fumbled with it for a moment. Not because they were shaking. No, it had more to do with the fact that he rarely zipped it up on his own anymore.

"I'm not too keen on helping with that zipper, Judge." The ruffling of cloth in front of Balk's bellybutton had apparently caught the old deputy's attention. "You just let me know, though."

"I usually ask my secretary to get me started."

"I figured."

"It's that obvious?"

A pause. "I wouldn't say that."

Balk stopped jimmying with the zipper for a moment. "Then what would you say?"

"I wouldn't say anything, Judge. I don't concern myself with any of that."

"But you seem to keep your ear to the ground around here, right?"

The old deputy looked away, unwilling to acknowledge the understatement. In the small space in which they were standing—a vestibule of sorts—there weren't many places to go with the eyes. He finally looked back over at the judge.

"What I meant to say," Balk added, "was that you seem to know what people are talking about around here. What they are seeing."

"It's my job to know, Judge."

Balk nodded. "So, do you assume that other people are seeing what you've noticed between me and—"

"I don't ever assume anything." He said this as he shook his head. "It keeps things much simpler."

"Never?" Balk wanted to call *bullshit.* "You're telling me you don't act on hunches?"

He continued shaking his head.

"I need to talk to Sheriff Dawson," the judge added with a smile. "We may need to get you back for a refresher in Policing 101."

"I doubt he'd do that, Judge." His tone remained humble, respectful. "I'm just a glorified rent-a-cop at this stage of my career."

Balk wasn't used to dealing with people who didn't seem to like compliments. His lawyers all needed to hear the sound of their own name every hour on the hour, but not this man.

"But you used to be in the field, right?"

"Sure. I used to do the real work, but I made my decisions on what I saw. What I smelled, heard, touched—you know what I mean, Judge?"

Balk listened.

"I didn't assume to know what those wildcats were thinking when I arrested them." He seemed to consider his words. "Like I don't assume to know what you're thinking."

Balk actually believed the man. Yet, he couldn't remember the last time one of his own decisions wasn't supported by *something* beyond the facts. After more than half his life in the profession of judging and lawyering, it seemed impossible not to make decisions without relying on his assumptions. There were simply too many factors to consider. Motivations. Agendas. Optics. Then the clients—their lawyers, even—they all seemed to have a game running on some level. It's just the way things were, and Balk had recognized this long ago. Without certain assumptions, he couldn't exercise sound judgment.

"Well, I guess I don't have that luxury." Balk's words sounded more like an admission. "I should've assumed you knew something..." his words trailed off as he wondered who else might know about Sheila, maybe even the senator.

"Don't be worrying about me, Judge."

Balk nodded toward the door. "There're people on the other side of that door who don't see things the same way."

The judge waited for some kind of response, but the man only stared back at him. His willingness to show restraint certainly agreed with Balk. His unwillingness to commit to how much it was he knew, well, that was exactly the kind of thing that kept a man up at night. Maybe the deputy only knew about a little hanky-panky—maybe he knew more. But an old-school lawman like that, one affectionately referred to by most as *Tracker,* doesn't come by a name like that for no reason. And because of this, Balk had to assume that the head of courthouse security had more than just a good feel for what happened throughout the building. He had to assume that the man knew everything—including the secrets.

"There it is!" Balk finally pulled the zipper up to the neck of his robe, shaking his head at his own ineptitude. "I guess I'll need to start practicing at home more. Nobody wants a judge that can't work his own fly."

"Ain't nobody fixin' to believe that in this county, Judge."

Balk slowly looked back at the man. He knew the surprise showed on his face, but it turned to a grin when the old deputy began to laugh. He'd never heard the man laugh. Its heartiness, though, only spurred the judge to do the same. They laughed together for another moment—until the side door opened from inside the courtroom.

"Judge Balk, sir—"

They both startled at the voice.

"—we're ready for you in here."

Balk glanced over at the door. The face of a courtroom deputy looked in on them with a puzzled expression.

"Give me a second."

The judge rubbed the wetness from his eyes, nearly grinning as he looked down again at his robe. His appearance was in order.

"Thanks for the company," Balk said, turning to the old deputy. He meant it.

"Of course, Judge."

Balk hesitated, then gave his own impression of that conspirator's grin he'd seen earlier in the day. "How about we keep my zipper issue between you and me, okay?"

The man nodded. "Your secrets are safe."

Balk paused, noting the plurality in the man's reply. An extra consonant. His training as a lawyer wanted to question. *Was it secrets that you said? As in, multiple? Let's have it stricken from the record if you may have misspoken.* But there wasn't time. Balk instead settled for a handshake, before turning back to the door.

"I'm ready. Go ahead and have them call it."

The courtroom deputy nodded, then turned away from the opening in the door. Within a matter of seconds, Balk knew the opening boom of *State of Georgia v. William H. Collins* would sound throughout the entire courtroom. The first step in a process that would take the judge closer to the last trial of his career—at least, that's what he assumed. Balk only hoped to see it through to the end.

And not be left to face a trial of his own.

19

"All rise!"

Maggie was on her feet at counsel's table, ready. The gallery behind her slowly followed, lumbering together as one mass of bodies. The pew-like benches under them came to life, voicing loud objections to the courtroom's exceeded capacity. Similar murmuring could be heard from the spectators in the gallery, echoing their own creaks and groans as they stood. Maggie wasn't concerned with the grumblings of those malcontents who waited behind her. What she worried about was the one who stayed silent among them. That coward—hiding in plain sight—who liked to leave nasty little threats for her to find. They stuck to her windshield. Fell into her office mail. Floated from her gym locker. And now—they even showed up in court.

You'd better quit, bitch. Maggie hadn't stopped thinking about the opening lines in the note—the one she'd found only a few minutes earlier. Recognizing it right off, taped to the inside of the red binder on her table, Maggie had quickly tucked the note back inside. She'd read it once, of course, but that was all it took to sear the note's image in her mind. Black ink, same scrawl as the others: *I hope to visit real soon. Bet that's what you want, isn't it? I'll be watching. XOXO*

Maggie tried focusing on the familiar terrain in front of her, still finding it difficult to push the thoughts back from her mind. The creep's note had her on edge, but that's what this guy wanted. And yes, Maggie knew it most definitely was a *He*—without question. She could feel the charged-up language in every note. There was joy he took in leaving these ugly little messages for her to find, and today made it four in all. *Four.* But this note—it was the first of the four that actually made her believe he was in fact lurking somewhere nearby. She'd felt it when the binder opened, like he'd chosen a seat right behind her so that he could watch. No doubt he'd enjoyed it, too. Maybe it'd even turned him on, watching her, his heart racing.

Ick.

Maggie couldn't help but glance over her shoulder one more time. Something the spectators along the front row likely found strange. The prosecutor's attention on the gallery, as opposed to the important case in front of her. Still, one by one, she went again along those in the front row. Each one, face after face, she tried to commit to memory. If he'd been bold enough to sit that close, then she'd see him. And Maggie rarely forgot a face.

"Holy sh—" Maggie half-exclaimed, jerking back around when a hand touched her shoulder.

"Whoa, sorry!" Michael Hart almost put an arm up to block her reaction. He stared at her a moment, then asked, "Are you okay?"

"Yeah, of course." Maggie nodded as she said this. His eyes were on her. "I'm good, Mike."

He looked unconvinced. "Okay. You sure?"

"*Yes,*" she said, realizing she wielded a knife-like tone. Deep breath in, then out. "I promise, I'm good."

"Be better than that," he whispered. "Be great."

Maggie rolled her eyes. "Thanks, Super Mike."

Hart didn't fire back, instead he nodded to the opposite wall. Maggie turned and saw that the judge had finally stepped into the courtroom. *About damn time*, she thought, taking in one more deep breath. Then, she noticed it—a thin folder that'd appeared in front of her on the table. She stared at it for a moment.

Hart noticed.

"Everything's in there for today," he whispered, pointing to the folder. "Holler if you need anything."

"I already have everything printed." Maggie paused. "It's—in the binder."

"No need to fool with that, Maggie." His face looked like he was trying to be helpful. "But do what you like, just remember we're on the same team here."

Maggie tamped down a horrible, unwarranted suspicion that suddenly came to mind. *Maybe he thinks I haven't found his note yet? Or he's worried it might pop out in the middle of the arraignment.* She stopped herself from going further. No, Hart was a lot of things—competitive, boastful, maybe even resentful of her for hijacking this case—but he wasn't that creep who'd been tormenting her. *He couldn't be.*

"Thanks for doing that," she finally said, without looking at him. She didn't want to. "You're right, same team."

Maggie turned and watched as the judge took long, intentional strides toward the bench. Balk carried with him his usual presence, one that seemed to demand order as soon as he walked into a courtroom. But having known John Balk for more than a decade now, Maggie saw that he possessed something more than just a good courtroom presence. There was a uniqueness to him—a kind of magnetism that was unmistakable. It had nothing to do with his looks, as he wasn't all that handsome. It had to do with the fact that he was memorable. Balk had that knack for making an indelible mark—good or bad, right or wrong—on anyone who met him. He wasn't flawless, of course not, and he seemed to make poor choices at a personal level. *Who didn't?* But what made Balk special—what made others feel as if they might one day be characters in his memoir—was the same quality that made Maggie memorable.

"The Superior Court for Blake County is now in session!" called the bailiff from the front of the courtroom. The judge stepped up to the bench, drawing every eye to the man in the robe. "The Honorable John J. Balk is presiding."

"Be seated!" Balk bellowed. "Everyone, let's be seated."

The benches throughout the gallery began their same routine, as did the spectators who took their time returning to their seats. The judge, waiting, it seemed, for the courtroom to quiet, looked directly over to Maggie. His eyes stayed with her, even as the noise in the room began to dwindle. He seemed to recognize the weight that was on her, acknowledging in his way that it was one that rested on them both. It was a weight that they shared—*that's what he'd say, droning on and on*—but it was one that would only continue to shift. Because he'd soon be gone—this trial would soon be over—and the history of this place would fall to her. If she wanted it, along with its burden.

All Maggie had to do was win. After that, no one could ever take it from her.

Not Collins. Not some faceless creep. No one.

20

John Balk felt the eyes watching him with curiosity as the courtroom continued to settle. His own attention hadn't left the table reserved for the State, though, more specifically its special prosecutor. Shoulders back, chin high, Maggie Reynolds wore a confidence that he'd long admired. She stood in sharp contrast to Collins's supporters, the devotees in the gallery who whispered to her back. Maggie seemed to ignore them and eventually noticed his gaze, offering him a nod as she took her seat. Balk could only assume she recognized the weight of the moment.

Her moment.

His gaze left hers and went to the small notebook at his desk, a Moleskine that kept his bench notes. As was his custom, Balk opened it to a fresh page. Date: *1/12/24.* Hearing: *Arraignment W.H.C.* Then jotted down a few preliminaries. The eyes from the gallery stayed on him as he did this, of course. The judge was who most of the people believed they were supposed to be focused on. Yes, it was his courtroom, but the judge knew he only played a role in it when it came time for a trial. His lines were often predetermined, and his place on the stage put him deceptively at the front of it all. Wearing the robe, slamming the gavel, and barking at lawyers was only appearing to lead the event. *All part of the ruse.* It trapped jurors, spectators, clients—even some lawyers—into thinking that it was the judge who led the trial. *Not true.* And the trial attorneys who understood this—the ones worth their salt—never spoke of it. But *it* was what determined the outcome.

Balk scratched: *The unspoken truth.*

Eyes down, fountain pen still at work, the judge finally heard the first sounds of the gallery's impatience. Rustlings had started—murmuring, chuckling. Blatant disrespect. It pulled the judge's focus to the crowded room. He reached for his gavel. But instead of slamming it, he pointed the hammer-end toward a thicket of supporters seated in the rows behind the defense table. The room went silent.

"I'll say this once," Balk growled, meeting several stares with the gavel. "I'll have order."

He glowered for another few painful seconds, then placed his gavel at the edge of the bench.

The ruse continued.

"Is the State ready to proceed with arraignment?" Balk spoke directly at Maggie.

She rose. "The State is, Your Honor."

He couldn't help but notice that Maggie didn't stand directly behind the prosecution's table. Halfway into the center aisle, she seemed to be tugging against an anchor still submerged under her old table.

"Please state your name for purposes of the record."

"Maggie Reynolds, Your Honor, specially appointed to act at the State's behalf."

Listening, Balk glanced occasionally at the slip of paper in front of him. He'd forgotten about it until a moment ago, when it fell from inside his Moleskine. It was a checklist with several perfunctory questions that needed to be asked, one that effectively punctured a tire under Balk's strategy to push the arraignment hard around the oval.

"Are you currently in the State's employ?" Balk asked.

"No, Your Honor. I'm in private practice."

"At your own law firm?" Balk checked this item from his list, one of many he already knew the answer to.

She nodded. "Yes, Your Honor, Reynolds Law."

"Are you in good standing with the State Bar?"

"Yes. Here in Georgia, as well as Florida and Alabama."

Balk squinted his eyes to read the next question. "Have you, your firm, as well as any of its lawyers, complied with all requests—" Balk paused, nearly stumbling over the words, "that were made during the course of the mandatory Conflict Check?"

"I have." Maggie paused for a moment, then added: "As the Court may know, I'm a sole practitioner."

"It does." Balk cleared his throat for the next question, one he didn't know the answer to. "The compensation drawn from this appointment, it's in line with the schedule published this past fiscal year for—"

"Your Honor." A rare interruption. "I've actually waived any compensation."

A few remarks from the curious rippled through the gallery. Balk was surprised, too. Maggie had certainly done a service to the community while she worked as a public defender, but she was in private practice now. She had her own firm, with bills to pay and employees to take care of. Lawyers in the private sector amassed huge numbers of *pro bono* hours through varying methods, but the sole practitioners weren't usually in a position to completely pass on a check. It was an interesting decision, he decided, but certainly not one that'd cause the special prosecutor to go tossing her couch for spare change.

"I hope the State remembers they only get what they pay for..."

Balk's comment landed a chair over from where Maggie stood. The collegial jab spurred a few laughs, including one from its intended target—Michael Hart.

"I've not heard the slightest demur, Your Honor." Maggie's smile pleasant, professional. "So, they're taking me on at their own peril."

"That they are, counselor." Balk absorbed her smile. *I'd say we all are*, he thought. *And for free. I never thought I'd see that day.* The judge found his place on the list. "Let's see—have you taken the necessary oath for your appointment?"

"I have." Maggie picked up a thin folder from her table. "I have the original certificate here, Your Honor. A copy of the same is on file with the clerk."

"Any objection?" Balk glanced over at the defense lawyer, Ryan Park.

Maggie held the manila file out for her inspection. Without reviewing its contents, the young defense lawyer only shook her head. Balk waited another moment. She needed to stand and voice her decision for the record.

"It should be noted," Maggie began, slowly, "I've shown defense counsel a folder containing the original certificate, one issued upon my appointment as special prosecutor." She then tied a nice, tight bow on the issue "with opposing counsel offering no objection to the fact that it bears an authentic signature, date, stamp, and seal."

Park didn't add a word.

"Very well," Balk said, "It's so noted."

The folder returned to the State's table. "With thanks, Your Honor."

The judge had reached the last item on his checklist. He only needed to memorialize the reasoning for this *special arrangement*—which was essentially an outsourcing by the State, one that gave free rein to a small-town mercenary in her pursuit of the senator. Balk considered the wording for a moment, then asked, "What's your specific directive in this appointment, counselor?"

"My directive," Maggie began, ready with her answer, "Is one authorized by the Prosecuting Attorney's Council of Georgia, done so with the consent of our state's attorney general." Her voice carried, wall-to-wall. "And is one that has vested in me the express power to lead the investigation *and* prosecution into one matter..."

Maggie paused for a moment, only to reach for the cup of water at her table. She carefully sipped, while glancing over at the table for the defense. Park—seated alone—now had another perfect opportunity to offer her first words onto the record. Still, nothing.

"Madam Special Prosecutor," Balk prodded, implying that she should move along, "Which matter is it that you've been appointed to?" Before she could answer, he leaned forward to add, "And how about you save us all the suspense and tell everyone the status of that matter? Although, I'd venture to guess we all know by now."

"Certainly, Your Honor." A small grin as she placed her cup back on the table. "I've been directed to serve as lead prosecutor, in connection with any and all state-based offenses committed by William H. Collins."

Maggie glanced at opposing counsel. Park remained on mute.

"Offenses that were," Maggie corrected, eyes back to the judge, "*allegedly* committed."

"Status?" Balk asked.

"Right." Maggie smiled again. "The matter was presented to this very county's grand jury. A true-bill indictment has been returned."

"Thank you, Madam Special Prosecutor."

Maggie nodded but remained standing.

"Ms. Park," the judge began, directing his words again toward the defense lawyer. She had to say something in response. "Having reviewed the basics surrounding the special prosecutor's qualification in this matter, are there any items you'd like noted for the record?"

She rose. "No, Your Honor. The defense is satisfied."

Balk nudged her. "Nothing that the Court might need to inquire into further?"

"No, Judge." Then she sat.

Balk nearly asked: *Are you sure?* But thought better of it. Her approach confused him. And while his own early mentors didn't demand that he understand the technicalities involved in creating a record for appeal, they at least explained the basics to him. To hook a case like this one, Park had to be far beyond the basics of trial strategy. Yet, she looked too young. *Too green.* And the judge usually liked to take care of his less experienced lawyers. He'd throw a life jacket when they needed it because he didn't want some baby lawyer, early in, taking on water to the point of sinking their client's trial *and* arguments on appeal. He couldn't throw her a line on this grand a stage, though. She either knew the rule—*If in doubt, object!*—or the senator already had something else in mind for his choice in defense counsel.

21

As the judge finally reached the long-awaited arraignment calendar, an unmistakable groan drew his eyes to the back of the room. He watched as one of the thick, nineteenth-century double doors opened at the main entryway to the courtroom. A man eased from behind it, seemingly unnoticed by all else. The politician acknowledged the judge's gaze with a wink, then leaned at the edge of that historic doorway.

"Thank you for joining us, Senator Collins." Balk tested his range in the role of the affable judge. "You've made it just in time."

A flutter of activity started in the galley. The faithful turned to get a glimpse of the senator, as did members of the media. The judge allowed their whispers, a few *rah! rah!* mutterings, to continue as the senator took measured steps toward the front of the courtroom. His lawyer stood from her seat, then stepped to the waist-high bar that ran behind her table. She pushed its gate open, leaning close to her client to offer a few hushed words when he walked by.

"If you need to confer with your lawyer, Senator, please feel free to do so."

Ryan Park started, "Your Honor, we might—"

"I'd say we're doing okay for now, Your Honor." The dutiful Park only nodded in the face of her client's interruption, stepping aside as the senator continued. "May I approach?" he asked.

The judge met the senator's eyes. The man had enough experience in a courtroom to know he didn't *have* to speak to the judge. In fact, the Fifth Amendment—with its unique privilege—provided a compelling argument that the accused, well, remain silent.

Balk glanced to his lawyer. "Ms. Park?"

She didn't get time to answer.

"It'll only take a moment, Judge."

Balk sighed at this. "Of course, Senator."

As the judge waited for the accused to come around to one side of the bench, he heard the stirring of voices again in the gallery. Balk could only assume that some were out there muttering about the varying misconceptions that surrounded *Taking the Fifth*. Of course, there were other protections that flowed from the Fifth Amendment. But it was most often associated with some combination between the protection against self-incrimination, and the unique privilege that *Number Five* afforded anyone who stood accused at trial—the right *not* to testify.

"Let's try and have order, ladies and gentlemen." Balk directed his words at the conversers throughout the gallery, but his tone of impatience was intended for Collins. The man stood in conversation with the clerk of court, and both appeared delighted to waste the judge's time as they talked about the awful weather from earlier in the day. "Mr. Collins?" Balk nudged.

He held up a finger. "I'm coming, Judge."

Balk took in a deep breath as the politician continued to jabber. Most defendants didn't have the experience the senator had. In the hundreds of criminal trials that the judge had conducted, he'd watched defendants take the witness stand, and plenty more make the decision to *Pay the Nickel.* And he'd seen every single one of those people struggle with that decision.

To testify, or not to testify?

The dread usually crept into their faces once the judge explained to them that *they* had complete command over this decision. He'd learned, from those moments, that the defendants didn't really want the power to make such a decision—one that might decide their own fate. They said they did, but then they'd start to appear uneasy once they felt the weight of it all. Balk knew that wouldn't be the senator, though. He understood power, and there was little doubt he'd felt the weight magnify before making major decisions. But it was also the senator's experience that just wouldn't allow him to see that there was power in his silence. Still, it wasn't too late.

For the both of them.

Bill finally approached. "Good afternoon, Judge."

"It's nearly evening, Senator."

"Ah yes." He extended a hand up, stopping it at a height that caused the judge to lift from his own seat to reach for the hand. "Well, I just didn't get the chance to check in on you earlier this afternoon." He held his grip tight around the judge's hand as he continued on, speaking at a volume meant for more than just the judge's ears. "And I just wanted to make sure that you were doing okay, Judge, and that my men handled everything just fine for you."

Balk had little option but to acquiesce to the display. Had their parents not already passed, they'd have moved onto their health next. It was local custom to do so, complete with a hearty greeting that usually one passed along to the other's spouse. *Those still alive.*

"I'm just fine, Senator."

Bill paused a moment, waiting it seemed for the judge to address the other prong of concern.

"And your agents," Balk added with reluctance, "Please thank them again for me. They seem like they're good boys, all of them."

"Good." Bill nodded at this, releasing the judge's hand. "They sure enjoyed meeting you, Judge."

"I bet."

"And how about Donna, how is she?" Bill asked, unhurried. "I haven't seen her in—goodness—it'd have to be five or six years now."

Balk started to respond, then heard that unmistakable groan again at the back of his courtroom. Much louder this time, as both of the tall doors opened at the main entryway. A group of men—several in uniform—started into the room. The gallery received another bolt of energy at the sight of the new arrivals. Several BCSO deputies struggled with a pair of federal agents, both in handcuffs. Still in dark suits, their loose ties and untucked dress shirts added to the image of wild defiance. The duo shoved at their handlers, trading words for all to hear.

"Bill—" Balk growled, turning back to where the senator stood. He'd disappeared, though. "Bill!" Louder this time as Balk stood from his chair. He scanned the room and found the senator working his way toward one of the courtroom's side doors—one that Sheriff Dawson waited by. The sheriff opened the door for the senator, and out they went.

The judge turned his attention back to the rest of the frenzied courtroom. He watched as the lead agent in custody—Collier O'Conner—found his footing on the center aisle's hardwood. Just past the main entryway's threshold, O'Conner dipped low and used his leverage to shove a deputy back against one of the doors. *Smack!* The door's strike against the nearby bench rattled the room, causing a mixture of both fearful and delighted screams in the gallery. The second man—without a toothpick in sight—copied his lead and dropped low to initiate a similar move. The courtroom deputies poured down the aisle, soon obstructing the judge's view of the melee.

"Order!" Balk yelled, his gavel hammering. "Order!"

The ruse turned to full-on farce, as spectators and reporters jockeyed with one another for a view of the downstage. Plenty more hustled for the exit.

"Order!" Spittle sprinkled the desk in front him. "Come to order!"

Wham! Wham! Wham!

A hand grabbed the judge by the arm, beginning to pull at him. Balk turned and saw the face of the old deputy. He needed to run.

Again.

22

Maggie waited in the secure corridor. Michael Hart stood nearby, leaning against a wall with his tie undone. Both had their eyes down, cell phones out. It seemed neither had much to say at this point. They, along with Ryan Park, had to be ushered out of the courtroom when the judge made the call. Another delay. Another lockdown. The *ping! ping!* of a phone notification broke the silence. It sang from somewhere at the other end of the hall.

At least they had service.

Although Maggie had her phone set to silent, her eyes were on its screen when the banner appeared. It notified her of a new message from her assistant—one of several, she was certain. The small team at Reynolds Law had been floundering as of late. With Maggie devoting nearly all available hours to her *pro bono* gig—work that she went unpaid for, *officially*—her assistant and paralegal had been left to cover the bulk of the firm, including most of her profitable cases. All cases had to be pushed, all had to be continued, to make space for Maggie's work on the senator's trial. Her employees worried. About her. About the firm. About their jobs.

Maggie ignored the message from her assistant. She wasn't worried about the firm. About the money. *It'd be there*. Maggie didn't have this in writing—no fee agreement had been drawn up—but the word of an Acker was as good as gold, as far as she was concerned. Which was all that mattered, because only Maggie, Charlotte, Grace, and Cliff knew about the understanding. Their *Fett Agreement,* at least that's what Cliff Acker jokingly called it. But the terms of it were simple: Maggie delivered a conviction in *State v. Collins*. Full stop. Payment upon delivery hadn't been discussed. All she had was the word of each Acker.

The bounty wouldn't go unpaid.

Another message rolled in from a different number—one Maggie didn't have saved in her contacts list. She recognized the number as Charlotte Acker's recent burner, though. Opening the message, she saw it included only the shared link to a user's social media account—*@DarlingInDefense.* Her thumb hovered over the link for a moment, then another message arrived from Charlotte. It read: *Watch this ASAP.*

"Where did Park run off to?" Maggie asked, almost immediately after the video began to run on the screen.

Hart didn't say anything.

"Mike?" she prodded, glancing over at her co-counsel. "You still awake over there?"

He turned. "What's up?"

"Do you know where Park went?"

His eyes went back to his phone. A SportsCenter update played quietly. Checked out, he replied, "Went to find the restroom, I think."

"That little snake," Maggie murmured, shaking her head. "I *knew* something wasn't right."

Hart chuckled at this. "Defense lawyers, right?"

"Be serious, Mike." Maggie turned her phone so that he could see what she saw. "Look at this."

He pocketed his device. "Maggie, if the shoe was on the other foot, you'd—"

His words trailed off as soon as the face on the screen registered. She held a button down on the side of the iPhone, sending the volume to the max. It seemed the words that Park couldn't find in the courtroom earlier, had all been saved up for her followers on social media. The video message on the screen came from the platform's story feature. Followers of Ryan Park's account—*@DarlingInDefense*—had the option to catch her filming real-time *stories* from the day or watch them later when she saved them to the account as featured content. The video playing on Maggie's screen showed the platform's live-stream icon in the corner—which meant that Park was filming at that very moment.

"That number at the bottom," Hart murmured, "is that how many people are watching?"

"Yeah." Maggie suddenly felt small. "Crazy, right?"

Almost a million people had already tuned in. Maggie listened as the defense attorney continued an update on her defense of Senator Collins—a sort of play-by-play that sounded a lot more like an attack on Maggie. *It's time to name names, and call a spade a spade, because Maggie the Marvelous is no more.* Park obviously didn't have any interest in building a productive working relationship. *She's a sell-out who isn't playing by the rules anymore. Have a listen, friends.* The audio switched to a recording of Maggie and Park talking with one another in the courtroom. Their first conversation—a private one that Park had someone behind the scenes cut pieces from. *Fixing cases and hiding her agenda,* Park added. *It's shameful that you're willing to target an innocent man for your own fame.* Hearts floated up along one side of the screen as people *liked* the video. The number below the icon for viewers' comments grew every few seconds. *Friends, I'll be back in a minute. Remember*—a link popped up, prompting viewers to kick in on the defense fund for Senator Collins—*We the People have to help keep Bill free so that he can help keep us free.* Maggie couldn't watch anymore.

She looked at Hart, and noticed that he'd stopped watching, too. "What're you doing?" Maggie asked, noticing that his fingers typed furiously against the screen on his cell phone.

"I'm trying to get in touch with Judge Balk's secretary. I think Sheila will be able to help us get to the bottom of—"

"No." Maggie held up a hand. "I want to do something else."

The fingers stopped. "Like what?"

Maggie thought for a moment. "Don't you think the acoustics in that video sounded pretty good? Like, singing in the shower good?"

He nodded.

"It's like you told me earlier."

"That she went to the restroom?"

A nod. "And I'm pretty sure I know which one, too."

Hart stared back at her for a moment, then started shaking his head. "Uh—uh, I don't like where this is going—"

Maggie grinned as she looked down at her phone. She shot off a quick text message.

"Because whatever you're thinking, Maggie, it's not the way to handle something like this."

She knew what a hard *no* sounded like from her old adversary. This wasn't it. "I need you on this, Super Mike."

When he paused to think, Maggie turned and started walking. She knew she had him.

"Fine," Hart groaned, starting after her. "I'm only going because someone needs to watch out for *our* case."

Hart's long legs caught up easily to her. Once they were side-by-side, she started humming the Batman tune.

Hart laughed. "Settle down, Maggie the Marvelous."

"It has a good ring to it, Mike. I'll admit that."

23

When Maggie opened the secure door at the rear of the courthouse, Ben Moss was waiting right where she'd asked him to. He stood with his back to her, talking with a group of five other people. The young reporter looked out of place among the rag-tag bunch, a contingent of bold outfits in heavy make-up, five o'clock shadows and well-worn blazers. Maggie caught the attention of one of the other men in the group. He tapped Ben on the shoulder, mouthing something to him as he pointed in Maggie's direction. Ben looked over at her but turned back to the group to confer a moment more.

"Come on!" Maggie called.

He eventually left the group on the opposite sidewalk, half-jogging as he crossed the one-way street that ran along the back of the courthouse.

"You ever patient?" he asked, stopping short of her and the doorway.

Maggie noted an edge. "*Thank you*, Ben, for getting here so quick."

"You told me you had something good." He seemed to force the sullen expression. "So, what's up?"

Maggie leaned to one side to get a look again at the group across the way. "Is that everyone?"

"You texted me, Maggie. I grabbed who I could."

Maggie waited a moment to respond. It didn't bother her one bit that

Ben didn't seem to appreciate the ask. The reporter knew that a story came with her request—like last time—so the package deal wouldn't get left on the table. She'd made the terms simple. He wouldn't get an exclusive, and the story needed to be out immediately, as-is. Her words: *the more people on this, the better.*

"You couldn't find anyone else on Varsity?" Maggie asked.

"That group doesn't even dress out with the JV." Ben started to make a move to walk past her through the door. "If that's not what you need, let's leave them out of it. I can handle—"

She stopped him with her hand. "Are they at least legit?"

"Are they real reporters, you mean?" Ben smiled.

"I'll take that they are, then."

The still-twenty-something reporter had hit a few primetime spots with his recent reporting and investigation into Senator Collins. The surprise indictment out of Blake County wasn't on any other news network's radar. When the heavies began scrambling for something on it, the young reporter's phone started ringing. It seemed everyone was willing to scoop the hot story from a hungry guy like Ben Moss. And it didn't hurt that he had more than just the knowledge. Ben had a face for being in front of the camera—which Maggie guessed he'd been hearing more and more about lately.

"Come on, Maggie." Ben reached a hand over her shoulder and placed it against the heavy door. "I need to get at it first—whatever this is."

Ben couldn't hide that the recent attention had added some swagger. That subtle shift probably felt good—deserved, even—and it was a feeling that Maggie remembered well. If Ben's star continued to rise, then she knew the reporter's confidence would track it. Maggie only hoped that he didn't lose sight of what mattered down below. *Like she had.*

"You want in on the story or not?" Maggie asked.

He kept trying. "You know I do, but—"

"No." Maggie pushed her palms and fingertips together into a tight steeple. She tapped the reporter once on the chest with the points of her fingers. "This is the deal, *Ben.* You play nice with your friends over there, or there's no story."

Ben took a step back from her. "All right."

Maggie started a slow clap. "Good."

"Anything I need to know?"

Maggie paused. "What do you know about the defense attorney involved?"

"That she's hot."

"Anything less obvious, like something that I can't see with my own two eyes?"

"Fourth place." Ben kind of bit back this knowledge. "She's a former Miss Iowa, probably could've taken the crown from what I've gathered. She made out better than anyone, though."

"Okay."

"You don't remember her?"

Maggie shook her head.

"Six years back, her response to the *On-Stage Question* during the Miss America competition went viral. She became like," Ben paused, "a kind of sensation on social media. She really ran with it after that, too. Now she says all kinds of controversial shit, while promoting products, and usually does it while wearing very little—"

"I get the picture."

"I don't think you do, Maggie." Ben stared at her for a long moment. "She's in the millions of followers."

"So?"

He laughed. "Ryan Park has more people who know what she ate for breakfast than we can even imagine. With that kind of following, she gets all kinds of advertising dollars thrown at her. Think about it, Maggie, she got into this case like three hours ago, and now millions of people already know. Most of them don't even care that she hasn't ever tried a freaking case!"

"Good." Maggie preferred to continue to ignore this blind spot in her strategy. "I'll look forward to seeing how well she does at trial."

"That's the thing." Ben placed both hands on her shoulders as he spoke. "She's already started."

She looked away. *He's right.*

He waited a moment, then asked, "You want to hear the good news?"

"That she's a former Olympian, too?"

Ben smiled, then turned to whistle toward the B-Team across the road. It got them moving.

"The good news is that those instincts of yours are spot on—"

Maggie listened.

"Because your first reaction to her video wasn't, *Let's go cry to the judge.* Instead, it was to turn around and throw a little bit of your own noise back. And this is only the first round."

Maggie nodded.

"How about it, then?"

"Make sure it's loud, Ben."

He didn't say anything else as he turned to greet the others. Ben seemed to be drawn to using his bonus confidence for good. She knew that's how it started, though. It propelled you forward, moving you toward your ambitions faster and faster with the winds of approval. This made it easier to get where you wanted to be, and even easier to jump off course.

"Where to?" Ben asked, turning back to Maggie.

"Take the stairs behind me and head up to the second floor. Mike Hart from the DA's office will be at that door. He'll unlock it for you and tell you where to go."

All nodded and started toward the stairs inside. Ben waited to go last, shelling out fist bumps to each of the group.

Ben held one more out to her. "You coming?"

"I need to get help on something else, first."

"Anything I can do?"

"No, you're helping enough already. And I'd prefer to get with the sheriff on this one."

Ben lowered the fist to his side. "Your husband." It wasn't a question.

Maggie nodded. "At least, I'm trying to keep it that way."

Ben turned and hustled up the stairs without another word.

24

"Judge!"

John Balk heard what sounded like a far-off cry. Somehow, the voice struck him as muffled, while also familiar in a sense. He turned a bit, easing away from the sound.

"Judge, come take a look!"

The voice still sounded obstructed, but it was clear enough now for the judge to recognize its owner. Instead of calling back to it, he drew on a recent memory, one he tried to stay with as the soprano urged him, over and over by name.

"John! John!"

Clearer now. Strained. And he wondered why she chose to call to him in such a manner.

Once more: "Balk!"

The judge started at the harsh sound of his last name. He opened his eyes as Sheila turned the corner into his chambers. Visibly upset, she asked him to get up from his desk and follow her to the front of the suite. When the judge shut his eyes earlier to rest, he'd not expected his secretary to come barreling in only a few minutes later.

"What is—" Balk cleared the grogginess from his throat. "What in the heck, Sheila?"

"Get up, Judge. You need to handle this."

Balk started to stand. "What could've happened in the last few minutes that warrants this—"

"It's nearly six, Judge."

"No." He'd cleared the courthouse of non-authorized personnel at ten minutes before five. Shaking his head, Balk looked down at his watch. *5:59 p.m.* He cut his eyes back at her. "Why didn't you wake me, Sheila?" The judge's voice rose as he asked this.

"You're not going to blame your nap on me, are you?" She started to shake in her response. He had her working overtime at this point in the day, but it wasn't for no good reason. "You asked me to not disturb you, remember that?"

"Jesus, I meant for a little bit! Not—"

"Don't direct your tone at me like that." She turned to start back through the doorless doorway agape in his chambers. "I'm not here to listen to your accusations, and certainly not while you take His name in vain—" Sheila's voice faded as she headed down the hall.

"Stop!" Balk hollered.

No response.

The Baptist in Sheila only came out on occasion, but it was usually when something had her bordering on hysteria. He started around his desk, heading toward the doorway. His shirt had come untucked during his slumber, and he worked to get the tail of it back inside his pants as he made his way to the front of the suite of offices. He turned the corner to the waiting area and saw that Sheila already had the front door wide open. It framed a portion of the commotion that waited out in the hall.

"What's going on?" Balk asked. He pointed toward the loud voices, as if his question might possibly reference anything else.

"I tried to tell you." Her tone cool. She was reaching for her coat behind the door. "Now, I'm leaving for the day."

Balk didn't try to stop her.

25

Tim started up the secure stairwell toward the second floor of the courthouse. Two of his deputies followed close behind, their boots thudding in and out of sync with each other's. Tim could tell that the men were tired. He'd prepared all of his deputies for a long, wet day on the courthouse square. Not one like this, though, with most of the BCSO still out pulling overtime. Half continued poking around the county for *Mr. Blanks* —their mysterious shooter who'd fired no bullets—and the other half remained in place around the courthouse to deal with security. Not to mention the reporters who wanted more access. The spectators who lingered about the building. And the two federal agents Tim wanted kept on-site, *quietly*.

Tim stopped as he reached the metal door at the top of the stairwell. Blake County's newly appointed sheriff was certainly getting his unexpected shot at proving he deserved the job. Which is why every day—until this one—he'd kept that opportunity front of mind, and focused almost exclusively on what was best for the reputation of the BCSO. He enjoyed the challenge. Hit the gym daily. Had even started taking Spanish lessons. All because Tim wanted to serve *every* community, the right way. And he felt confident that he could, but he wasn't sure where that fit in with days like this one. It wasn't the chaos. Nor the media. No, Tim worried about the games—the ones that he and Maggie loved to run together, especially while she worked a big case.

"You have the time, Sheriff?" called up one of the deputies.

Tim glanced at the time on his wristwatch. *Right on schedule,* he thought, *so long as nothing's changed.* He called back to the deputy, "It's five-fifty-six, Cardenas."

"It's *Cardenas*, Sheriff." The deputy focused on the phonetics of his last name. He emphasized the roll of the *R* as it met the *D*, then for some reason pronounced the *E* like an *A*—finishing it all with at least three extra *S's*. The deputy smiled at this, easing up the last step with a cockiness in his gait meant for someone well above five-five. "Go ahead, try again."

Tim cleared his throat. "*Carrr-day-nahsss.*"

He laughed. "You're halfway there, Sheriff."

"Which half?"

"You just keep studying. You'll pick it up, Sheriff, at least that's what my sister tells me."

"I'm trying."

Tim looked down the flight of stairs as he heard his oldest deputy bringing up the rear. The *thud, thud, thud* of the man's heavy soles seemed to scrape every step along the climb. Tim noticed the hand holding tight to the rail as he made his way up, only leaving it as he'd cleared the last step.

"You need us to take a minute?" Tim asked him.

"I tried to learn Spanish once." Tracker waved his hand as he ignored the question, breathing hard. "It just didn't take."

"I'm not sure it's taking to me, either." Tim paused. "But at least Cardenas's sister is a patient teacher."

Tracker eyed him for a moment, then glanced to the young deputy. "She's not as squatty as Eddie, right?"

Cardenas took obvious offense. "I'm sturdy, *viejo.*"

"And I'm handsome, *pendejo.*"

"For a guy that's like a hundred, maybe."

Tracker only smiled, straightening his back so he could momentarily reach full height.

"Man, stop it, Tracker. The best athletes of all time were built just like me. Think about it, Messi, Pele, Maradona—"

"I don't know any of them." Tracker seemed happy to annoy the young deputy. "Besides, the greats have names like Namath, Montana, Marino—"

Tim put a hand up. "Let's finish this another time."

Both shut up and looked to the boss for direction. Tim pulled his cell phone out, checking to make sure nothing had changed. Nothing new from Maggie. Not since she came by fifteen minutes earlier to see him again.

"Okay." He turned to the two deputies. "I need you both to walk toward the judicial suite and check on the judge. I called his office before we left, and no one seems to be answering."

Cardenas chuckled. "Maybe he's missing, again."

"Calla." Tim said this with his hand pointed at Cardenas. It was one of the first few words the sister encouraged Tim to learn. And she was right, her little brother needed to just *shut up* at times. "You want to work with me, you keep it in line when it's time to."

He nodded. "Yes, Sheriff."

Tim wanted to smile at the young guy's sense of humor, but Deputy Eduardo Cardenas needed to learn to play it straight. He already worked hard, complained little, and had a great attitude—the early recipe for a solid lawman. And it didn't hurt that he had a great family around him, too. *Really great, actually*. The BCSO needed ten more deputies just like him, as did policing in general.

"Are you coming with us, sir?" Tracker asked.

Tim waited a moment to answer. He leaned against the lever on the metal door, cracking it enough to hear the sounds of loud voices not far down the hall.

"That all depends, Tracker. I'm going to need to see about breaking up whatever this is first."

26

Balk stood just outside the open doorway of the judicial suite. The judge's modest offices sat on a second-floor, front-facing corner of the Blake County Courthouse. The northwesterly facing corner, in fact, with a view from the judge's chambers that was probably the best in all of Blakeston's historic downtown. And the judge appreciated this, of course, but the placement of the suite itself was still something he'd never quite liked. Because for the sitting judge to reach their own courtroom, they had to walk from the doorway where Balk stood, and they had to cover the full length of the hallway outside. Which wouldn't be all that bad if the rectangular court building wasn't so large. The courthouse ran nearly twice as long as it did wide, with two second-floor hallways that'd cover the length of a football field, corner-to-corner. Much too far for a judge to walk anywhere in his courthouse without interruptions.

Now, the judge thought, staring down the length of that hallway, one he had to traverse to get to court for the arraignment, *why should I have to deal with this?* A small group of reporters, maybe fifty feet away, seemed to be trying to badger the senator's young defense lawyer. *Trying,* being the operative word.

Balk saw a very different defense lawyer. This one looked surprisingly calm, collected.

"Why are you recording conversations with the prosecution?"

"When did Senator Collins hire you?"

"One question at a time!"

"Have you ever tried a criminal case, Ms. Park?"

Balk listened, impressed with the confidence in her response.

"Where is your client now?"

"Is Collins evading custody?"

"Ms. Park, do you plan to represent the agents involved in the courtroom brawl?"

"Does the senator plan to hire more lawyers?"

"I'll answer your questions—some of them, at least—but not like this!"

Balk recognized that the last question seemed to have struck a chord with the young lawyer. Otherwise, she'd not appeared flustered whatsoever. That didn't mean that the press wasn't still trying to gang up on her, though. And the judge didn't like seeing the Fourth Estate beating up on one of his fellow members of the Bar.

Besides, it was on the way.

The judge turned and reached inside the doorway. He lifted his black robe from a nearby coat rack and closed the door behind him. As he slipped the gown over his shoulders, he turned to start the walk to the courtroom. The judge glanced down at the front of the robe, then pulled the zipper to his neckline with steady hands.

"Would you look at that." Balk murmured. "First try."

Lifting his eyes, the judge refocused his attention on the faces in the group ahead. It seemed that none of them had noticed his presence in the hallway, yet. Their attention still rested squarely on the defense lawyer, Ryan Park, who continued to look very comfortable as she took more questions from the semi-circle of reporters around her.

"Ms. Park!" called out a young reporter, readying his next question. Balk recognized him as a local. "What caused you to go on social media—this early in the case—only to accuse the prosecutor of misconduct?"

"It's Mr. Moss, right?" Park asked. "I don't see your press badge, but I know your face."

"That's right, Ben Moss." Instead of a press badge, the young reporter held out a tablet in one hand. He had it turned so that its screen faced the defense lawyer. "The video I'm specifically talking about is this one you posted on—"

She placed a finger to her lips. "Mr. Moss, if you'll let me answer, please."

"By all means."

"I don't agree with the premise of your question because I'm not accusing *the prosecutor* in the DA's office of anything. Mr. Hart and his colleagues are hardworking public servants. They're no different than my client. Nor have I gone on social media with the sole purpose of attacking anyone. My client's supporters need to hear the truth about this case, Mr. Moss."

"Come on, Ms. Park," he griped. "Do you need me to play the video for you to jog your memory?"

"Next question."

"Then what caused you to attack the special prosecutor?" The follow-up to Moss's question came from a man who stood at the other end of their little semi-circle, a snarky sounding reporter with a patchy neck beard. "Specifically, Maggie Reynolds."

The judge continued to wait at the edge of the group, listening. He wasn't sure what it was that these reporters were asking Park about. She hadn't said more than seven words their last time in court. Soon, two of the reporters in the group turned and acknowledged him. Ben Moss was one of them.

"Can I see that video, young man?" Balk's eyes were on Moss as he asked this.

"Of course, Judge." He passed his tablet over without even pausing to consider the request. "It's already cued up. Just press play there at the bottom of the screen."

The judge was about to start the video when he heard the defense lawyer call to him.

"Your Honor," she said. "I know I've not spent a lot of time in *your* courthouse, but I wasn't sure what the policy was as far as media having access to this restricted corridor. I was back here working—well, on the case, and they all just kind of showed up."

Balk looked up from the screen and met her eyes. *A striking blue.* And they looked like they wanted him to help. The judge turned and glanced around the group. The other reporters seemed to be waiting for the answer, too. It appeared to the judge, though, that the six of them had converged on the young defense lawyer and employed a kind of bull-in-the-ring strategy. Obviously, Park didn't seem to have shied away from it in the least, but that didn't make it right. Or in line with the media policy in *his* courthouse.

Balk asked the question to the group. "Who authorized the extension of your media access to include this corridor?"

Every face in the semi-circle turned to look away from the judge, except Moss.

He was who spoke up first. "I didn't get permission, Judge."

"I knew that was the case," Park added. "I didn't want to miss an opportunity to talk about my client's innocence, but this just felt wrong the whole time."

Balk *hated* when lawyers grandstanded for the media—and Park certainly was—but he was willing to give her a pass in this situation, in this location. It wasn't a place where the media was *ever* allowed entry. And these local reporters—Moss especially—knew that.

"Anyone else not authorized to be here?" Balk asked.

Park couldn't help herself. "And to be clear, Your Honor, I certainly didn't authorize any of this."

Balk nodded to her. "I believe you, Ms. Park."

"Thank you, Judge."

As the judge prepared to turn his wrath onto the group of journalists, he began handing the tablet back to the young reporter.

"Hold onto it, Your Honor." Moss held both hands behind his back, unwilling to take the device. He held eye contact with the judge as he said this. "I think you should give it a look. I can pick it up from your office another day."

"Mr. Moss, that won't be necessary—"

The judge stopped when he heard the loud voice begin at the opposite end of the hall. Still holding the tablet, he turned to see who it was that was yelling at the group with such authority.

27

Tim pushed through the metal door and let it fly. It swung around wide on its steel hinges, slamming hard against the wall behind it. He was already into the corridor, eyes on the gathering a hundred or so feet away. With as much force as he could muster, Tim shouted, "Listen up!"

Every single face in the group turned his way. As Tim started toward them, he leaned into his take on *bad cop*, a persona that he always found uncomfortable having to go to. He knew that he possessed the physical tools to make the role sing, though. At six-two, he'd built a sturdy taper from throwing the weight around for two decades. He also had the look of someone who might enjoy knocking heads every now and then. Which he did for a time, back in college, with other blue-chip athletes vying for time in the Auburn secondary, then later on, in his early years with law enforcement. He didn't miss the shots to the head or taking the lead spot in a raid on a crack house, but he had the look of someone who wasn't afraid to. And because of this, Tim still remembered the intensity it took to play at a high level, the tone one had to strike when that battering ram crashed through the door of a drug den. And Tim knew that when he brought this out of himself, that's when people started to get uncomfortable.

"This is a restricted area of the courthouse." Tim continued to stalk toward the group, his deputies easing up on both sides. Given that he'd not prepared them for this kind of approach, Tim guessed they were almost as surprised by it as the group of reporters waiting in the hall. "Anyone authorized to be in this corridor should have a badge from the first-floor security desk."

"I don't recall issuing a single one this week, Sheriff." The old deputy understood the job, and the improv that needed to take place when one lawman *dirtied up*. "But I wouldn't put it past me to forget a thing or two. I'm getting on up there these days..."

Tim and his men stopped near the edge of the group. He saw then that Judge Balk had started to ease out from the other side and looked like he wanted to say something. Tim didn't want any interruptions.

"Deputy Cardenas." Tim put a hand on his young deputy's back, speaking loud and clear for the judge's ears. "Go check in over there with Judge Balk, please. Make sure he knows the status as far as getting his courtroom organized."

"Yes, Sheriff."

Judge Balk nodded at this suggestion, then stepped away from the group as the young deputy made his way over to the man in the robe.

"As far as the rest of them," Tim said, turning to the old deputy. "How about we see how well that memory of yours is holding up, Deputy Buck?"

"Fine idea, Sheriff."

Tim pointed to an open stretch of wall that ran along the interior side of the secure corridor. "If any one of you've not been given explicit permission to be in this part of the building, step to that wall right there."

"Right over here, folks." Tracker waved a hand at the open space. "Come on, I know at least one of you aren't supposed be here."

The reporters looked around nervously at one another. It seemed they were waiting for someone in particular to take the first arrow. Soon, a few hissed in the direction of the youngest reporter among them. Tim ignored this for the moment.

"Ma'am, I'm Sheriff Dawson." Tim made eye contact with Ryan Park as he spoke directly to the defense lawyer. "You're one of the attorneys involved in today's arraignment, correct?"

She returned a stiff nod. No words.

"Your client, Senator Collins, is waiting in the courtroom for you now. I believe he'd like you to join him when you're ready."

Another nod as she collected the briefcase that waited beside her feet. Her eyes drifted to one end of the corridor. "Which door should I use to get to the courtroom?" Park didn't look at him when she asked this.

Tim turned and pointed in the direction he'd come from. "It'll be your next door on the left. I can have Deputy Buck show—"

"No."

She was already walking.

Tim watched the attorney as she walked away. Not to appreciate the view, though. It was to see if she was going to stop up ahead before heading into the courtroom. It seemed as good a place as any to record more content for her adoring followers on social media. Park stopped close to the door, then pulled her phone out. She pressed it to her ear first.

"I assume you'll take care of this, Sheriff?"

Tim turned at the voice. The judge stood there with a hand already out, one that waited expectantly between them.

Tim smiled. Took the hand. "Of course, Your Honor."

"Good."

There was a reason the judge sought him out, and Tim waited for him to tease the topic of interest. When the man didn't do so immediately, Tim glanced back down the hall one more time to steal another look in Park's direction. She was gone.

"She's something, right?"

Tim didn't need to see whatever grin was on Balk's face. He kept his eyes at the end of the corridor. "Something indeed."

"Walk with me a moment, Sheriff."

Tim looked over now and saw that the judge hadn't waited for a reply. He'd already started to ease down the hall, away from the group of journalists. Tim followed.

"What can I do for you?" Tim asked.

Moseying a bit further, sheriff and judge stopped just out of earshot.

Balk spoke in a low voice. "The federal boys." It was a question, of course.

"I've got them both in custody."

"And?"

A pause. "No warrants have been taken."

"Yet?"

"That New Englander tuned up one of my rookies pretty good. Chipped a tooth. Bloodied his nose. Might've broken it."

Balk appeared to sort of weigh this information, sucking at a tooth as he looked toward one end of the hall. He took in a deep breath, let out a long sigh. "And the other one?"

"Well, Judge," Tim paused a moment. He could tell that the big man faced some kind of dilemma in all this, but he wasn't sure why. Tim decided to leave an opening in his reply. "The other one wasn't as spirited. Not sure what we'll do with him yet."

"I'll be honest, Sheriff." Balk stopped, then turned his eyes back on Tim.

Tim didn't look away. "Please do."

"I've got enough problems already with the coverage happening around this trial." He motioned in the direction of the reporters who still waited down the hall. "I mean, these folks will do anything for an angle."

Tim waited. He knew that if he did so long enough, there'd eventually be an ask.

"I guess what I'm saying is," Balk lowered his voice even more, "that it'd be nice to have less problems to worry about."

"I couldn't agree more."

"Yeah?" Balk asked. "Look, I don't want to be stepping on toes. I understand you have your people to answer to. Your rookie who's hurt is—"

Tim shrugged. "He's a young guy."

"Tough?"

Tim nodded. He knew that this was how politics worked in a small town. "He's real tough, Judge. And prideful. That's what gets these guys out of bed some days."

"Give it some years, right?" Balk laughed.

"Right."

"It's settled, then." Balk sounded relieved. "I won't speak of it again. Just if there's a problem, you let me know."

"Sure, Judge."

This seemed to be enough to satisfy him. Tim noticed the judge glance down at his wristwatch and decided to pivot on the subject.

"When would you like to call things to order?"

"Give me ten, maybe fifteen minutes, Sheriff." Balk said this as he turned a large tablet over in his hands. "I need to hit the head, then I should be ready."

Tim knew that Maggie would be pleased with this answer.

"I'll send Deputy Buck over shortly."

"Fine."

Balk turned and headed in the direction of the only men's room on the corridor. He already had his eyes down on the tablet in front of him, one hand fidgeting with something on the screen.

Tim looked back at the group of reporters. He scanned the faces, and really only knew the one that Maggie always talked about. Tim decided in that moment that a little shove couldn't hurt.

"You." Tim pointed at the young reporter in the group. "Are you supposed to be in this area of the building?"

"Of course, Sheriff."

"Yeah?"

He didn't respond. He only ran a hand through his hair, probably making sure the Stamos look remained in check while he waited for Tim to take another few steps closer.

"Who was it that gave you permission?" Tim asked.

A shrug. "I'm bad with names, Sheriff."

Tim smiled. "Okay."

"Wait." He stepped a little closer as he seemed to think about this. "I do remember her name. She asked me not to tell anyone, though. That's how she is sometimes about things."

Tim usually didn't like playing the bad cop. "Is that so?" he asked, suddenly inspired by the undertones in what was being suggested.

Another hand through the hair. Another smile with the intent to insinuate there was something more that Tim didn't know.

Tim looked away. "Anyone else have a name they can give me?"

No one else in the group said a word.

"I guess that's okay, though." He turned to Tracker. "No real harm was done, right Deputy Buck? How about we let them go?"

"It's your call, Sheriff."

"That it is."

"So, we can go?" asked another reporter in the group.

Tim nodded to her, then pointed at four others. "Each of you can hit the door. Make sure you talk with Deputy Buck next time you need to be up here, please."

A few half-hearted thanks began as they started for the end of the hall. The young reporter turned to move with them.

"Not you."

"What?" he shot back.

"Deputy Cardenas over there will take you downstairs. He'll write you up with a notice, and then remove you from the building."

"Remove me?" His tone stepped up several notches. "I'm a freaking journalist, Sheriff. I'm the lead on covering this trial—"

Tim ignored him. He looked to the young deputy. "Cardenas, can you handle this?"

"Yes, sir."

"I'm not being handled by anybody."

Tim stepped toward the reporter, who took two back.

Cha-Cha.

Another step. Another two back.

"Come on, bro, this is—"

Tim's smile widened. "Bro?"

"Tim—I mean, Sheriff."

"What's your name?"

A long pause.

"You want to go for obstruction, too?"

He shook his head. "I figured you knew it already."

Tim shrugged. "I'm bad with names."

"It's Moss."

"Alright, Moss. How about you come see me in a couple of weeks? We'll talk about getting you back in the building before the trial."

He looked away, continuing to shake his head.

"Or not."

"Sure." No eye contact. "I'll be by on the twenty-sixth, Sheriff."

"Make an appointment first."

Tim turned and started toward the courtroom.

28

When the judge took the bench, he did so with the expectation that nothing would go as planned. It was how he really should've approached his entire day, at least from the moment he stood to leave the breakfast table. Showered. Shaved. Dressed for his day. Balk actually *assumed* then, at that moment, that he'd seen the worst of his day. A Divorce was what she wanted. His wife, Donna. She'd told him at breakfast, as he ate the same meal that he ate most mornings. Eggs and bacon. Biscuits. Her sister's peach jam. *A divorce, Donna?* he'd asked. *Yes.* It was all she told him. Which was more than he deserved.

"Good evening, ladies and gentlemen." Balk allowed his voice to sound tired because it—*he*—was tired. "It should be no surprise to anyone that we've had a long day here in this building. I know for many of you who've taken an interest in this matter, that it's been a long day for you as well."

The judge looked down only for a moment at the desk in front of him, lifting from its surface a single sheet of paper—that day's arraignment calendar.

"I'd like to move through this evening's calendar efficiently." Balk turned his eyes to the lawyers first, then the faces out in the gallery. "I'll walk through a few formalities with the representative for the State, and then I'll ask the accused, Senator Collins, to stand for purposes of his arraignment."

At this point in a normal court calendar, the judge usually thanked those who were present—the lawyers, their clients, a handful of family members—then moved forward with the business of the day. However, given the events of *this* day, Balk felt that it seemed more appropriate to expound upon his gratitude.

And shortcomings.

"Thank you all for being here, and I welcome you to this courtroom." Balk hesitated—*there were other ways to do this*—then started to drive forward. "My belief is that this courtroom is open to the public, and I intend to keep it that way for as long as I'm seated up here. The delays that we experienced today probably could've been avoided. But closing the doors to this room, hiding this process from the public—I won't have it. Maybe doing so would've prevented us from being where we are right now, but at what cost?"

Balk knew his answer. It faded in the rearview.

"Now, our judicial system isn't perfect." A satisfied smile crept into his face. "But it has improved over time, and it will continue to do so for as long as we remain steadfast in the pursuit of justice. We must continue this endeavor, without compromise for the sake of convenience or our own self-interests. But for this to remain possible, fervent transparency *has* to remain the court's guiding principle."

Balk surveyed the scenery before him, especially the faces of those seated along the front row. He saw a few who were nodding, acknowledging him, his words.

"Without transparency, the People, the lawyers, and the accused cannot seek justice for *all*, nor vindication for the *few.* The light of transparency isn't meant to only be directed at one corner of this courtroom. To uncover only certain things that might be hiding in this process. No, it's a light that's meant for all of it."

The judge directed his attention to the accused—Senator Bill Collins.

"Even your judge."

The senator looked back at the judge with a curious expression. He seemed to recognize that the judge didn't plan to stop.

"That's right."

Balk waited for the senator to move. Nothing.

"To ensure that there's transparency in this courtroom," the judge added, pushing on, "we must first look to the bench. Because if I'm not completely forthcoming, I shouldn't *expect* to find a courtroom with lawyers, and witnesses, and defendants who respect this process."

The senator finally moved. Leaning over to one side, close to his lawyer's ear, he whispered to her.

"So, in the spirit of fostering transparency in this courtroom, among all of you, I need to offer an apology."

Balk put both hands up for all the room to see. Momentum carried him now.

"A single arraignment—a reading of the indictment, followed by a simple plea of *Guilty* or *Not guilty*—this has been the entire focus of today."

The judge pressed forward. He couldn't turn back. Not now.

"Yet, all the while, I've been struggling with my own guilt. I've been demanding respect for this judicial process, while not being completely transparent myself. I've—" Balk pressed the pedal to the floor. "I've been hiding the fact that—"

Park stood and pulled her client away from the road at the last second. "Your Honor, if I may!"

The young defense lawyer's crisp, confident tone leapt from the version of her that Balk had only been introduced to in the hallway earlier. Quite different than the Park who'd appeared in his courtroom the first time. While she stood tall, waiting for the judge to address her, Balk couldn't help but think about that third version of Ryan Park he'd been introduced to recently. He wondered if she would've made the decision to step in for her client, thus avoiding the carnage. Balk doubted this—as she could've shown the aftermath to her millions of followers.

"You may not, Ms. Park." Balk pointed to her seat at counsel's table. "I'll allow you to address the court when I call Defendant Collins's case. Until then—sit."

"I'd like to speak on—"

"No." Balk replied, calmly. He kept his tone measured. "Now, sit down, please."

The judge turned back to the gallery, ready to resume his confessional of sorts, when another interruption cut in from the same place in the courtroom.

"John, then I'd like to be heard."

29

Maggie turned when she heard the senator interrupt the judge. He was already on his feet, addressing the Honorable John J. Balk in a manner that she'd never seen before. Not in this courtroom. Not in any other. Another *first.*

"Take your seat, Defendant Collins." Balk spoke in a tone that he often used when issuing orders from the bench. Calm, precise language. "This is out of order, and I'll not have your interruptions, or any other person's, interfere with the way that I intend to conduct proceedings in *my* courtroom."

"John, you're not the only one who has a right to be heard in this setting—" the senator's voice wasn't even close to calm.

Balk pointed with the gavel. "I've already instructed you to sit, Defendant Collins. I don't want to hear another word from you until it's appropriate for you to speak again."

The gallery couldn't contain itself at this point. Maggie turned around in her seat and saw that at least half of the spectators were on their feet. Noticeably fewer people remained along the benches, but the majority of those who'd decided to stay were clearly there to support the accused. It seemed it'd been well worth the wait for them because their senator stood defiant, ready to take on the trial judge at the front of the courtroom.

"I won't be muzzled, John!" he yelled. "I'm an innocent man, and I won't be treated as anything less."

Free Bill! called a single voice from somewhere in the gallery. A few of the brazen followed the statement with their own words of encouragement.

"Take that man into custody," the judge said, without pause. He pointed to a spectator in the back who was on his feet, possibly the one who'd called out first in support of Collins. "And that man as well," Balk added, once another man stood to protest. "Arrest that woman right there on the front row," Balk said, pointing almost directly behind Maggie. "All three of those men on the right." Balk didn't raise his voice more than was necessary. "Him. Her." Deputies scrambled as the judge added more arrests. "And those two over there, that's right."

Maggie couldn't believe what she was witnessing. The gallery wasn't close to under control, and the courtroom deputies didn't have enough restraints on them to make all of the arrests. They were openly arguing with people who didn't have any respect whatsoever for their authority. These were law-abiding citizens—which every one of them repeatedly made clear each time a scuffle ensued with law enforcement—and they all seemed more than willing to spend a night in jail if it helped demonstrate their loyalty to the cause. Maggie couldn't tear her eyes away from the scene, but then she heard the judge suddenly direct his words toward defense counsel.

"Ms. Park!" Balk called. "What do you think you're doing?"

Surprised, Maggie turned from the ruckus in the gallery and looked to her opposing counsel. Park was still seated quietly at the defense table. Legal pad in front of her. Laptop on the table. Her client was on his feet, standing in opposition to the process—apparently as some self-proclaimed sentinel for the wackos behind him. But neither the defense lawyer nor the senator seemed to be engaged in otherwise offending conduct. With the gallery on the verge of upheaval, and the accused well beyond contempt of court, Maggie wondered: *Why go after one of the lawyers, Judge?*

The judge remained focused on Park. "Counselor, I asked you a question. What do you think you're doing?"

Park offered nothing.

Maggie almost stood to ask the judge to consider a recess, maybe to reassess his approach and allow the deputies to organize the room. But when Maggie finally lowered her eyes to where the defense lawyer had her hands, she saw the offending item. Park clutched an iPhone in one hand, halfway under her chair.

"I'll have that phone." Balk said this as he pointed to his last available deputy. "Place it on your table, Ms. Park."

Park found her voice. "Cell phones aren't prohibited, Judge."

Maggie agreed with the statement. In fact, her own phone sat right in front of her. It was an essential tool for her practice nowadays. Maggie wasn't using her cell phone to record what went on inside the courtroom, though. She wasn't taking photos or videos, without permission from the judge. Maggie guessed from the judge's reaction that he'd taken time to look at her social media presence. All thanks to a hand-off from her favorite reporter, Ben Moss.

"You don't want to test this issue, Ms. Park." His voice kept an eerie, measured tone to it. Very un-Balk like. "It's within my discretion. Read the courtroom policy on electronic—"

She interrupted. "I'm not giving up my property."

Although the lawyer was being childish, Maggie really wanted to yell: *Judge, take the defendant into custody! He's the instigator. Not his lawyer!* But Maggie didn't want to risk her own rebuke in the judge's current state.

"Counselor, I'll hold you in contempt of court." Balk was leaning over the edge of the bench, pointing a finger down at her. "And if I do, the deputies will inventory your property. So, you can give it up now or—"

"Here." Park slammed the phone on the table. "May I sit?"

"Thank you, Ms. Park." Business as usual. "Please remind your client that he needs to also take his seat."

Park didn't respond to this, but the senator did.

"I'm not going to sit down, John." Unlike almost everyone else around the courthouse at that hour, the senator didn't look like he needed a rest. He looked fresh, energized. "I can't submit to this unlawful process, and I won't submit to the jurisdiction of this court."

Arrest him! Maggie thought, wanting to pull her hair out. *Him, he's the problem.* She was staring up at the bench as she thought this, shifting her eyes back and forth between the judge and the accused. Balk seemed to notice her, but he didn't react. Maggie had never seen anyone in a courtroom act the way that the senator was acting. On top of that, he was adding fuel to the fire by using the language of *unlawful process* and *won't submit* as he opposed the jurisdiction of the court. Maggie recognized the phrasing from a particular firebrand of the citizenry, one that had always been comprised of tin-hats and bumbling anti-government types. It shocked her to hear the senator appropriate some of the same language used by the *Sovereign Citizen,* but it worried her, too. It was a movement that most lawyers laughed at, but it was one that Maggie had always believed could be whittled down and introduced to the masses. All it needed was a little repackaging, rebranding. And if the senator's approach to the charges in the indictment—maybe even his trial, if they made it that far—was taken on from the perspective of the Sovereign, then she might actually find herself in some trouble.

The judge sat quietly at the bench. He'd been waiting with his arms crossed in front of him, staring out at the faces in the gallery. Maggie noticed that it took several minutes for the room to settle, but it was relatively subdued at this point. It seemed they were waiting for the man in the robe to make his decision. If the judge was considering taking a poll as to what to do with the accused, Maggie was ready to cast her vote for a cramped room at the county jail.

Judge: "Defendant Collins, I have only one matter on my calendar this evening. I'm prepared to call your case and allow you to leave this building, on bond, while awaiting your trial."

Accused: "I don't—

Judge: "Wait—please." Balk held up a hand. "I'm not finished."

Accused: "As you were."

Judge: "By my count, I'm holding twelve people in custody for offenses that amount to contempt of court."

Accused: "I'm prepared to be the thirteenth."

Judge: "You won't be."

Accused: "And why's that?" after a long pause.

Judge: "That's because I'm prepared to arraign you in the matter that's on the calendar for today, and then I'm planning to leave for the evening."

Accused: "Go on home, then."

The gallery liked their champion battling in open court. Their *ooohs* and jeers sounded pathetic from where Maggie sat. She couldn't quite grasp what it was that endeared the senator to so many, but the contingent sitting in the courtroom wasn't even a sample size that warranted studying. They'd fallen captive to the idea that he was doing something heroic for all of them. While in reality, Bill Collins was just another politician who required a fervent base. These were the outliers.

Judge: "That's the thing, I can't—"

Accused: "Until you handle my arraignment, I understand."

Judge: "No, not that, Senator." Balk's hand was up again. His face stoic. "See, my wife wants a divorce. In fact, she told me about it this morning at breakfast." He lowered the hand and placed it on his desk. "So, because of that, I've been told not to come back to the house, a place I've called home for the last twenty-five years."

Maggie wasn't sure the room could get any quieter. The judge's words sounded incredibly raw. Even those who'd jeered only moments ago, seemed to recognize what a sad realization this must've been for the man. It seemed cruel for any one of them—including the senator—to delay him in any way from ending what had most likely been the worst day of his life. Maggie waited in that moment with the rest of the room. She could feel the weight of the silence—until the *screech* of a chair on hardwood cut across the courtroom.

Senator Collins sat.

30

"I'm sorry, John."

Balk saw in the man's face that he tried to mean it. He sat now at his table with both hands clasped in front of him, clearly making a concession of some kind. But the judge knew the senator didn't do anything strictly out of kindness, so this act had to be the result of some calculation on his part. Not all that different from Balk's own calculation earlier—one that led him to a decision to resort to playing the game of chicken at the beginning of that evening's calendar.

"I'd like to get this day behind us." Balk spoke in the direction of the accused, but his words were meant for the man's supporters as well. "All of us."

"The State is ready to proceed with the arraignment, Your Honor."

The judge turned to Maggie. He wanted to step down from the bench and hug her. Instead, he nodded his thanks and turned back to the defense lawyer.

"What say the accused, Ms. Park?"

A stillness fell over the room while everyone waited at the edge of their seats, watching as the young attorney leaned close to the senator. The two conferred for a moment. A discussion, certainly. Not just the giving and taking of orders.

"I believe we might be, Your Honor." Balk sensed a request. "But with one condition that my client asks that the court consider. Respectfully, of course."

The judge could tell from Maggie's stance that she wanted to go after this request with a flamethrower. The defendant had no power in this setting. Zero. There wasn't a concession to be made. Not any kind of negotiation to be had. And even if that were the case, this kind of discussion was one meant to take place behind closed doors. Between prosecutor and defense counsel. Not the judge.

"I'll tell you what I'm willing to do, Ms. Park." He leaned back in his chair and looked up at the high ceiling above. "I won't listen to whatever request this is that your client has in mind. It'd be inappropriate for me to do so, and I won't allow it in my courtroom. However—"

Balk returned his gaze to the horizontal, then panned the room until he found the sheriff. The lawman acknowledged him with a nod, calm and composed as he listened from where he stood. The judge took this to mean that their understanding remained unchanged. He shifted his attention back to the lawyers before him.

"I'd like to extend an olive branch instead. Not to your client, Ms. Park, but to the people who've visited Blake County today."

This sounded like something that several in the gallery found interesting, mainly those who had a loved one currently sitting in the holding cell.

"Okay."

"Sheriff Dawson is standing over there on the wall that's to your left," Balk nodded in that direction, "And I imagine he hasn't been able to process everyone in his custody yet, so he might be amenable to allowing those two federally employed agents to catch a ride back home to DC tonight with your client."

Balk felt like a gameshow host as he held a hand up. *But wait, there's more!*

"And with that, I might also be agreeable to dispensing with any further proceedings for those who're now facing contempt matters due to what happened earlier in my courtroom."

Park waited to respond. As the senator whispered in her ear, she started to shake her head.

"Let me add," Balk said, feeling that he needed to close the deal, "If the accused is going to take the position that he *will not submit to the jurisdiction of this court,* then he needs to know that what he's really saying is, *my interests are above those of the people who came to Blakeston to support me.*" Balk lifted his eyes to the gallery. Most of them seemed to now be watching the senator very closely. "Take as much time as you need to consider things."

Park took in a deep breath. "My client wouldn't even consider his own interest over—"

"I know."

The senator waited another moment, then slowly nodded to his lawyer.

"Are we in agreement, then, Ms. Park?"

She stood. "We are, Your Honor."

"Good." Balk smiled. "Let's proceed."

31

Maggie grabbed the folder that Michael Hart had prepared for her. As she left their table and started toward the bench, she caught a look from another local lawyer seated out in the gallery. Jim Lamb, the old head who'd given Maggie her start at the Southwest Circuit's Public Defender's Office, shook his head from a few rows behind the defense table. The sight of her toting that simple, manilla bifold in her hand probably conjured up mixed emotions for her former mentor. Jim called the folders *manilla slims,* and they'd been synonymous with the local DAs office since long before Maggie arrived in Blakeston. Any lawyer who'd done their time as a PD in the circuit remembered what it was like to sit down and negotiate *jail* cases with a prosecutor. They'd slap a pack of *slims* on the table—indictment and plea offer in each—then they'd start negotiating prison sentences. The DAs had too many cases. The PDs had too many clients. No one seemed to have enough time. Once you did the math, it wasn't that difficult to understand how it all worked. Jim considered it his mission to make sure every new lawyer—every defender—understood that criminal defense work didn't have to be that way. And for a time, Maggie had agreed with him.

"I'll call the case," Judge Balk said, once Maggie neared the bench, "Then I'll leave it up to you as to who you'd rather have read the indictment. That's if he doesn't decide to waive."

Maggie noted the instructional tone. "I'll read it, Judge."

"You have it in your file?" he asked, helpful.

Maggie smiled before flipping the thin file open in her hand. She looked down at a copy of the original indictment. It'd been taped to the inside of the slim's front flap. "I have it right here, Judge."

Balk waited for another moment.

Although she wouldn't ever admit it, there were some first-day jitters creeping in before her initial foray as special prosecutor. She knew it wasn't the task of handling the arraignment itself that'd caused them. No, a bailiff could wheel her into the courtroom, still asleep in her bed, and she'd be able to hop right up, ready to handle one for a defense client. But looking at the courtroom from the other side's perspective, with wholly different responsibilities, wracked the nerves a little more than she'd expected.

"I know what you're doing, Judge." Maggie leaned a little closer, winked. "I'm fine. No need to check the saddle."

"I'm doing nothing of the sort."

Maggie nodded to him. It didn't surprise her that the judge was taking a couple of minutes to check on her. It was that area of the courtroom, close to the bench and out of earshot, where judges often coached up the new lawyers. The clerks might listen in, but they were in on helping run the training program. And although it'd been a long time since Maggie's first rodeo, Balk understood that this was a new horse for her.

She planned to hold tight.

"Defendant Collins, please stand."

Maggie was already in place, looking out at the courtroom from the area immediately in front of the bench. Ryan Park, and then her client, stood from their table.

"Again, good evening, Your Honor." Park offered no warmth. "As you know, I'm presently serving as counsel for Senator William H. Collins."

"Yes, thank you, Ms. Park. Are you aware of any housekeeping matters that need to be addressed?"

She paused.

"Aside from the matter of your cell phone, Ms. Park."

"Then no. There are no others, Judge."

Maggie watched Park work, and still just couldn't get a handle on her. She gave the impression inside of a courtroom that she was made of cool steel, but once outside, she sparked on command to a temperature that looked like it'd be dangerous to touch. Maggie wasn't sure which version the defense lawyer would come prepared to present to a jury. Even if Park tried to bring the heat, hopefully it wouldn't have the same effect on people that it did through the social filter.

"Madam Special Prosecutor, I'll hear from you. Any other matters that need addressing?"

When she heard these words, Maggie couldn't help but glance over again to where Jim Lamb sat in the gallery. He wore a faded, battle-tested courtroom suit with no tie. The old gruff didn't smile when he noticed that she looked his way. *No surprise*. Jim claimed for a time to have fully converted Maggie to the cause of indigent defense, but he probably knew deep down that she'd never truly made it through confirmation. Few did. His dogma and strict code of the true believer required selfless commitment to public service. It was a brand of lawyering for those who felt they waged a lifelong campaign against the State. Them against us. Good versus evil. Black or white. Maggie never saw it quite that way.

There was always some grey.

Jim looked away.

"No, Your Honor." Maggie glanced at Park. "I do hope that you return counsel's phone. I only just started following her today."

"I'm sure you do, counselor." Balk's comment spurred a few chuckles in the room. "I take it you're otherwise ready?"

"The State is, Judge."

Maggie noted the time on the wall. *Seven-thirty.*

"I have in hand..." the judge paused as he pulled a sheet of paper from in front of him, "The Blake County Superior Court Arraignment Calendar, for our January term of court." Balk sounded as if a weight lifted with each word that moved him closer to adjournment. "Listed here in position one, is Case Number Twenty-three, *CR*, Eight-eighty-five, *State of Georgia v. William H. Collins.*"

A clerk at a nearby desk hollered. "No waiver, Judge."

Maggie thought it was silly to hear the formality used in these arraignment proceedings, but it was in line with a policy the judge implemented long ago. No formal waiver had been filed. *Although Park tried, gamely.* But had a proper waiver of arraignment been filed in a timely manner, it would've excused the senator's appearance. No waiver meant he had to be present in court, which was what he'd really wanted all along.

Balk micromanaged. "Check the entry, ma'am."

Maggie turned back to the gallery as she waited for the clerk to confirm the next of their silly formalities. She glanced at Jim, again. He sat next to another man in a suit, one who seemed to have just joined him. He was younger than Jim and much flashier. They looked like the odd couple seated there together, quietly chatting away about something of particular interest to them both.

"I've reviewed the file, Your Honor," the clerk said, after finding what she needed. "Ms. Ryan Park, Esquire, does in fact have on file her entry of appearance." She paused. "Along with another lawyer—a Mr. Thomas K. Hackett."

Maggie turned to the clerk. "Who?"

Park answered for the woman. "Tom Hackett. Out of Boston."

Maggie nodded, trying not to show her frustration.

"Very well, thank you, Madam Clerk." Balk said this without any mention of the new lawyer. "Defendant Collins, please step forward."

As the accused started toward the bench, Maggie eased over to her own table. Michael Hart had looked comfortable all day in his role as a potted plant, but it didn't surprise her that he looked distracted when she approached. Maggie leaned down close and pulled his legal pad over to her.

"What is it?" he asked as she took the pad.

"The second defense lawyer, Mike." She flipped a few pages in his legal pad, looking for a blank sheet. "Do you know his—"

She stopped. The page wasn't blank. Only three lines at the top. Black ink. Maggie's heart pounded. She flipped on.

"Here." Hart reached for the pad. "Give it to me, I'll write the name down."

The creep's letters had a flare to them. Not the language. No. It was in the way he wrote the actual letters themselves. They each tailed off in the same distinct manner, like those three lines inside of Hart's pad.

"Does the State need another moment?" asked the judge. He spoke to her back. "My understanding was that you were prepared to move this along?"

"I'm—" Maggie stopped. Took one beat, then turned to face the judge. She stepped toward the bench. "I mean, we're ready."

Hart whispered to her. "The pad."

Maggie kept walking away.

"Hold on, Maggie," he hissed. "I need it back."

Maggie stopped where she stood, a few feet more from the table. She scribbled a name on the pad.

T.K. Hackett.

32

The judge called over to the special prosecutor once more.

"If there isn't a problem, counsel, then let's move this along."

Maggie spoke, still with her eyes on her legal pad. "There's not, Judge."

He watched as she wrote something more on the yellow paper. When she looked up from the pad, her face seemed to have lost some color. Usually, when the judge asked one of the lawyers whether there was a problem, it didn't have much to do with the wellbeing of that man or woman. It had to do with the flow of matters in his courtroom. *Usually.*

"You're sure everything's okay?" the judge asked.

Balk knew he couldn't pull the question back. No, he could only wait—for Maggie, Park, and about every other woman in the room, to finish their collective shake-of-the-head. Hoping for a merciful reply, he watched as Maggie turned and pitched the legal pad in bizarre fashion. The yellow sheets of paper fluttered like a winged Bobwhite, eventually falling short of the table reserved for the prosecution. Balk didn't dare ask his question a second time.

"*I am.*" Maggie smiled as she left the pad where it lay, walking toward the bench. "Thank you, though."

Balk cleared his throat.

"Okay, Senator Collins, this is your arraignment. I know that you have counsel standing with you, so I don't expect you to speak unless it is your desire to do so."

The senator nodded.

"Now, I've reviewed the calendar, along with a copy of the indictment. It appears they are in order, and that both were provided to you before today's proceedings."

Ryan Park noted her response for the record. Nothing for her client.

"Your Honor, I was handed a copy of both items, *today*."

The judge turned to Maggie.

"Madam Special Prosecutor, can you confirm that appropriate notice was provided earlier than today to the accused?"

Maggie pulled a thin file from under her arm.

"Of course, Your Honor."

Balk had little doubt that what he wanted memorialized from the proceedings seemed like overkill to most, but he'd never been seriously questioned about his impartiality in any case. *Ever.* But when that day arrived, he hoped he'd be around to answer those questions himself. And if he wasn't—he'd at least have the transcript to help answer for him.

Maggie continued. "It should be noted that Ms. Park was only handed copies of the indictment and calendar, *today*, because no one in the DA's office knew she was even involved in the case." A pause. "In fact, it appears Ms. Park only informed us of her involvement *after* she'd gone ahead and told her millions of followers that she planned to be here today."

The judge only motioned that Maggie move it along.

"Eight-forty in the evening, on December 8." A document crept from the manilla file in her grasp. "This is the entry of service, from last year. Notice of today's proceeding, a copy of the original indictment, and a spoliation letter—all served on the defendant." She held the document out in front of her. "May I approach?"

The judge nodded. He leaned forward to collect the paper.

"Manner of service?"

The judge had not yet looked at the document. Park interjected.

"Intrusive and unnecessary, Your Honor."

The special prosecutor spoke before the judge could entertain Park's theatrics.

"Personal service, Your Honor. Provided in a manner that is consistent with the laws in Georgia, and those in the District of Columbia."

Balk shook his head at both ladies, then turned his attention on the senator.

"Senator Collins, your counsel indicates that a copy of the original indictment in your case has been provided to her, and the State has provided me with sufficient proof to suggest you were personally served in this matter." Balk glanced quickly to the document, then back to the accused. "In December of last year."

The senator looked to his counsel, then spoke.

"That's right, Your Honor. I was ambushed with it during my staff Christmas party." He turned to look at Maggie. "A simple phone call and an email will be just fine in the future."

The judge dispensed his standard warning.

"Address the bench with your comments, please."

Park added her bit.

"It was inappropriate, Judge."

Balk only pressed forward in an even tone.

"Your outrage is so noted." He pushed the document aside, then folded his hands in front of him. "Now, Senator, you're entitled to a public reading of the accusations in this indictment. Do you wish to exercise this right or would you like to waive it?"

Park answered for him without any need to confer.

"My client maintains they are false allegations, and it's his desire that they be read aloud."

Balk nodded.

"Very well. We'll address your client's plea after, then."

Park had more.

"Along with his demand for a speedy trial."

The judge kept his eyes on Park, while pointing over at the special prosecutor.

"In due time, counsel. Now, is there any objection to the State handling the reading of the indictment?"

Park leaned close to her client for a moment. Nodding, listening to what was whispered in her ear.

"To clarify, would my client object to Maggie Reynolds reading these false allegations in open court?"

Frustrated, the judge leaned to look over one side of the bench.

"Madam court reporter, strike defense counsel's last question from the record."

The senator spoke before the judge could turn to reprimand his young lawyer.

"Maggie can read it, Your Honor. In fact, I'd prefer it."

33

Maggie opened the slim folder once more. She drew her three-page indictment from inside it, like an arrow from a quiver. Her target stood no less than ten feet from her. Turning just a bit, to make sure that the senator could see her, Maggie felt the twinge of another *first.*

The opening shot.

Maggie began. "May it please the court—"

The judge leaned back in his chair, comfortable, it seemed, with the fact that his day was almost over.

"I have in hand, a two-count *criminal* indictment." She lifted it up, pausing for the gallery behind her to get their looksee from afar. "In each count therein, Defendant William H. Collins is named as the lone defendant."

Maggie felt the emotion swell. *Pride.* An unexpected kind, and different from that which she'd grown accustomed to. The pride that she knew best was the type that generated expectations, self-importance. Her role as special prosecutor certainly carried with it expectations, but it was one that also demanded a unique responsibility. Maggie took pride in this. *Surprising.* Given her own self-image—one she'd crafted and built around defending people who'd been accused by the government. One might think that the pride Maggie held for her newfound responsibility—a by-product of her about-face, no question—should've juxtaposed that sense of self. *It didn't.* Instead, the indictment in Maggie's hands fit neatly on the shelf she'd set aside for her accomplishments. She'd traversed an enormous hurdle for her clients—the Ackers—by hijacking an almost exclusive function of the executive branch—criminal prosecution. And with the tools of the government in play, Maggie was beginning to view the power they held differently. She was beginning to view the people who wielded them, differently. It was they who had a responsibility. It was they who had the burden. And Maggie took pride in the fact that it was now hers to own.

Maggie tiptoed into a bit of grandstanding. "A true bill, this indictment was returned in open court on Friday, December 1, 2024." She let herself move a little, loosening up her trial muscles. "All grand jurors who engaged in the deliberations were properly qualified, then administered their oath." She pointed the senator toward the rows at the front of the gallery. "Blake County citizens heard testimony in this very room, from the very witnesses that you'll find at the top of page two in this document."

The witness list offered little information, but it read like a set of directions through Maggie's past. The waypoints in a life that she'd never planned on returning her to Blakeston, planted for so long. Her work with the local public defender wasn't supposed to be anything more than a resume builder, a steppingstone to a bigger, grander life. But then the Lee Acker trial came along—her first shot at a title. And it gave her a chance to go in search of that better life—for a time—but Blake County kept calling. Homesick for a place she wasn't from, Tim convinced her that she could find what she wanted anywhere. Convinced her that she could find that feeling of purpose, anywhere. Maggie thought about this a moment, staring at Tim's name at the top of the witness list. *He was right.*

Witnesses:

1. Tim Dawson, Blake County Sheriff's Office.
2. Grace Acker, individual.
3. Cliff Acker, individual.
4. George Dell, individual.
5. José Valdez, individual.
6. Alex Olivera Calderon, individual.

7. Kelvin Ramirez, Houston County Sheriff's Department.
8. Kevin Bond, Blake County Sheriff's Office.
9. Charlotte Acker, individual.
10. Lawton Crane, individual.
11. Liam Hudson, individual.
12. Colt Hudson, individual.
13. Deacon Campbell, individual.
14. Charlie Clay, individual.
15. Cam Abrams, Georgia Bureau of Investigation.

"For purposes of the record," Maggie said, "I'm directing the defendant and his counsel to the second page of the indictment." Maggie turned the page. "There you will see the allegations, numbered as counts one and two."

Maggie had crafted an indictment with only the heaviest of allegations. She could've pursued more, under RICO statutes and other devices prosecutors held in their arsenal. Doing so had become the expectation, in fact. Indictments included the meat, then layered on plenty of ticky-tack violations—the *malum prohibitum*—thus providing cushion for negotiations and increasing the likelihood of a conviction at trial. But Maggie didn't want a backstop, and her clients had asked for only the unforgivable—the *malum in se*. And the heaviest of sins were certainly there, right at the top of page two. Maggie stared at the first: *Count One—Conspiracy to Commit a Crime, to wit: the MURDER of Lucy Kelley Collins.* Then, close to the bottom of that same page, began the second: *Count Two—Conspiracy to Commit a Crime, to wit: the MURDER of John A. Deese.* The substance of the allegation ran through to the following page.

Maggie cleared her throat, then directed her voice at the senator.

"As to Count One, the Grand Jurors aforesaid, in the name and behalf of the citizens of Georgia, do charge and accuse William H.—"

"Wait!" Collins held up a hand. "I need you to give me a moment, please. Can you do that?"

Maggie nodded slowly at the act. She waited a moment, as requested, then began again.

"The citizens of Georgia do charge and accuse William H. Collins with the offense of conspiracy to commit a crime, to wit, the Murder of Lucy Kelley—"

"Hold on!" Collins sounded even more distressed now. He put his head in his hands. "I'm going to need another moment."

Maggie stared at the man. She felt herself beginning to stew at the sight of him. Probably a good thing, since his victims were who she was really supposed to have in mind. *All of them.* Maggie liked to think that Lucy Collins and John Deese—both unlikable in the small moments they'd shared together—might actually be delighted by the selection of Maggie as their advocate. They were the victims in this case, and the senator ended their lives to ensure his own survival. Today, Maggie wanted him to hear about it, maybe even cause a question to percolate somewhere in the back of his mind. *Will my knack for self-preservation prevail?* Maggie wanted him to question it, and his decisions. For the Ackers. For Lucy. Even for John.

"Okay." Maggie sighed. "Ms. Park, let me know when your client is ready."

Park stepped across Maggie's path without acknowledging the words. "Judge, would you permit a brief break for my client?"

"No, Ms. Park." Balk looked at both the defense lawyer and her client. "This is it, right now. The indictment will be read aloud for you, or you can review it later at your leisure."

"I can't listen to her speak, Judge." The senator wasn't looking at Maggie. "I won't take this kind of slander in my hometown. Not from some out-of-towner. No, sir."

Maggie couldn't believe it. She was certain that this was exactly how little Charlie must've felt each time he tried to kick that football. *Whiff!* But she could feel it, her moment being ripped away all the same. And with her nice running start, she'd fall, just like Charlie. A good, public fall.

"I won't have it." The senator said again, shaking his head. "Not here."

Balk slowly glanced over to Maggie.

"No way, Judge." Maggie protested. "The defendant asked for this, and he can't—"

"Yes, he can."

That's all he said.

34

The judge thought about stepping down from the bench, for good. *Y'all can have it*, he'd say, while leaving for the main doors. *I'm done with this case. I'm done with this robe. Adios.* But he knew that wasn't possible. Not yet. The senator had proven to the judge, along with anyone else who'd been paying attention around the courthouse, that he was capable of tipping the scales in whatever way he liked. Even if Balk really wanted to walk, he knew the politician would find a way to drag the judge back into the fray. No, he wasn't leaving—no one was—until the senator said so.

"Now, as to the matter of obtaining the defendant's plea." Balk allowed the statement to drift, waiting there for the man who pulled the strings. "I see no reason we shouldn't move forward."

The senator only nodded.

"Good," Balk said, glancing down at his copy of the indictment. He then turned to speak over the side of his desk, toward his clerk. "Madam Clerk?"

"I'm already on it, Judge."

The original indictment waited in the clerk's file. Once a defendant entered their plea—*not guilty* or *guilty*—the clerk would then have the accused sign the original indictment. This signature on the charging instrument served an important purpose because it ensured that the accused had in fact received notice of the allegations being made by the government. It also provided the defendant with a chance to see who it was that'd played a crucial role in the bringing of their charges. Co-defendants. Witnesses. Grand jurors. Prosecutors. Defense lawyers. These names all appeared together on an indictment. Even in a modern world, where email and e-signatures sufficed for billion-dollar business deals, this requirement that the defendant ink the indictment himself—an arcane holdover from the Founders—was still one meant to *hopefully* prevent nefarious conduct by those in positions of power.

"My clerk over here is going to get the original indictment from her file, Senator." Balk spoke to the man in that moment the way he spoke to any defendant at their arraignment, like a third grader. "She'll place it on that table beside you. Then, once you've entered your plea on the record, she'll have you sign and date it. Understood?"

"Let's get on with it, Judge."

Balk nearly laughed at this. Instead, he started through the very dry procedure of addressing each individual count in the indictment. "Okay, Defendant Collins, as to *Count One* in the indictment, Conspiracy to Commit a Crime, that is, the offense of Murder, how do you plead?"

"Not guilty."

"As to Count Two in the indictment, Conspiracy to Commit a Crime, again as such, the offense of Murder, how do you plead?"

The senator took a long pause, and Balk, along with probably almost everyone else in the courtroom, slid to the edge of his seat.

"I'm not guilty, Judge." Bill said this with a face that hinted he might have his first little request for the judge to consider. "But—I'd like to deal with this case in an efficient, expeditious manner."

Balk nodded at this, thinking. He waited as the clerk placed the original indictment on a desk beside the senator. The senator slowly turned, then signed it to complete the first step in the process.

"The plea is entered, Your Honor."

Balk half-thought the courthouse personnel who remained in the room might start slapping hands, congratulating one another for surviving the day. The moment, though, felt as inconsequential as it always did. It was a routine matter that should never have brought on the kind of hysteria that'd transpired. *For what purpose,* he wondered, *and to what end?*

The senator cleared his throat. "I'd like to discuss the scheduling of my trial, Your Honor."

"Your attorney will receive a notice with all those predetermined dates for this term of court.

Balk spoke directly to the senator. "I believe she intends to make a demand for a speedy trial, so I'd let her advise you—"

"Ms. Park will be handing everything over to Mr. Hackett." The senator turned and pointed toward the gallery, a few rows back on the defense side of the room. A well-dressed man nodded back at this from his seat, one next to a local lawyer who Balk knew well. "He'll be filing the formal motions and all, but I assumed that with the special prosecutor here, and Mr. Hackett, that we all might come to an understanding today."

Balk paused at the suggestion.

Collins pushed on. "It's like I always say, Judge, good understandings make for long friendships."

"This is inappropriate, Senator."

"My wanting to know when the trial is going to be set for?" Sounding incredulous. "My wanting to accommodate you, my lawyer, me—"

"I'm happy to oblige, Judge." Maggie stepped a little closer to the bench. It was just her and the senator beside one another, with Park easing away. "And I like to work fast," Maggie added, "so let's set it for trial."

Balk didn't like this one bit. He shook his head at Maggie. She knew better. The defendant was entitled to receive all of his discovery in the case today, then had a ten-day window to file any pre-trial motions. These were meant to challenge certain issues, preserve items for appeal—the list went on and on. And that window of time didn't even apply to motions *in limine* and other items that might need to be dealt with once all of his pre-trial rulings had been made.

The judge sighed. "Senator, I'll schedule a status conference to discuss this."

"Why the delay?" he asked, raising an eyebrow.

Balk couldn't. "Have Ms. Park reach out to my office."

"Ms. Park is no longer formally involved." He smiled, a curt reminder. "However, Mr. Hackett over there is in total agreement with this course of action."

The judge looked out at the attorney in the gallery. He appeared attentive to the matter, even from where he waited.

"Mr. Hackett?" Balk called over. "Please step inside the bar and approach the bench."

He stood. "Of course, Your Honor."

The gallery took notice of the Boston accent immediately. The impeccably dressed attorney dropped his *Rs* hard, making *course* sound like *'carse,* and *honor* sound like *'anar.* Nothing remotely close to the southern parlance most of the region's lawyers leaned into when arguing inside the area's courtrooms. This contrast also drew even more attention to the senator's not-so-subtle roster change. One suited up lawyer walked through the gate at the bar, while another finely polished attorney packed up her briefcase at the defense table. It was that *Clean out your locker* moment, and all the fans seemed to just move on with the new configuration of their team.

"Good evening, Your Honor." He reached a hand high to shake the judge's. Silver cufflinks peeked out from under the edges of his azure blue jacket. "I'm Tom Hackett. I'll be stepping in for *BC*."

The senator placed a hand on his lawyer's back. "Thank you for coming, *TK*."

The judge watched the new lawyer. Although he sounded far from home, he knew the appropriate order of business for an unfamiliar courtroom. He followed his introduction to the judge with a polite, professional one for the special prosecutor. Then he turned to briefly acknowledge the nearby clerks, court reporter, and closest courtroom deputy.

"Mr. Hackett, your client has asked to discuss the potential scheduling of his trial."

Hackett nodded, listening quietly with the senator at his side. At the rear of the courtroom, Ryan Park was just as quiet as she slipped out through the main doorway.

"And as you probably know, these matters can be hard to predict at this early stage. I'll have the official notice mailed to your office and it'll include my trial dates for this term."

Hackett smiled. "Your Honor, you'll have to excuse my client. He doesn't realize your courtroom isn't Washington."

The judge liked the man's opinions already.

Hackett continued. "Me, personally, I'm all set with what's been done today. If we can't specifically set it for a certain date, given opposing counsel's schedule or the court's, there'll be another day to—"

"It's not that." Maggie stepped in. "I'm ready next week."

Hackett whistled. "I don't know about that."

Balk nodded to his new ally. "This place can certainly move faster than most small towns, Mr. Hackett. I've never once heard our special prosecutor use those exact words from your side of the aisle, though."

Maggie offered a grin. "I'm newly reformed, Judge."

"That's what I hear." Hackett leaned away from the senator, whispering not so quietly toward Maggie. "But I'm told you'll still be a bit of a pissah."

Maggie laughed. The judge saw that her new adversary had the endearing qualities that made trial work enjoyable for the lawyers who worked against each other.

"Unless we have a more realistic proposal," the judge finally added, "it's hard to do anything more today."

"How does four weeks sound?" asked Hackett without pause. "I have an entire two weeks open, and that's plenty of time for me to get ready."

Maggie took her cell phone out.

"I don't know, Mr. Hackett." Balk said this as he waited for Maggie to add something more. "That seems awfully quick."

"I'll be ready, Judge." Maggie said this as she looked up. She knew that Balk liked to start his longer trials on Tuesdays, if possible. "That would be starting trial on Tuesday, February 13."

The senator added his wishes. "The sooner, the better."

The judge knew that it would take weeks for the dust to settle after the day's events, and he couldn't even begin to think about what potential controversies might surround the trial itself. Although it appeared the politician's forecasting, when it came to Maggie's willingness to move forward at a record pace, had been sourced from solid data. *But what did the senator gain from that strategy?* He mulled this over for another moment. *And what did Maggie possibly have that he wanted the jury to hear about?*

Balk shook his head. "I'll consider it."

"Thank you, Your Honor," Hackett quickly replied. His client looked unhappy at his side. "Does this conclude the day's business?"

Balk looked at Maggie. "Unless there's anything to add from the State?"

"No, Judge. Thank you for considering our request."

He looked back at Hackett. "And nothing from the defense?"

"No, Your Honor."

"Okay—"

"When will *I* know about the trial?" asked the senator.

Balk stopped himself before he said something he'd regret. Neither lawyer added anything to suggest they didn't want to know the answer themselves, though. Before the judge could collect his thoughts, the senator asked again.

"John?"

"A trial in four weeks?" Balk shot back, his tone ragged. "That's really what you want?"

A diplomatic smile at this. "If the court would be so inclined."

"Four weeks it is, then." Balk growled. "You're excused."

The judge turned and looked out on the courtroom. He didn't care to add any remarks for the remaining agitators in the gallery. Or the media. He imagined he'd soon see them all again.

Wham! Wham!

"We're adjourned."

INTERLUDE

Quitman County, Georgia
Georgetown

"How was the drive up?"

A latch behind the screen rattled, then a spring creaked, expanding with the flimsy door that opened away from the porch. The judge held it open with one hand. He extended the other for a handshake.

Ben Moss took it. "Not too bad, sir. I took thirty-nine the whole way."

The judge waved him through and onto the porch, before letting the door loose. *Clack*! Its sound left the porch and started for the lake. The judge stood there with him, looking out to where it faded. Morning sun and calm water. Eventually, Alabama.

"Be careful heading that way at night." The big man pointed to a truck just off the porch, its smashed headlight and nineties-something grill bent in. "Big buck got me on it late last Thursday. A few miles out of Fort Gaines."

Ben only nodded at this. He didn't know much about trucks. Deer.

"Come on."

The judge pointed to a doorway on the inside wall of the porch. Ben followed him through it and into the kitchen.

"I'm out of coffee. And unless it's Sunday, while my wife's at church, I don't go into town. Divorce lawyer told me not to."

"I'm not big on coffee."

"No?"

"No, not really." Ben said this as he glanced around at the dated kitchen. Plates in the sink. Two folded up thirty-packs. Otherwise, clean. "I'm not a Mormon or anything," looking back to the judge.

"Name a great newspaper man who is."

"Brannan."

"Who?" he laughed.

Ben smiled. "I thought we might be doing a Jeopardy thing."

"It was going to be a joke." He shook his head. "Damn, son."

"Yeah?"

"Yeah." A wave of his hand. "But it won't be funny now."

"Probably not." Ben grinned. "Who said I wasn't joking?"

They stood there, still in the man's kitchen. The casual judge in his jeans stared back at him, until he finally started to chuckle.

"Was it an old guy joke?"

"You told me you wanted to talk about retiring."

The judge nodded at this. Ben didn't see a man that looked comfortable with the idea.

"You're right, Moss. That I did."

They sat on red Adirondack chairs.

"I'm going to record this."

"That's fine." The judge chewed his cigar. "I'll take a copy."

Ben placed his phone on the table between their chairs. He added preliminaries. The sound of an outboard hummed. Water lapped against the dock below them.

"Why did you choose the law?"

He smiled. "It was just an aspiration. No real reason other than that."

Ben sat on the question. The judge lit the cigar.

"I was the proverbial country boy, and back then the folks from that part of Blake had a whole lot less than they have now. My mother and father both worked to make ends that rarely met, but stuck it out to watch a son finish high school. Then college."

He puffed.

"I applied to law school, and they took me. That was that. It wasn't anything inspirational that happened."

"It was financial, then?" Ben asked.

Balk sort of laughed.

"So, it wasn't?"

"How old are you, Moss?"

"I'll be twenty-seven next week."

"You seem pretty sharp." He smiled. "*I*, however, didn't have a lick of sense when I was your age."

"But you were a lawyer by twenty-seven?"

"Of course." He waved a hand, clearing smoke that lingered. "I was on my way to being a fine one, too, but smarts and sense aren't the same."

"I'm sitting at your lake house, Judge. It seems like those financials eventually worked out."

The judge didn't respond. And Ben didn't push, yet. They had all day to look at the lake.

"I guess they did, Moss." Definite melancholy. "But what I'm saying is, of course my twenty-something mind saw the law as a financial decision. That's what we all see at that age. And I was worse off than most—not because I came up poor—but because I was *certain* about the things in my life. I thought I knew all about it. *I didn't*."

Ben nodded, listening.

"Which isn't to say I didn't have some wonderful surprises. It's been a privilege—write that—but becoming a small-town lawyer shouldn't ever be a financial decision."

"So, what kind of decision should it be?"

"Not financial." He laughed.

Ben stayed with it. More ash grew from the cigar. A bass boat soon eased by, sparkling.

"See, the young lawyers I meet—" He paused to wave at the fishermen. "They tend to already be hard-working, competitive to some degree. People who like to win, you know? They think they'll go to a town and make a million dollars like that." He snapped his fingers. "And some do, eventually."

"Is that a bad thing?" Ben asked.

"Don't be coy with me, Moss."

Ben smiled. "The boring answer is that those young lawyers won't ever be happy. Right? Blah, blah. That's a piece you can get anyone to write. The money comes, the money goes. Some lawyers leave, some lawyers stay. Find happiness..."

"My Sunday school class would like it."

"She's getting that in the divorce."

"Don't get too smart, Moss."

He snubbed the cigar, but Ben didn't think the judge was done talking. Not yet.

"I looked into you, Judge. Forty years in the profession. Fourteen in private, then twenty-six on the bench. You got over the money, and found something else to sustain you, right?"

"You want me to tell young lawyers it'll get better." He sighed. "Is that the angle?"

Ben shook his head. "Hell no."

"Good. Then what is it?"

"I want my story to be about why *you* stayed, Judge."

PART II

THE TRIAL

35

DAY ONE

Maggie stared at the line of binders. All were red with color-coded sections inside that met her meticulous, and rather specific, trial-prep technique. Maggie was the first to tell a new attorney that they *had* to be willing to improvise once they planted their feet in front of the jury box. And she felt that the attorneys who *really* tried cases for a living—the ones who just couldn't live without it—that they embraced a similar philosophy. Because there reached a point in every trial when one just had to flow with it. A time when the best just reacted in the moment, riffing to the music that only they could hear playing in the room. It was an artform for those who were of this mindset—without question.

But *trying* cases wasn't like *preparing* cases. And anyone who planned to sit with Maggie at trial had to understand the distinction between the two. Because when it came time to prepare a case for the courtroom, there was no flow. No art to speak of. It was an exact science for Maggie, one with a trial-prep technique that she'd developed through trials and countless errors. It was the only way, and she knew what worked best.

No one else.

From where Maggie stood, she could already tell that someone had been through her binders the night before. *I swear to Clarence freaking Darrow.* Maggie took a deep breath in. *I'll kill him.* She turned for the door.

"Mike!" she shouted. The sound of her voice disappeared into the quiet hallway, one that connected to most of the offices in the DA's suite. She took another step, out into the cluttered back space of the offices, waiting for him to poke his head out from inside one of the doorways along the hall. "Mike Hart!"

No answer.

She shook her head, then glanced at her watch. *Seven-forty-five.* No one was in the suite yet, and she only had a little over an hour before they began their first day of trial. Maggie started back into where the binders were set up to grab her cell phone. *No one else would've been in here last night.* She picked up her cell phone from the table. *This is different than before.* Which it was, certainly. But still, she'd torn down the road of making rash assumptions about Hart once already. And while him messing with her trial folders wasn't the same as her accusing him of being that little note-leaving creep, it wouldn't look good to be wrong again.

Still, she unlocked her phone. Found his contact. Pressed call.

Ring, ring, ring. Voicemail.

Maggie immediately started calling again. While she waited, she glanced around her tiny office space and it reminded her that *he'd* done her wrong, too. She knew it was counter-productive to replow old territory in her mind, but it still made her angry. She and Hart had a deal, before Maggie took on the role of special prosecutor. *In writing, no less!* With terms that clearly stated that she'd be permitted to conduct *all* business (e.g. investigation, preparation, negotiation, *basically insert any term ending in -ation*) wherever she so pleased. Expansive language, certainly, but it was an important part of the deal. Maggie was at her best when she worked and prepared in her own law office—Reynolds Law—a building that was only two blocks from the courthouse. Maggie's preferred space for trial prep operations, though, couldn't have felt farther away on that morning.

Voicemail, again.

She hit the button once more, thinking still about the reneging on the agreement. *No, no,* everyone who knew the rules at *PAC*—the Prosecuting Attorney's Council of Georgia—got together and picked her and Hart's agreement apart. They'd insisted that it was absolutely imperative that the work of the special prosecutor remain untainted—thus separate from the work of her law practice. They handed her a crappy little office, tucked in the back of the second-floor DA's suite, then followed their decision up with an email that stated: *Reynolds Law is off-limits for all matters dealing with State v. Collins. Happy hunting, counselor.*

Maggie stood in her windowless office. Phone pressed to her ear. The call connected.

"Where's the fire?" Mike asked.

"Where're you?" she shot back. "Because I'm standing in my little closet office—oh, I don't know—getting ready to meet with the judge and pick a jury in the courtroom next door."

"Take it easy, Maggie." He sounded calm, probably well rested, too. "I'm pulling into a spot by the building now."

"Were you in the files after I left last night?"

Silence, then a car door slammed on the other end of the line.

"Mike?"

His tone changed on a dime. "Are we really doing this again?"

"Look, this is different, and I've apologized for—"

"How many times do I need to tell you?" he cut back. "I'm not trying to sabotage this case, Maggie."

"What was I supposed to do, Mike?" she yelled back into the phone. "That creep's handwriting was in your legal pad. We both saw it!"

"And *my* handwriting was on all the other pages, but instead of considering that, you just preferred to jump right to assuming I was some kind of freak-o stalker."

"I'm sorry, Mike."

"Right." He laughed. "Then quit accusing me of this shit."

Maggie paused. She wanted to tell him that this was a different issue, again, but he didn't give her time.

"Forget it. I'm heading up."

Click.

36

DAY ONE

9:45 a.m

The judge pulled into his designated parking space alongside the courthouse. *He was late.* And in between the swipes of the windshield wipers, he tried to tell if one of the courthouse deputies waited for him under the nearby portico. He pulled his cell phone out from inside his jacket and dialed courthouse security. Pressing the phone hard to one ear, all he could hear was the sound of worn rubber on the glass, kicking back-and-forth, back-and-forth. But even the wipers couldn't overpower the noise from the heavy rain. It'd been that way for the last twenty minutes, since he'd crossed the county line at Blake's northern edge. Pounding the roof, blurring his windshield, making it nearly impossible to make up for lost time.

"Dadgummit," he muttered as the call went unanswered.

Balk turned as best he could, then reached over the back of the seat. As he started to pick through the cluttered mess in the rear of the truck cab, he tried to remember the last time it'd been cleaned out. *Maybe last summer?* Which was probably about right, because up until a few weeks ago, the '98 Chevy had been *just* the family's lake wagon. And during those weekends spent together on the lake, the Balks—plural, then—had used the truck for little more than hauling the boat around the area, maybe an occasional ride into town. *Not anymore, though.* Balk—just the one—now spent *all* his nights at the lake, and the Chevy had become his daily driver.

"Dadgummit," he said again, louder. No umbrella.

The judge cursed his wife as he turned back around in his seat. He knew that his favorite golf umbrella was right where he'd left it, neatly tucked under the driver's seat of his Lexus. But the sedan was probably still in the garage at their house, right where he'd parked it. *A stupid mistake.* One he'd made a few weeks ago. His wife had called him, needing to borrow the Lexus. *Her car was in the shop.* Balk dropped it by the house that next morning, a Tuesday. Parked it in the garage for her and left without saying another word. She filed her divorce action that Wednesday.

Balk smiled. His wife had pulled one of those same tricks he dismissed on an almost weekly basis, in *other* couples' divorces. *Settle down, Mr. Smith,* he'd say, *your wife may be divorcing you, but she's not conspiring to do "X" with the intention of deceiving the court.* But Balk knew that Donna had in fact done just that. And it was the phone call that gave her away, the one when she'd asked to borrow his Lexus. It'd sounded so sweet on his ears that day. Too sweet. *Of course,* he'd replied, their courtship salvageable. Already having been sent to Siberia, he was living up at the lake for an indefinite period of time. The truck was already there. *I'll just drive the Chevy, Donna.* Smiling through the phone. *It'll do the wagon some good to run a little bit.*

And run the Chevy had—lake to courthouse—with plenty of windshield time for the judge to ponder whether she'd really taken his Lexus just to spite him. Having listened to him complain night after night at dinner, his incessant talk about the underhanded games that muddied his divorce court days. It'd probably just been something she felt needed to be done, out of obligation, for the betterment of the legal profession.

Knock! Knock!

Balk turned at the sound. A deputy stood outside the truck. Umbrella and a rain slicker. The judge motioned for him to back up, then swung the door open.

"You're late!" was the first thing the deputy said.

Balk didn't want to clock anyone that early in the day. Instead, he thanked the man, then kept his mouth shut while they walked along together under the one-man umbrella. As they hustled toward the courthouse, Balk thought again about the deputy's remark. The judge couldn't remember a time when he'd arrived late on the first day of a trial. In fact, he was almost certain that he'd never been late on any day of trial in his forty years of practice.

Never.

Balk wasn't one to believe in omens, karma, or anything that far-out. But he did believe in the *yips,* thanks to the Fall Classic of ninety-six. And a bad case came on suddenly, and it wasn't something that one shook off in a day.

37

DAY ONE

10:00 a.m

The judge started into the courtroom from his usual side door. He found the large room as expected, nearly empty. He could feel the energy beginning to build in the nearby hallway, though. It was starting to fill with activity in the arrival of potential jurors, those who'd been summoned to serve in the upcoming trial—*State v. Collins.* Each would've received a notice in the mail, explaining the basics. What to wear. What not to say. Where to be. And what time to be there—ten-thirty.

Balk glanced at his watch. The jurors wouldn't be allowed inside for another thirty minutes, hardly enough time for what he needed to accomplish with those who were already seated in the courtroom. They weren't jurors, though. They were the parties, along with their lawyers. And they were waiting on him to begin the morning's status conference. After all, it was one that he'd demanded they all appear for—at nine-thirty.

"Good morning to you all," the judge said, taking his place at the bench. "We need to be quick, but I'll allow each of you to give me one lashing for my tardiness."

The group offered smiles, but the judge could tell from their faces that the tension of the day weighed heavily.

"I do apologize to each of you," he continued, running a hand through his drying hair. "Let's just say that it has been a morning."

They offered nods, almost in concert, but no complaints whatsoever. The judge knew his own tardiness could've been avoided. Still, he'd raked lawyers over the coals many times for being late to his courtroom. Their lack of regard for the time was usually treated as a serious affront, when he really knew that most had just made the same kinds of mistakes he had that morning. Forgetting to check the fuel level in the Chevy added ten minutes. His dress socks weren't fully dried, which added another five. The rain—*did you see that rain, Your Honor?*—made for a longer than expected commute into Blakeston. *No factor* was what he always told the lawyers who arrived late with excuses. *No. Factor.* It was a strict approach that he applied easily to others, while apparently not himself. And this was something the judge had not questioned himself about in a long time...

And there was no excuse.

The judge looked down at his notes for a moment. Neither party seemed interested in engaging with the bench.

"Well," Balk finally said, looking back at them, "I do appreciate you all being here as planned. I had some trouble with the weather this morning, and I hope to not let it happen again."

The senator smirked from his table.

"As you all know, the jurors will be arriving shortly." Balk nodded toward the main entryway. The clock above it. "Before then, I'd like to again consider any motions by either party."

Tom Hackett stood at his table. "Judge, I spoke with the special prosecutor—" He paused, careful in his choice of words. "While we had a little extra time this morning. I believe we're pretty much in agreement on things."

"No other motions from the defense?"

"Like I've said in our earlier phone conferences," Hackett glanced over at the senator, "We've reviewed our packet of discovery, and found no real challenges to the State's evidence."

"With merit," Balk added.

"Of course, Your Honor. I wouldn't waste the court's time arguing any meritless challenges."

"And you've compared *your* packet of discovery with that which is in the prosecution's own file?"

Hackett smiled. "Judge, I've been practicing for twenty-two years. The first boss I worked for wanted me clipped for trusting without verifying. It's an experience that I won't soon forget."

Balk nodded. Silent. He wasn't sure if Hackett meant the first law partner he'd worked for, or one of his first clients.

"To clarify, Mr. Hackett." Balk looked down at the surface of his desk, then pushed open the flap on his copy of the clerk's file. "By my count, there've been zero motions filed by your office."

"Aside from my standard omnibus motion."

"Right."

Balk paused for another moment.

"Your Honor?" Per usual, the special prosecutor saw the gap in discussion and went for it. "I understand the defense hasn't yet addressed an issue in—"

"Which one?" Balk asked, smiling.

Maggie continued. "I have several statements made by the senator on the date of his arraignment—"

The judge nodded emphatically, listening.

"And I'm not sure whether we could address those matters today. I do intend to use them at trial, Your Honor, and Mr. Hart and I have already briefed this issue to—"

"There's not an objection to those statements coming in." Hackett still stood at his table. "It's a matter of record, as far as I'm concerned."

Balk looked back at Maggie. "You have your answer, Madam Special Prosecutor."

As she started to sit, the judge thought about the fact that prosecutors—even *special* ones—couldn't offer up to a jury the obvious fact that a defendant has elected to remain silent. It didn't matter if this happened in police custody, out of custody, or in the courtroom itself. Arguing the fact that a defendant hadn't said anything in their own defense at trial, even mentioning it, was off limits. It suggested guilt—and risked a mistrial, even sanctions.

Maggie returned to her feet. "Actually, Judge, I'm not sure I do."

"The defense isn't making any pre-trial objection to the statements being offered at trial, counselor." Balk turned to look at the defense lawyer. "I did hear that correctly, right Mr. Hackett?"

He was back on his feet. "That's correct. No objection."

"Right," Maggie said, before Hackett returned to his seat, "But if the defendant elects to *Pay the Nickel*—"

"He won't." Hackett said this without any hesitation. Seated now. "I assure you."

Balk waited for another word from the defense lawyer, but Hackett simply stayed in his seat. Of course, everyone knew that when a defendant *did* remain silent in his defense, the twelve jurors who deliberated couldn't overlook the obvious. The words from Hackett regarding his client's wishes sounded definite, decided. Like the Fifth Amendment's protections weren't even something he'd been able to get the senator to consider.

Maggie started to return to her seat. "I'll take that direction, then, given counsel's assurances."

The doors at the main entryway opened. A courtroom deputy asked if he could start filling the gallery with jurors.

"Anything more at the moment?" Balk asked.

Nothing.

"We'll return at eleven to begin jury qualification. Both parties are excused until that time."

Balk stood and made his way off of the bench. As he started toward the side door, he couldn't help but feel out of his normal routine. He was tight, like a reliever stepping to the mound after a long rain delay.

Don't be late, John.

The judge stopped at the sound of the senator's voice. When he turned, he saw that Bill Collins was already halfway across the room. Balk hoped the words had in fact been spoken by the senator. If not, then he had bigger problems.

38

DAY ONE

11:00 a.m

They called the jurors by name, handing them numbers with jimmy-pins as they walked through the main entryway. A pair of ladies with clipboards then directed the jurors down the center aisle, organizing them sequentially, right-to-left along the pew-like benches. This order allowed for the lawyers and judge, looking out on them from the front of the room, to view the pinned numbers on each person's chest, starting from left-to-right.

That's eighty! hollered a woman from the door, pausing the cattle call. One of the clipboards responded: *Hold the rest!*

Maggie had a list in front of her with basic information about the two hundred potential jurors. Beside the numbers 1-through-200, the list provided each juror's name, gender, date of birth, address, and race, if available. When Maggie heard the call from the door, she took an orange highlighter and struck a line below position eighty on her list.

Maggie saw Hart reach for a highlighter on the table. "Use orange," she reminded him.

"Right."

"Pink for the defense." Maggie didn't look up at him as she spoke. "Yellow for us."

She and Hart sat beside one another at counsel's table. They'd moved their chairs around to the other side, though, the edge of the table that usually fronted the bench. With the judge to their back, they could sit facing the gallery, working at the table throughout the selection process. Maggie liked to spend as much time as possible watching the faces of those on the panel, so she worked from a rather large visual aid when she picked her juries. It was positioned on the table in front of them now. Two poster-boards, lined and gridded out to match the rows of benches in the gallery. Each square on the board reserved for a prospective juror. All of them blank, for the moment.

Once the judge began qualifying the jurors, he'd start to whittle down the potential eighty for a variety of reasons. Maggie and Hart had worked together, preparing the square cards with the preliminary research for the entire *venire*—the panel of prospective jurors. So, for example, once *Juror No. One* was qualified, they'd add the square for *Conner Mangrove, M, Age 39, White, 2738 Five Forks Road* to the posterboard that corresponded to whichever side of the courtroom's center aisle he sat on. The square then matched his seat in the room. This made it easy for Maggie to reference who he was, along with whatever information they had on him while she worked. Each card also included the same three points of information from their in-office research: rent/own home, occupation if available, and a simple *Y* or *N*. On Mangrove's card there was a *Y*—which meant he was one of Ryan Park's three million-plus followers on social media.

When the judge took the bench, he started right in with his greeting to the panel. Maggie knew his routine by heart. She listened to him thank the courtroom deputies, bailiffs, and volunteers, then made his customary joke. The punch line ended with him saying: *But that's the last time I'll have my pastor sit in on a month-long trial!* The jurors always liked it, lightening the mood in the room.

"Madam Special Prosecutor," the judge called over, moving to the next item on the agenda, "If you'd like to offer a very brief introduction, you may do so."

Maggie rose from her chair, ready with the words. She usually kept her remarks short at the beginning of selection. Not once had she ever worried about her introductions coming off as stiff, though. That lack of warmth, creativity, was always covered by the prosecutor.

"Good morning, ladies and gentlemen, I'm Maggie Reynolds." She used an open palm to motion to her co-counsel. "Seated at the table with me is Michael Hart, Chief Assistant District Attorney with the Blake County DA's Office. Together, we represent the State in this matter." She paused a moment, nodding to several people she knew from the gallery. Letting them take her in. "I see some familiar faces, and I'm pleased you're all here." Smiling. "And I'm always reminded during *voir dire,* that even in a small town like Blakeston, that there are many people I've still not had a chance to meet. I know we'll get to some of that later today, and I look forward to it."

She looked over at Hart. A silent offer for him to add anything. He shook his head from his seat at the table, then looked away. Maggie hoped the jurors didn't sense that coolness between them.

"Mr. Hart and I look forward to trying this case," smiling again as she turned her focus back to the gallery, "and we appreciate your time here today."

Easy. No time wasted. Everybody's happy.

"Thank you, counsel." The judge then turned and made the same offer to the defense lawyer. "Mr. Hackett?"

"Of course, Your Honor." Hackett got to his feet and walked closer to the gallery than Maggie had been standing during her introduction. She couldn't see his face, but she guessed that he was smiling. "I'll go ahead and get this out of the way, ladies and gents."

His accent grinded the ears.

"I'm not from Blakeston." He let the chuckles sputter, then put a hand under his chin as he walked along the bar. "I know, I know. I hide it well. But I'm from Boston, in fact." More steps along the rail. "Lived there my whole life, actually. Not for everyone, but I love it. Been that way since before I can remember."

He seemed to think about this, before turning to point to the senator.

"And I represent Bill Collins, over there at our handsome table."

Hackett turned back to the gallery, giving them what Maggie guessed was another grin. "I know you all—*y'all?*—no, I can't." A flip of the hand, egging on more laughter at his expense. "But I know you people know him well, so I won't try to tell you his story." Hackett then leaned closer to the group, whispering loudly. "And we won't even get into the whole Washington thing."

They liked this, so he let the chuckles roll for another moment before lifting his hand to point again at his client. He slow walked it back toward the table.

"But there was a lot about Bill that I didn't know until recently. And we've connected on a lot of things since I started working his case—not sports, or politics, or religion, well—" his hand went to his chin again, allowing time for the laughter to ripple some more. "But really, what I've noticed most in our conversations together, is the affection he has for this place." He paused. "It couldn't remind me more of the way I feel about my own place in this world."

It seemed most of the eighty were nodding, listening.

"Personally, I don't think I could spend the kind of time away from Boston that Bill has spent away from his home. It's a special thing, really, having a hometown. Not everyone has one, right?" He shoved both hands in his pockets. "I'm one of the lucky ones, too. God, I know that. But the trade-off is you get homesick, right?"

He cleared his throat, waiting. More heads nodded.

"So, I just wanted to convey to you all—on behalf of my client—how much this place means to him." He turned again to the senator. "Right?"

Rare speechlessness. The senator looked out on them with a hand to his chest.

Hackett started for his seat.

"We'll talk more soon."

When he reached his table, the senator stood. Both of the men then turned to face the flag at the corner of the room, waiting for the judge to begin. Hackett had certainly gathered his intel on Balk's routine. He knew exactly what followed the defense's remarks—the Pledge.

"Ladies and gentlemen," Balk said, "if you'll now please stand and face the flag."

Maggie felt stiff as she stood from her chair.

39

DAY ONE

2:30 p.m

The group of eighty prospective jurors had been reduced to sixty-four. They'd moved quickly through the standard questions for the panel, with the judge employing his direct approach to any soft-shoeing or time-wasting by anyone who hindered his process. Those who remained on the benches, were then pointed out the door for an hour lunch, with assurances from the court that they'd resume jury selection at two o'clock.

Maggie sat at her table, trying to discreetly watch the interactions among the remaining sixty-four. She did her best to not give them the impression that they were the attraction at the zoo. It was difficult, though. The positioning of her seat invited awkward eye contact with anyone who looked her way, but she refused to keep dodging eyes for the sake of avoiding awkwardness. Appearances mattered greatly when it came to first impressions—even more so for women who tried cases before juries.

All rise!

Everyone in the room seemed to exhale in unison, *finally!* They lifted slowly, still weighed down by the mid-afternoon drowsiness. Several faces on the panel weren't making attempts to hide their frustration with the judge. Maggie didn't usually take this reaction as one that was wholly negative. It was an emotion she liked to have in a few jurors, at least it was when she picked cases as a defense lawyer. Now, though, she wondered whether she might need to be careful with these kinds of jurors. People sometimes associated the judge and prosecution with one another. Some even viewed the two as one and the same. Frustration with the judge sometimes meant retaliation for the State. If she wound up with a few impatient jurors, she'd need the judge to make a better effort to be on time.

"Good afternoon, ladies and gentlemen, and I apologize for the delay in getting us all started again."

The judge offered this from his place at the bench. When he glanced over in her direction, Maggie noticed a redness on one side of his face. It was difficult to tell because he'd started the day with a kind of wind-blown look already, but the face certainly looked redder on his right side.

She stood. "Judge, may I approach?"

He looked toward her, rubbing that side of his face before he answered.

"What is it, counselor?" he asked, already ticked about something.

"I'll be brief, Your Honor."

He nodded and Maggie started up to the bench. Hackett followed.

"What's this about?" Balk asked, once they were close enough out of earshot.

Hackett only listened in, comfortable it seemed wherever he needed to be.

"I just—" Maggie paused. She knew her words might not be received well. "I just wanted to make sure everything was okay."

"Everything's fine."

She nodded, considering him from their close distance. There was a tiny impression on the judge's face, hidden in the redness.

"Anything else?"

"You're sure?" she asked, casually brushing a hand along one side of her face.

Balk gritted his teeth. He seemed to accept the jab, maybe remembering he'd asked the same of her. "I'm fine," he reiterated, but the tone was the lowest of his options, one meant to ease under the radar of the clerks nearby. "I bumped my face during lunch. It's nothing."

"I missed what you said, Judge." Hackett leaned closer to them. "Sorry."

Maggie held up a hand.

"What is it?" Hackett asked.

"It's nothing," Maggie replied. "I thought the judge had a reaction to something he ate. There's some swelling."

Hackett nodded.

"Anything else?" Balk asked, eyeing Maggie.

She shook her head.

"Good. Don't come up here just to waste this kind of time again."

Maggie walked back toward her table. Hart looked at her with interest, but she wasn't about to discuss this with anyone else. Not until she had a chance to speak again with the judge, alone.

40

DAY ONE

6:30 p.m

Tim slowed as he neared the intersection.

"You want that window down, bud?"

He mashed the button, lowering the window halfway on the truck's passenger side. The dog hopped from the floorboard onto the seat.

"That's what I thought."

Panting still, the two-year-old hound lapped at the night air. Tim lowered his own window. The cross-breeze brought a chill into the cab.

"It's a little cool tonight, right? I hear we might even get a freeze."

The dog looked at him, then shoved his head back out the half-open window. The dark stretched farther at one edge of the two-lane. Tim's eyes went there, the road bearing north while it headed for rural Blake County. Riding it south, though, the road brightened as it carried one back into Blakeston.

"I used to live in town, did I tell you that?"

Tim shifted his eyes to the left, toward Blakeston. Headlights from a car grew in the distance. He waited until they passed, then lifted the lever for the blinker.

"You wouldn't have liked that." He scratched at the deep red coloring behind the dog's ears. "No, you're a country dog, right?"

The dog looked back at him, happy.

"That's right, bud. We're country dogs."

The red waggled at this, recognizing the playful tone in his new owner's voice. It called for more affection, and the dog nuzzled at Tim's hand. Slobber and drool.

"Let's go eat."

Tim glanced once more into town, then eased the truck out into the road. Almost two months had passed, and he still wasn't used to taking that right turn.

Home was back south.

41

DAY TWO

Maggie went to the back door of her house. She peeked through the blinds to the patio, then pulled back the deadbolt.

"Morning," Ben said, once she'd opened the door for him. He held a small bag. Two cups from the downtown coffee shop. He smiled at her from the bottom step. "You're looking nice, by the way."

"You're late."

"Only by two minutes."

"Try five, Ben." Maggie waved him in. "I have a lot going on today, and a jury that's far from selected. I'm shaving minutes as we speak."

"Here." He handed her a coffee cup. "Dale told me this was your drink."

Maggie took it from him. She never went to Beans on Broad during a trial week. Too many distractions, and the close proximity to the courthouse made it easier to get tied up with jurors or a witness. She turned and led him to the kitchen.

"Grab a seat over there."

"I picked up some of these, too." The paper bag crinkled as he pulled out his loot. "Two of each, approved by Dale."

Maggie looked at the two B&B biscuits. The pair of heart-shaped scones next to them. Her favorite barista knew she didn't eat the scones, and he probably would've told the reporter that she didn't eat biscuits on trial days.

"They only had the hearts," he added, only clarifying this once she'd not stepped to grab any of it. "I asked and they told me this was just a Valentine's Day thing."

"This is very sweet." Maggie knew what this was, and she couldn't help but feel like she was now talking to a puppy. "Thank you, Ben."

He turned after she said this, walking toward the kitchen table to take a seat. A notebook came out. His cell phone behind it. The coffee became an afterthought.

"You must not go there much."

"What?"

"The shop." Maggie nodded at his coffee cup. "You didn't grab a sleeve for your coffee."

"Oh." Ben kind of stared at his cup for a moment, until a silly grin crept in. "It's apple juice, actually."

Maggie laughed.

His face grew pink, smile widened. "I'm not embarrassed."

"Your face says otherwise."

"Nah, Maggie. Maybe by that—" Ben waved his hand at the heart-shaped bread. "But I'm a proud juice guy. I don't need that black cup of death you're drinking over there."

Maggie shook her head. "Don't be embarrassed by who you are."

"It's all good." He opened the notebook in front of him, pouting. "You're busy, so let's get to it."

She sipped at her coffee. Waited until he turned and looked at her.

"You done?" she asked.

"What—"

"Don't get offended." Maggie pointed to his face. "I see—"

"I'm not offended."

"Good." She kept her finger pointed at him. He needed some unsolicited advice. "That's good, because if you can find a way to stop doing this whole thing—whatever it is—then you're going to *kill it,* Ben."

He nodded, listening.

"But if you don't—" Maggie lowered her finger slowly, walked toward him. "You'll find a way to stay that nerd that you think you are, and that's what'll screw up your shot."

Ben looked a little nervous when she reached the edge of the table. "And just to be clear—I'm talking about your career." She picked up one of the scones that lay on top of the B&B bag. "Not anything between you and—"

"I know." Ben said this quickly before he looked away. "I know."

"Okay."

"But just to be clear, nerds are cool." He pushed a hand through his new hair before turning back to face her. "Damn cool."

"One hundred percent. But it's on you to own that."

"Okay." He sighed. "For the record, though, I'm already killing it."

"Not *killing it*, though."

Ben shook his head. "Enough of that. I know I'm on borrowed time."

"That's right." Maggie began working on her own hair. "You have ten minutes."

Ben opened to a page in his notebook, one already filled with his scribbling. He turned it around and handed it over to her.

"What's this?" she asked.

"Those are notes on a series of land deals that happened back in the late Nineties. I got some help with the title search, and we pulled up a few parcels of interest." He pointed to three lines on the page. "These were all joint ventures between Bill Collins and another local, E.B. Acker—"

Maggie listened as she tried to remember how long the Acker family's lawyer, Bruce Tevens, had practiced in the area. *At least since the mid-Nineties.* She'd have to ask him.

"Now, you may not recognize E.B., but he was a big-time farmer, timber man, and—"

"Charlotte's grandfather."

"That's right."

"Did a lawyer by the name of Tevens prepare the deeds for those transfers you mentioned?"

"No, he did not." Ben smiled. "It was John Balk."

"Okay—"

"And before you say what I think you're going to say, hear me out." Ben got on his feet. "We pulled every deed and Balk prepared them all. But—" he raised a finger. "We also found a *lis pendens* that'd been recorded on one of them."

Maggie shrugged. Real estate work wasn't something she'd ever touched, but she was at least familiar with a *lis pendens.* They were often filed by lawyers who wanted to keep a piece of land from being transferred or sold while they had a lawsuit pending. The real property always had to be connected with a case, because a clouded title caused by a *lis pendens* made a piece of real estate essentially worthless. And a legitimate *LP* could remain in place until the conclusion of a lawsuit, which meant years and years in some cases.

"Ben, you'll have to excuse me, but I'm not all that alarmed by a lawyer having to file a—"

"This is different." He pointed to his notebook again. "Balk filed the *LP.* Balk filed the lawsuit connected to it. And Balk handled all the conveyances."

"Did he file the lawsuit for Collins?"

"Nope." Same smile. "For E.B."

Maggie had a bad feeling. She looked over at the clock on her stove. *Seven-thirty.*

"Am I out of time?" Ben asked.

"Not quite. Tell me as much as you can for the next few minutes."

Ben reached for his juice. "You may want to sit."

42

DAY TWO

9:45 a.m

The judge checked the clock above the courtroom's main entryway. From his end of the room, he could make out everything on the face of it, except the thinnest of the hands. His eyes not being able to see it, though, that didn't affect this little second hand in the slightest. It continued marking the seconds of the day. And would. Around and around, until the mechanics of the clock itself didn't allow it to keep pace any longer. But time continued. *Why shouldn't it?* It was unyielding, inflexible, even unapologetic—which was why it eventually won.

Always.

And Balk believed that the people who were able to grasp this terrifying aspect of time—early enough in their life, like the senator—didn't run from it. *Give it time. Time heals all wounds. Time will only tell.* The judge had understood the rationale behind these sayings, especially when people brought them out in difficult times, but it'd taken him most of his life to appreciate the powerful concept found in each adage. He'd told himself he couldn't leave. *But time went on another thirty years.* He'd told himself that his mistake had trapped him. *But time pushed on while he stayed chained.* He'd told himself that he could wait it out. *But time kept on while he waited.*

Balk's eyes went to the defense table, where Bill Collins sat patiently. He seemed to sense in that moment that the judge's gaze was on him. He looked back toward the judge, then pointed to the watch on his wrist.

"It's nine-forty-five, Judge—"

It was the voice of one of the clerks. It jerked him from his thoughts, mercifully.

"Do you want me to go ahead and call the roster?" she asked.

"Yes, ma'am."

The woman walked to the edge of the gallery and began calling through the names of the prospective jurors. He'd excused sixteen from the original eighty they'd started with yesterday, then after lunch, the challenges made by the lawyers caused him to exclude another five from the *venire*. Which meant that at nine-thirty that morning, the remaining fifty-nine potential jurors were supposed to be seated in the gallery and ready to continue with jury selection. When the clerk finished with the roster, Balk waved her over.

"We've got about five missing, Judge."

Balk sighed. "About five?"

"Sorry, Judge." She seemed nervous. "Five of them aren't here. I'm not sure where they are."

"I don't expect you to know—" Balk paused, his frustration was being misdirected. "But—thank you. That's all I need right now."

The woman returned to the workbench below and the judge moved his eyes to the gallery. As he considered his words for the group, he heard whispers from the clerks below about him being *mean*.

"I know this isn't what you all want to hear," Balk began. "But it appears, ladies and gentlemen, that we have a few people running behind this morning." Groans followed this. "I know, and I'm sorry."

A man raised his hand from the front row of the gallery.

"What I'll do, everyone, is call a fifteen-minute recess. Y'all can have an early comfort break, and we'll hopefully resume this process once a few phone calls have been made."

"Judge!" the man called from the front row.

"Sir, I'm sure one of the bailiffs will be able to help."

Balk was reaching for his gavel.

"Hold on, Judge," the man pressed, louder now. "I know where they are."

Murmurs started in the gallery, but it seemed that most of the jurors wanted to ease out into the hallways for their break. Balk looked over at the old deputy. He stood from one of the seats in the empty jury box, then nodded back to the judge.

The man still waited at the waist-high railing. Balk saw the number on his chest. *Number One.*

"Sir," Balk pointed to the jury box, "Deputy Buck over there will speak to you."

"Yes, sir."

Balk called out once more to the rest of the group, most already exiting. "Be mindful of the time, folks. Fifteen minutes!"

Wham!

43

DAY TWO

10:00 a.m

The walk seemed to take a little longer than usual. Behind him, the lawyers followed in silence. There was a feeling that the trial might not happen, and it seemed to still be marinating with the differing expectations among them. The thought certainly wasn't beyond the realm of possibility, at least for the judge. He wanted to hear it from the mouth of Juror Number One, though.

Balk pushed open the door to the judicial suite. He found the old deputy standing in the waiting room. The juror sat in a nearby chair.

"Mr. Mangrove?" Balk asked.

"Yes, sir."

"Come on."

The deputy motioned with a hand for him to follow and they all started toward the judge's chambers. The office felt quiet to the judge, and he assumed the others had noticed this, but no one mentioned it.

"Take a seat in that chair over there, Mr. Mangrove."

"I'm not trying to get anyone in trouble," he said, sounding like a kid in the principal's office. "I just thought, you know, someone needed to say something."

"Hold on, sir." Balk held up his palm to the man as he said this. The desk phone rang. Before he picked up, he motioned to the lawyers. "Maggie, Mike, Tom, y'all go ahead and sit, please."

The phone rang again. He picked it up. Listened.

"Let's be quick, now," he told the woman on the line. "Plenty of people are waiting on us."

He placed the phone on the receiver.

"Is everything okay?" the juror asked.

"No, not really." Balk said this with a chuckle. "We're waiting on my court reporter, though."

"Oh."

The deputy's radio squawked. The lawyers worked from their cell phones. The juror seemed to only sit there and sweat.

They could hear the woman coming from down the hall. She sounded... steady. She reached the doorway and came on in. Roller bag in tow.

"I'm here, Judge." Nothing more.

"Dee, set up over there, please." Balk pointed to the conference table off to one side of his chambers. "We'll go on the record as soon as you're ready."

She didn't move fast. She didn't move slow. And once the ratchets and zippers and cords were done with, she nodded to the judge. Nothing more.

"We'll go on the record," Balk began. "Juror number one, please give me your name."

"Conner Mangrove, sir."

The judge administered the oath.

"I do."

"Okay, Mr. Mangrove, you're in my chambers inside the Blake County Courthouse, with Maggie Reynolds and Michael Hart, for the prosecution, and Thomas Hackett, for the defendant. Standing here is Deputy Marlin Buck, BCSO, who I believe you spoke to earlier about some strange communication that you received yesterday. Correct?"

"That's correct, sir. I spoke to Track—Deputy Buck—and explained to him that I'd received a message to my phone last night, encouraging me to cut out on jury service this morning."

"To break the law, then?" Balk wanted this nailed down.

"I understand it to be, sir. That's what it said on the summons I got in the mail."

"Okay." Balk approved. "Do you have a copy of this message?"

"No, sir."

"Why's that?"

"It disappeared—it, well the app—that's how it works sometimes."

"I see."

"And it wasn't from an account I recognized, Judge." He seemed genuinely nervous. "I saw it and didn't pay it any mind."

Balk looked at Maggie. Then Hackett.

"Any questions?"

Hackett stepped quickest. "What did it say, exactly? The message."

"Basically, that—"

"I don't want basically." Hackett wielded his edge like a butterfly knife. "I want exactly."

Balk gave the man some cushion. "As best you can, please."

"There was a quote with it."

Mangrove paused as he seemed to think on it for a moment.

"It was something about giving up freedom for temporary safety."

Hackett nodded. "It's Franklin, I know it. What else did it say?"

"That if I was a believer in the cause—that I'd do the right thing and disrupt the trial."

"That's *exactly* what it said?" Hackett pressed.

He nodded.

"Let the record reflect that juror one nodded in response to the last question."

Maggie didn't let Mangrove breathe. "Did you respond to the message?"

He paused, too long.

"I take it you did."

"Objection." Hackett.

Balk noted the timely objection on the record. "You can respond, Mr. Mangrove."

He looked down at the ground. "Yes, ma'am."

Dee called over from the table. "Speak up, sir!"

"I said, *Yes*."

The silence sat there, offering the juror a chance to elaborate. He didn't.

"Okay," Maggie said. "What'd you send back?"

"I asked who this is. They responded with a link. I clicked on it."

He paused.

"And?"

"Nothing. It jammed the app up on my phone. When I logged back in, it was gone."

"What do you mean by *it*?" Hackett cut back in on the dance.

"It. You know? The message. The link. The profile of the sender. All of it."

"I find this hard to believe." Hackett turned his back to the man. "I don't have any other questions."

"Maggie?"

"Do you know if anyone else received the message?"

He shook his head. "I don't, ma'am."

44

DAY TWO

11:00 a.m

"I'm open to suggestions."

Maggie couldn't bring herself to do it. She crossed one leg over the other, willing to wait for someone else in the room to quit. Hackett had grown equally quiet with the judge's opening. It seemed to her that he didn't want to scrap the current panel either.

"I certainly could take it upon myself to excuse this batch of jurors," Balk mused. "But then there could be the same problem with the other one-twenty who've received a summons..."

The judge seemed to want someone to suggest the nuclear option to him.

"It's one juror." Hackett sounded confident. "Twenty years ago, if someone would've made that kind of claim." He laughed. "I mean jury tampering isn't unheard of, but my God, let's at least have something more than a message that just goes *poof!*"

"I've been in this seat longer than twenty years, Mr. Hackett." The judge sounded thoughtful. "The world has changed a lot faster lately. Technology made things possible that I never would have imagined at forty."

"You're right, Your Honor." Hackett seemed to adhere to every rule a trial lawyer needed to follow. "And I couldn't agree more. However, I don't understand this stuff. I get messages from people I don't know, sure." He slipped his hand inside his jacket. Removed a cell phone. "I just can't keep believing that *anything's* possible when we're talking about these things. Proof, I still like it right there." He smacked the phone against the palm of his other hand. "If my proof is just *one* guy? Uh-uh."

Balk appeared to absorb this, then: "There might be more than one, counselor."

Hackett stuck to the rule. "You're right, Judge."

"Maggie?"

The judge had his eyes on her. She didn't look away, but she did pause to wonder why Hart didn't have an opinion about anything. *Strange.*

"I think it's still early, Judge."

He didn't look away.

"My suggestion would be—" Maggie paused. "My request, rather—would be for Juror One to be excused."

"With the thanks of the court, of course." Hackett added this, helpfully. "If what he's saying is true, then more of them will surface. If he's a fabricator...well, he earned himself a couple of days out of the office."

"So, this is win-win for the both of you?" Balk asked.

"I hope not, Judge," Maggie smiled, "because I call those ties."

Hackett nodded. "Same. In fact, I only like two options. I win or we both lose."

Balk smiled. "I take it you're a Sox fan."

"Is that a question, Judge?"

"It's an assumption."

"Well, it's a damn good one." Hackett leaned forward, animated. "I'll say this, I love the Sox, hate the Yankees, and if that ever changes, I'll walk my pale you-know-what right into the January Charles."

"I'm sure that won't happen."

With Hackett and the judge content, talking baseball, Maggie glanced over at Hart. Even before her accusation—one she still felt was fair, in that moment—she'd recognized he wasn't the same lawyer when he sat second-chair. And while Maggie doubted her own ego would allow her to move a seat over in the courtroom, her instincts told her that wasn't all of what was going on with Hart. Which was good, in some ways, because Maggie wasn't sure there was more room for him at the table. But Hart was supposed to want a greater role. Being a prosecutor was part of who he was, and it bothered her to see that he'd somehow forgotten this.

"Mike?"

"Yeah?"

Maggie paused. He wasn't even looking at her.

"Look, I still don't know who sent me those notes. It's like, whoever is doing this, they wanted to set you up and—"

Hart cleared his throat. "Look, it's fine. We're past it."

"No, we're not."

He turned now and looked at her.

"We're not," she said again, "because that creep is still somewhere around here, laughing about how clever he is for dropping his handwriting in your notebook."

He seemed to consider this. "He probably is. The freak."

"Right?" Maggie reached over and nudged Hart's shoulder. "We shouldn't be pissed at each other."

"You're right." He nodded. "He doesn't know it yet, but he fucked up when he tried to pin his little game on me."

There he is. Maggie wanted to hug him, but Hart was already starting to get to his feet. He turned his attention to the judge.

"Judge, may I be excused?" Hart asked. "I actually need to take care of a few things before we get back to the courtroom."

"Of course, Mike." Balk was smiling. "I'm planning to have the panel break for lunch anyway. We'll resume after."

Hackett stood to make his exit also. "I need to handle a few matters myself."

"You're excused." Balk nodded. "We'll talk Yankees soon."

"I won't bring up ninety-six, don't worry."

"You just did, you jerk."

Hart and Hackett both slid out the door. One looked happy as a clam, while the other looked ready to box.

It was quiet in the judge's chambers, with just Maggie and the judge facing each other over the desk.

Balk cleared his throat. "Anything else?"

"There is."

He sighed.

"Did you give your secretary the day off?"

He nodded.

Maggie gave him a look. "During a trial week?"

A shrug.

Maggie decided to risk it. "I bet that bruise below your left cheekbone has something to do with it, one I'm pretty certain came from a ring."

Balk ran a hand over his face. Shook his head.

"Sheila's ring?"

Still nothing.

"Put your nickel on the desk right there, then." Maggie crossed one arm over the other. "That is, if you're not going to talk to me about what really happened."

"I told you—" he started.

"Don't tell me you fell, Judge." Maggie hoped he saw that she was concerned. "Tell me what happened, please?"

Maggie kept eye contact with the judge for a long moment. He eventually looked away to pull the drawer out from his desk, sighing as he placed a silver coin on its surface.

"Is that Jefferson?" she asked.

He nodded.

Maggie was the one who shook her head this time, standing. "Really?"

He didn't respond.

"I'll grab you some concealer at lunch." She headed for the door.

45

DAY TWO

2:30 p.m

"That's another four that are missing, Judge."

Balk motioned for his clerk to come closer. She hesitated. Took a few more steps, until she stood right up against the bench's wood exterior. Her short arm stretched high to hand the judge her clipboard.

"That's nine total, then?" he asked.

"Yes, sir."

"So, that takes us to fifty-one out there in the gallery."

"Yes, Judge."

The judge thought as he looked down at the list. Circles had been made around each missing juror in red pen. He counted them himself. *One, two,* through nine. All of his defectors were men. And they'd soon be down to fifty, once he cut Mangrove loose.

"Okay." He looked back to the clerk. "We may just need to lock the rest of this group up at the county jail, then we'll at least know where they all are." He smiled. "How's that sound?"

Her laugh sounded louder than he'd expected. He looked at her a moment more, wondering what else she hid behind that meekness.

"Oh, I don't know if I'd go that far, Judge. The sheriff might not like having all those people to feed—"

"The sheriff's a friend."

"Right." Her smile was nervous. "Of course."

He smiled. She was the type he'd always gone for over the years. A little younger. Lacked confidence. Saw his job as something grander than it really was. He scratched his cell phone number on a piece of paper. Tucked it behind the last page on the clipboard.

"Make a copy of your list here for the lawyers." He handed her back the clipboard. "You text me the amended version when you have it prepared."

"Sheila always likes me to email things—"

"She's out of the office this week." Balk tried to sound casual. "And I'm bad with email. Text is better."

Another nervous smile. "Okay, Judge."

"Both of you are serious about moving forward with this panel?"

Balk stood in the secure corridor with the lawyers. He'd felt certain one of them would feel uncomfortable enough at this point and demand that they get a clean slate of jurors.

"They were probably deadweight, Judge." Hackett didn't seem bothered one bit. "Good riddance, as far as my client's concerned."

"Aren't these jurors standing in solidarity with *your* client?"

"Maybe, but my client doesn't want them." Hackett pointed at the wall behind him. It divided the corridor from the courtroom. "My client wants people who are willing to serve on that jury. Not whiners, like these nine no-shows."

"I'll admit that it's concerning," Maggie added, "but I see Mr. Hackett's point. People who want to dodge the defendant's trial, just to prove a point, well—that won't interfere with my work."

"Give me the first twelve." Hackett sounded confident. "Another four-pack to serve as alternates."

"You don't really mean that?" Balk scoffed.

"I don't." He smiled. "I do, however, want to avoid losing the whole group. I refuse to assume these messages taint every prospective juror."

Balk still couldn't get over the way the defense lawyer said *juror.* It sounded like *jur-raw*. He also couldn't get a handle on who Hackett thought he was fooling. Someone was obviously out there trying to cook his *raw* jurors. The judge just didn't know who the senator had doing it. His guess was that Hackett probably knew *something* about what was being done, but not enough to be considered a person who was involved in its planning or execution. The Boston lawyer had been around long enough to know how to avoid *actually* helping his clients commit crimes—which jury tampering certainly was. And while the attorney-client privilege applied to almost anything discussed between the senator and his lawyer, Hackett couldn't rely on that privilege in the same manner if he were to end up charged with a crime. To ensure that didn't happen, Hackett probably insisted on staying out of the senator's scheme, thus maintaining plausible deniability.

But the senator once had another attorney—Ryan Park—whom he'd made an overly public dismissal of on the day of his arraignment. *Unnecessarily public, even for Bill.* And Park had a healthy appreciation for the power that lay in digital influencing. Which made Balk wonder if the senator only wanted everyone to believe he'd quit using the young attorney's expertise, and whether Park was bold enough to risk her law license in such a manner.

Balk decided to test his theory. "Mr. Hackett, why shouldn't I assume the whole pool has been tainted?"

"That's simple." Hackett looked up and down the hallway once. "If you were to assume that, Judge, then the next logical inference will be that my client directed said tampering. A slippery slope, I'll just add."

"You want twelve jurors from that group inside the courtroom, then?"

"Yes." Emphatic. "I'd strike a jury today."

"Maggie?"

Balk turned to her. He wanted to help her, but he knew this was where her aggressive nature proved to be a liability. Prosecutors had high conviction rates because they picked their cases carefully. She'd taken this one for another reason.

Maggie didn't hesitate. "I'll run with this panel."

Balk turned at a sound from Hart. He thought the man was finally going to chip in—maybe throw the judge a life preserver—but the lame prosecutor didn't have anything to say. He was apparently only clearing his throat as he flipped through a stack of documents, ones that appeared unrelated to *State v. Collins.*

"The media will get wind of this." Balk shook his head, sighing. "Deputies will be sent out to pick these jurors up and one of them will probably start spouting their delusions."

"Fine." Hackett didn't blink. "I'll stand out on the front steps and call those jurors cowards myself."

Balk didn't doubt it.

46

DAY TWO

6:30 p.m

Gravel crunched as Maggie pulled up the drive. The lights on her SUV bobbed along, drifting to one side when the Rover dipped its tires into a washed-out rut that snaked the driveway. She came to a stop in front of the rental house. It was only her second time visiting it over the last two months. Her first at night. A light looked to be on above the side door. Maggie cut the engine, stopping at the sound that greeted her.

Wow-wow! Arroo-ooo!

She opened the door, and the sound of the dog grew louder.

Wow-wow! Wow-wow! Arroo-ooo!

The dog looked out at her from a front window on the house. She could almost hear the blinds bending and slapping together from the big head that shoved them around, trying only to get a better view.

"You're new." She said this once she came around the front of the SUV, although she guessed the dog couldn't hear much from behind the window it peered through. "You're a good-looking boy...or girl, either way."

Arroo-ooo!

Maggie nodded emphatically to the dog's reply. He'd stopped dancing, though, hearing something else of interest. Maggie turned and saw headlights making their way toward the house. Tires on the black BCSO truck crunched along the same route she'd just traveled.

As she watched it approach, she tried to lean casually against the back of her SUV. Other than the flats she'd switched to, Maggie still wore her courtroom attire. Jury selection usually called for skirt suits. She'd not strayed from that rule today. Muted purple, with matching pencil skirt and double-breasted jacket. No flashy jewelry. A good choice that gave her a polished, approachable look for a day in the courtroom when jurors needed to feel comfortable speaking to her.

She was ready to get out of that outfit.

"This is a surprise."

Tim smiled at her as he stepped out of the truck. She returned one of her own.

"Good surprise?" Maggie walked toward the truck. "Or should've called ahead surprise?"

He turned to pull a bag out of the truck, waiting to respond until he could get his things in order. Maybe his thoughts.

"Good surprise, of course." He pointed toward the side door, holding his gym bag in the other hand. "Do you want to come in for a minute?"

A minute.

Maggie craned her neck a little. The dog had left the window. "Can I meet whoever it was that was eyeing me earlier?"

"Sure. He'll love you."

She followed him to the side door of the house, bracing herself for the big dog to come flying out. Instead, the door opened, and the red hound eased out to inspect their new visitor.

"You're sweet," she said, rubbing his head. "What's your name?" She kept massaging his ears, seeing that she'd already found a happy spot. "*Maybe*, your roommate will tell me what to call you."

"It's still up in the air."

"What?" she asked, offering Tim a playful look. "Up in the air, still?" Maggie shook her head and looked back down at the dog.

"That just won't do. You're too old to not have a name. And too handsome."

"He came from the shelter with one," Tim added, "but I scrapped it."

Maggie laughed. "It couldn't have been that bad."

"It wasn't for me, let's say."

Maggie turned to him, still smiling. "What was it?"

"Reb."

She went back to rubbing the dog's head. "He's right, that won't do. We'll have to find you something new."

"You coming inside?" Tim asked.

"Sure. I'll just let Reynolds use the bathroom, and then I'll be right in."

He kept walking into the house. She only heard one word before he went through the door.

"No."

Maggie sat on a stool at the breakfast bar, watching him as he started to heat up a skillet. Two cartons of eggs came out of the fridge, along with a half-empty gallon of milk. He wore gym shorts and an old hoodie. She could tell the last couple of months had involved serious time with the iron.

"You want some eggs?"

"I think I'm okay."

He paused. "I'll make extra."

She grinned behind his back. He popped the hood up on his sweatshirt and got to work cracking eggs. The red dog paced for a moment, then found his way over to lay at her feet. He even seemed to notice the comfortable silence in the room. She'd missed it, so she wanted to wait a bit before coming out with why she was there.

"We got our jury seated today."

"I heard." He spoke with his back to her. "Word on the street is that y'all might've set the record up there."

"You could say that."

"We picked some juries quick, Mags. But dang. What was it, under three hours today?"

"Something like that. Balk had already handled the prelims the day before."

"What's the rush?"

The eggs went into the pan. He turned around to face her, leaned against the counter. While he waited for her to answer, he uncapped the milk jug and took a swig from it. The fact that he didn't use a glass struck her as a not-so-subtle nod to the fact that he was slowly reacclimating himself to life as a bachelor.

"When did you get Reynolds?" she asked, tabling the jury discussion.

"Stop." He laughed. "He'll get a name when I'm ready."

Maggie didn't want to push it. They'd had some rocky moments arguing around the subject of kids. She didn't want to venture close to those waters. Tim turned around to check on their eggs.

He handed her a fork and sat down beside her. The plate of eggs between them. Cheese on hers.

"Are you going to tell me why you're here?"

"I wanted to see you."

He picked up some eggs with his fork. Chewed. "And?"

"I came across some stuff today."

He took another bite, listening.

"And it's hard to organize in my mind where it all belongs, given the trial and everything. It helps when we talk."

"I thought it might be something like that."

"But I also just wanted to see you." She took her fork and picked up a bite for herself. "It's one of those—"

She stopped when she felt his hand on her back, knowing then where it would lead. They sat like this for a moment, deliberating. They needed to talk about what was happening. With the trial. With the judge. With their marriage.

But she turned only a little, an invite to come closer.

They could talk later.

47

DAY THREE

As the judge crossed into Blake County, he took in the morning sky. Its brightness sharpened the familiar terrain, calling his eyes to the rarely noticed. Patchy colors on the ageing barns. A single cow wading in a pond. The saplings that peeked from the wiregrass, struggling under the tall pines. Beauty surrounded him, and he acknowledged it, alone.

It wasn't enough.

His cell phone rang. He reached for it in the cupholder. It was a local number, but one he didn't recognize.

"This is John."

"Good morning, Judge. This is Ben Moss."

Balk paused to glance at the time on the dash. *Eight-ten.*

"This a bad time?" the reporter asked.

"You caught me driving." Balk slowed as he entered the city limits of Blakeston. "I hope you're calling me to say you have that article ready."

"It's close."

"Moss," he growled, "you know what they say about close."

"That it only applies if it's high school?"

"Quit being a smartass."

Although the judge talked tough to the reporter, he smiled on his end of the phone.

"I'll give it my best, sir."

"You called me. What do you need?"

"Right. So, I'm boning-up on some of your basic background, mostly for the fluffier side of the piece and—"

"It'd better be goose down."

"Very goosed, Judge. But I need the details to work with. Every lawyer has a website nowadays, telling the world how freaking amazing they are—except you."

"What do you need to know?" Balk asked. The truck's tires started to bump along the brick streets of the downtown. He'd be arriving to the courthouse earlier than the lawyers, and certainly before the jurors, who were due at nine. "Hustle. I don't have much time."

"Tell me about your practice before you were a judge?"

As the question was asked, Balk drove by the downtown building he'd once shared space in. Him, and two other lawyers, Three-fifty a month, each. And they ran their practices together at that address for over a decade. The secretaries came and went, usually because they couldn't afford to pay them enough, but the three lawyers stayed at it for some good times in that building. Not because they made bunches of money. No, they were just ham-and-eggers, like most of the other twenty or so lawyers in Blakeston at that time. Just waking up each day to chase that case, *that client* —the one that'd set them up for the long-haul.

"I had a fairly robust general litigation practice." Balk spoke matter-of-factly. "Handled a lot of domestic and child custody work. Took in a few minor criminal cases here and there. Nothing nasty, of course. I hit the Winn-Dixie a few times on some slip-and-falls. Had several good car wrecks over the years. That sort of thing."

"Well-rounded, then?"

Balk turned into his designated parking space at the courthouse. "Of course. It's the way lawyers were trained to practice back then. Not many lawyers can manage to do that anymore, though. It's a shame."

"Anything you didn't do?"

"I'm sure I took some one-offs here and there, but those areas I mentioned to you were my bread-and-butter."

"Good." The reporter paused. "Let's see—"

Balk glanced again at the time. *Plenty.*

"How about clubs and organizations?"

"Look, I'll have my secretary send you something today, okay?"

A pause. "Sure."

"I need to run, Moss. I'm sure I'll see you in court today."

"Actually, Judge—I have a little problem with my access credentials."

"What kind of problem?"

Another pause.

"Spit it out, Moss."

"I've come to find myself at odds with our sheriff. He hasn't been too happy with me since the day you arraigned Senator Collins, mainly because I was with a group of reporters in the courthouse's restricted corridor without—"

"I remember it." Just like he remembered that it was where Moss tipped him to the fact that there was another side to the senator's lawyer, Ryan Park. "Why didn't you mention this when you visited the lake?"

"To be honest, Judge, I didn't want to. I worried it'd affect your decision on having me do the story on you."

"Have you made a complaint?"

"No."

"That's good, Moss. Don't make one. I'll handle this with one phone call."

"That would be—"

"Don't mention another word about it." Balk figured he could afford to be magnanimous with the young reporter. "That's how these things work."

"Thank you, Judge. I'll owe you one."

Balk paused at this. "Sure. But be careful with who you hand those favors out to."

"Of course."

Balk hung up, then stepped out of the truck, heading toward the building. He wore his best suit. As he walked, he decided that good publicity around his upcoming retirement might be just what his reputation needed this week. After a little good press, and once the trial was behind him, he'd be good to go.

That would be enough.

48

DAY THREE

9:45 a.m

Mindful of her surroundings, Maggie tried to appear calm while she waited to stand for her opening statement. It wasn't easy. Having waited this long, coiled in anticipation, she could finally feel the wheels inching forward. A trial moved slowly at first. But Maggie knew from experience that just getting it to roll a few feet always proved to be the hardest phase of all. Once she had it moving, though, the trial began to pick up speed. And she'd always been quick enough in the courtroom to flow with a trial, to keep up with it, to push it—until she could hop on and drive.

Almost time for the first push.

Maggie looked over for a moment at the senator. The image of him bothered her. His occasional laughs. The way he acted unconcerned with her. Unconcerned with any of it, really. She didn't understand. Maggie had represented people accused of all manner of crimes and they all were nervous about it. They'd instruct her—beg her, on occasions—to please, *please* go meet with the hammers who handled the prosecution for the State. It was a common theme among her clients. They couldn't go another night without sleep. Another day looking over their shoulder. Another minute—without knowing *something.* Not the senator, though.

No phone call. No plea bargaining. No dance request. Nothing.

"Does the State wish to present an opening statement?"

Maggie nodded at the question. *Silly.* Every trial lawyer wanted an early crack at the jury.

She stood. "Yes, Your Honor."

"You may proceed."

Maggie stepped around the table. She smiled at the jury as she did this, hands clasped at her waist. She needed them to see her without notes in her hands. Without gadgets to mesmerize them. Only the truth—one that they had the privilege to decide.

"Ladies and gentlemen of the jury. Good morning, and welcome back."

Maggie looked on at the twelve faces. She slowly went by each, one after another. It was her routine—*not superstition*. She spoke each juror's name in her mind as she passed their face. It was her way of silently acknowledging them, and it refocused her attention on the twelve most important people in the room. Five women. Seven men. All knew the senator, and about the incident on the day of his arraignment. Five were Black. Seven were white. All claimed they'd treat Collins like any other person who sat accused at trial. Eight had voted for him. Four had not. And All claimed to have no opinion as to the matter of guilt or innocence. *It was time to see.*

"I have one request for each of you today."

Maggie turned, making a demonstration out of pointing toward the senator.

"The *defendant*." She hit the word hard, emphasizing his place in the process. "He's seated there at the defense table. Blue jacket. Red tie."

Still pointing.

"When you hear the evidence presented during this trial, I want you to give him...the *benefit of the doubt*." She lowered the hand. Kept her eyes on the senator. "It's the least we can do, right?"

She glanced back at the jurors. They all looked confused, watching her as she acted as if she planned to sit down at her own table. She walked toward it. Slow. Quiet.

"Hold on." Maggie smiled as she turned back to the jury. "I actually have a second request."

She noted the chuckles in the gallery behind her.

"See, you may not know this, but today is my first real day in *this* job."

Several of the jurors smiled back at her.

"And since this is all new, at least from my perspective, I'd like you to think about something as you hear the evidence presented to you during this trial."

They waited.

"Whenever I see a case, any case, I think: Where are the holes?" Another pause. "It's just how I'm wired. It doesn't matter if I'm standing where I am now, or back on the other side of the room. I'm obsessed with finding them."

Maggie saw one juror writing a note. *Good.*

"I look for them because I know they are always there. Always."

"I look for them, because the government, with all its resources, all its people with experience—all its *power*." She slowed, letting them get comfortable with the word. "Yes, even with all that power, the government *still* misses something in every case."

She shrugged. "It's the truth. I'm here representing the government, of course, but I know the way they work. And I want you to look at this case the way that I do, so you need to know that they leave a hole in every investigation. All of them. They leave a hole when a witness goes missing. Another one when a DNA sample gets messed up at the lab. Another one when the investigator is feeling lazy. And sometimes, they leave holes that *We. Can't. Even. See.*"

"Why?"

A juror mouthed it.

"Power." She nodded to him. "Because that's what happens when you have power."

Maggie angled toward the gallery—her thirteenth juror.

"And the power feels good, right?" Maggie flexed an arm. "Really good."

She lowered the arm and placed one hand on her table. "And I'm seeing it, feeling it. I mean, look where I am right now. I have all those resources at my disposal. Investigators. Experts. Technicians. Some really smart lawyers who care about this stuff."

"I have all of it!" she yelled toward the gallery. "All that power!"

The room faded to silence. Maggie waited in it for another moment, then turned back to the jurors.

"So, what I'm asking of you." She slowly stepped closer to the jury box. "What I'm asking—is that when you hear the evidence from witnesses. When you see the photographs. When you hear the recordings. I want you to look at them like they are being presented by a powerful prosecutor for the government."

She held out her hands as if to say: *Me.*

"But." Maggie glanced over her shoulder, then back to the jury, "At the same time, I also want you to take that evidence and put it up against a man who is *equally* powerful—*if not more so.* And I want you to ask yourself one question when you do that."

Maggie stepped to the edge of the jury box, closer than she'd be at any point during the rest of the trial.

"Ask yourself—who really has the power?"

49

DAY THREE

10:00 a.m

The judge opened the Moleskine. He found the bench note that he'd started running for their third day of the trial. He noted the time from the clock above the entryway, then scribbled a few notes about Maggie's opening statement. Although he didn't include this in his note, Balk found the opening statement too short for his liking. He also wasn't particularly fond of her following the recent trend—the attorney who argued during their opening. But this had become so popular as of late, that a quasi-courtesy had developed between these advocates. It was one that discouraged the lobbing of objections when it came to the argument aspect of the opening *statement*, and had all but converted this phase of the trial to an opening *argument.*

But things were changing.

And trying cases nowadays was nothing like it was in the judge's earlier years. Back then, the judges adhered strictly to the rules that applied to opening statements. The prosecutors in those days couldn't say ten words in their opening that didn't include: *The evidence will show.* Now, the younger half of the Bar preferred the flash, the form over function. They didn't understand the days before the screens, tablets, and technology that were available now. Balk guessed that Hackett, although not as far along in years as the judge, was a lawyer who still remembered seeing cases tried the old way.

"Mr. Hackett, is the defense prepared to present their opening statement?"

He took a moment to stand. When he finally did, he stepped from behind his table to address the judge—and jurors.

"Your Honor, I'd like to reserve opening statement."

The judge nodded slowly at this. It'd certainly been some time since he'd seen an attorney elect to go this route.

"Okay, Mr. Hackett."

"With that, Judge, I'd like the court's permission to do so after the State has finished with its evidence."

He looked at Maggie. "Any objection from the State?" the judge asked, noting the surprise on her face.

"No objection."

"Very well, the defense reserves that privilege."

Balk turned and looked over at the jurors. He smiled at them. Teacher Balk was there to talk to them.

"Ladies and gentlemen, you've heard from the special prosecutor in her opening remarks. As the State has the burden of proof in this matter, she and her colleague, Mr. Hart, must present their case and evidence first. For that reason, they only have the option to give their opening statement at the very beginning of the trial."

He hoped no one raised a hand. It did happen on occasion.

"However, the defendant doesn't have a burden, during this trial, so he and his counsel will make a decision as to whether they want to present evidence *after* the State is finished with its case-in-chief." He pointed toward the defense lawyer. "What Mr. Hackett over there did earlier, was make sure he kept the option to present an opening statement for his client, *potentially* later on in this trial."

Balk smiled at the group when he was finished. No hands. *Good kids.*

"With that decision settled for the defense," Balk said, still focused on the jury, "we'll go ahead and take our first break of the day."

As the judge turned back to the courtroom, he thought about the advantage that this strategy gave the defense lawyer. *Not much.* Other than the fact that the defense had two bites at the apple. If Hackett offered an opening at the end of the State's evidence, then he'd get another shot at it with a closing argument at the end of the case. He only needed to offer a bit of evidence in between so that he'd be allowed to do so.

He looked at both lawyers, inviting any additional comment. "Counsel?"

Both shook their heads.

"The court will stand in recess."

All rise!

Wham!

50

DAY THREE

11:00 a.m

Tim slipped into the courtroom through one of its side doors. He couldn't help but smile when he saw the man who stepped to the witness stand at the front of the room. It'd been quite a while.

"Raise your right hand, please."

He stood tall in a dark suit. The tie looked expensive, as did the dress shoes. No doubt the watch was, too.

"Do you swear, or affirm, that in the testimony you present to the court today, that you'll tell the truth, the whole truth, and nothing but the truth, so help you God?"

"I will."

He sat.

Tim had once told the man that this day would eventually come for him. Open court. National stage. Maggie leading him through his story on the witness stand.

"Introduce yourself to the jury, please."

"Good morning, ladies and gentlemen," he said, somewhat sheepishly. "My name's Lawton Crane."

"Thank you for being here." Maggie had positioned herself behind a lectern, a clear barrier between her and the witness. “Is it okay if we just go with Lawton for today?”

“That’s fine.”

Tim watched as Lawton looked over at the jury again, then the packed gallery, and then eventually around to where Tim stood. If the uniform surprised him, he didn’t show it.

“Okay, Lawton, let’s get a few things out of the way for the jury, okay?”

He nodded. “Let’s rip the Band-Aid off.”

“Right.” Tim guessed that Maggie didn’t want to appear sympathetic in any way. Which was easy for her. He knew she had zero sympathy for what he did, still. “You’re a former lawyer?” she asked.

“That’s right. I was a practicing attorney until roughly two years ago, when I lost my license. First in Pennsylvania, then several other places.”

Lawton was a smart, also very stupid lawyer who Tim once dealt with on a case for Maggie. Tim was still leading her investigative work at that time, when Maggie took on Charlotte Acker as a client. The young, Blakeston native had been accused in the killing of Senator Bill Collins’s wife—Lucy Kelley Collins—and Maggie defended Charlotte in one of Blake County’s most infamous murder trials. And Lawton was involved, too.

Maggie kept the kid gloves on. “How about you tell the jury what happened with your law license.”

Only forty-one at the time, Lawton made the surprising decision to leave his position at a prestigious, Washington law firm to go play law professor. Lawton then stepped onto the faculty at Georgetown University, where Charlotte was attending law school. The two met while Charlotte was enrolled in one of Lawton’s courses. Eventually, one thing led to another, and office hours started taking place in the bedroom. When Charlotte was later arrested for killing the senator’s wife, Lawton was right there to help in her defense. They were closing in on the end of Charlotte’s murder trial when Lawton finally unloaded his own guilt. He’d been just another pawn in the senator’s game.

“I violated several ethical cannons.” Lawton sounded like a law professor. “I lied to a client, violated confidences, lied to the court, and was later convicted of a federal offense.”

“Did you serve time in prison after your conviction?” Maggie asked.

"Eighteen months. I also had to pay a fine, and I'm still on a form of supervised release."

Another softball from Maggie. "How about you tell the jury what happened with your conviction."

Tim knew that Lawton had been convicted, but he didn't know much about how the deal was brokered.

"I was originally charged in a conspiracy." He paused and looked over at the jury. "One that involved the murder of Senator Bill Collins's wife."

This, the gallery found interesting. Tim looked around as several people murmured and talked with one another at a normal volume. The chatter continued to rise. Tim knew the gavel was coming.

"Order!" called the judge.

Wham! Wham!

"I'll have order!"

51

DAY THREE

2:30 p.m

Maggie watched from her table as Lawton Crane returned to the witness stand. She'd spent the rest of the morning with him on direct examination, walking through his involvement in the efforts to frame Charlotte Acker. Lawton handled himself as she'd expected. He was a solid witness with a bad story. They'd prepared little for his testimony, though, because Lawton had extensive experience from his former life as a civil trial lawyer. He was also extremely bright, and skilled when it came to deceiving others. Maggie only hoped that this combination in Lawton would be enough to overcome that which made him a liability. But being the lawyer in the room, the one who gets to ask the tough questions, wasn't like being the one who has to answer them. And being under pressure, seated on the witness stand, could bring out the worst in any witness—especially someone with a quick temper.

"I'm going to stick with Mr. Crane." Hackett said this as he stepped into the well. "I'm Tom Hackett, and I represent Senator Collins."

Lawton sat up straight in the chair, waiting for a question.

"Okay," Hackett said, moving on. "I'm not going to pick through your troubles lately. The State tendered into evidence the certified copy of your conviction, and you explained earlier that you did your time."

Lawton still waited.

"What I'm interested in, Mr. Crane, is how the whole substantial assistance side of things worked out for you."

Most witnesses at this point, would start offering some kind of an answer. Maggie remembered Lawton as a trained heavy hitter, though, who knew the rules well. He wasn't going to cede an inch if he didn't have to.

"Mr. Crane?"

"Yes, Mr. Hackett?" Lawton paused. "Is there a question?"

Maggie couldn't say she'd never done something similar herself, but she at least recognized that every now and then, ceding an inch, was a whole lot better than taking it in the ear. She'd seen Hackett remove his knife once, using it to cut away at Juror One's story while they had him in the judge's chambers. That cross-examiner's blade was on the Boston lawyer, somewhere.

"Before you were convicted, Mr. Crane, you offered information in exchange for leniency at your sentencing, right?"

"That's right."

"How did this process—the *offering of information*—work in your case?"

Hackett stepped a foot closer to the witness stand. Lawton seemed not to notice.

"My attorney arranged for me to meet with the investigators. They—"

"Who?" Hackett asked.

"The investigators."

Another step.

"Okay, so the investigators interviewed you?"

"Yes."

"And you offered them this information?"

"Yes."

"Did they decide how much leniency you'd receive?"

Lawton looked annoyed already. "No."

"Who was in charge of that decision?"

"The judge who sentenced me."

"Judge King?"

"Yes."

Hackett glanced at the jury. "So, you told the investigators everything you told us today, right?"

Lawton paused. "Basically—"

Hackett showed his edge. "I didn't ask whether you *basically* told the investigators what you *basically* told us."

"I told them what I testified to this morning."

"Thank you." Hackett smiled. "Did you tell them anything else about my client?"

Maggie could see that Lawton had only two options: lie or explain to the jury himself that he'd lied earlier. He chose the first.

"No."

Hackett left his place and walked over to the defense table. He pulled a file out from his stack of trial materials, then turned to Maggie. He handed her a copy of what looked to be a transcript—one from Lawton's interview with investigators. She saw that in Hackett's other hand, he had two more like it. Maggie wanted to scream.

Hackett stood close to the witness stand.

"Let's get things straight, Mr. Crane."

Lawton's face did nothing to hide his anger.

"You lied to investigators, right?"

"I embellished."

"Is that a, *yes?*"

Lawton paused. "Yes."

"And then you lied to a reporter from the *Post*, right?"

"I told him the same story I told the investigators."

"A lie."

"An—"

"Mr. Crane, this story was a lie, was it not?"

A longer pause. "Yes."

"And then you lied to the judge at your sentencing?"

"I didn't lie. I remained consistent with what I told the investigators."

"You've already told us you're not a lawyer anymore." Hackett smiled. "What you haven't told us, is whether or not you lied to the judge at your sentencing. Now, did you—"

"I told him—"

"Judge King."

"Right, I told Judge King the same—"

"The same lie you told investigators."

Lawton was red-faced.

"Mr. Crane, don't make me hold your hand."

Lawton sighed. "I told the same lie to Judge King."

"There we go!" Hackett turned and went back to his table for a moment, returning the transcripts to where they came from. "Now, Mr. Crane, this lie was something you'd told another judge, right?"

Maggie couldn't help Lawton, but she at least had to do something. "Objection!"

"On what grounds?"

"The question has been answered. Defense counsel's belaboring—"

"Overruled." Balk turned to Lawton. "Mr. Crane, you can answer Mr. Hackett's question."

Lawton only nodded, his eyes down.

"Mr. Crane, do you remember my question?" Hackett asked.

Lawton didn't look up.

"Okay." Hackett's eyes stayed on the witness while he spoke. "Madam Court Reporter, can you read back my last question for Mr. Crane?"

"I don't need it read back," Lawton spat. "I heard you just fine the first time."

Nothing for a moment.

"Are you sure?" Hackett asked.

"Yes." Lawton finally lifted his eyes. He looked like he needed a drink. "I told the same lie to another judge, Mr. Hackett."

The defense lawyer made a show of picking up his legal pad, like he was actually going to write the answer down. He kept his eyes on the pad as he asked the question.

"Which judge would that be?"

"Judge Balk."

52

DAY THREE

6:30 p.m

Maggie opened the door to her office. Hart followed behind, toting a box of files with him.

"You sure?" she asked. She flipped on a light.

"Quit asking." Hart found a place on a side table for the box. "You being at the top of your game is more important than some stupid policy."

The two stood in the quiet of the lobby. As far as Maggie could remember, the local prosecutor hadn't ever actually visited her at the law office. They'd met plenty of times to discuss open cases, but it was usually in the DA's suite or off to one side of the courtroom.

"You don't have to rush home, do you?" Maggie asked.

"Not yet."

"Help me get this box back to my conference room. I'll grab you a drink."

"I don't even know what to call our day in court, Mike."

Maggie sat on one side of her main conference room's table with red wine in a coffee mug. Hart sat on the other side with a chilled Fat Tire.

"I call it leading with our chin." Hart smiled as he sipped from the bottle. "I expected Crane to come off as an arrogant, disbarred lawyer who screwed his client—"

"Literally."

"But I didn't expect him to get up there today and tell another bald-faced lie."

Maggie laughed. "Hackett ripped him for it, too."

"He deserved it."

Maggie sighed. "Yeah, but where does that leave us for tomorrow?"

Hart seemed to perk up at this. "You asking my advice?"

"If you can still remember how to *advise.*" Maggie paused. "Because I need your help out there. In here. With that creep, too."

He nodded. "I'm working on it."

She waited for him to continue.

"Put the Hudson boy up first. They'll like him."

"You're talking about Colt, right?"

Hart was taking a sip as he heard this. "Don't make me spit my beer out and have to say his daddy's name."

Maggie smiled. "Colt's just a little more likable."

"I'd give them the GBI agent after that. She's young, but she'll make Hackett work." Hart looked like he was starting to picture it in his head. "Then, I'd start working my way through our local guys."

"Campbell. Clay. Tim."

Hart shrugged. "You could run it either way. If you lead with Tim, he can set your stage for you. If you put him on at the other end, he can clean up any problems."

Maggie took another sip. She didn't regard Hart as a very creative trial lawyer, but that didn't mean she lacked respect for his approach. He worked cases like a brick layer. Brick by brick. And he knew how to stack the evidence up in a good, workman like manner.

"Where would you put Tim in the order?" she asked.

"I'd call him first." Hart sounded confident. "He's the strongest piece we have. He'll set the tone and show the jury the new BCSO."

"Good." Maggie saw that Hart's phone was ringing on the table. "You need to get that?"

When Hart came back into the room, Maggie asked, "Is something wrong?" His face wasn't relaxed like it was before.

He looked at his phone. "Everything's fine with this. I need to go get my kid from church. My ex had something come up."

Maggie nodded.

"I stepped into your little office kitchen, across the hall to take my call."

"Yeah?"

"Did you go in there to get our drinks?"

Maggie shrugged. "Yes, Mike. What's wrong?"

"Didn't you notice that thing on the fridge?"

Pinned under the magnet for *Stack's Sandwiches*, a local spot that the team from Reynolds Law loved, was a note. It read: *Thought you'd be here, bitch. You waited too long. It's time to come see you. It won't be in the morning with heart-shaped treats. It won't be at night while you're getting your sweets. Look for me in the day. That's when we'll play. See you soon. XOXO*

Maggie broke the awkward silence. "To be clear, Mike, I know this wasn't you."

"I believe you."

She only nodded at this, relieved.

"Have all the notes looked like this?" he asked, already moving on. "Same paper and all?"

"Pretty much."

"Pretty much is more than enough for probable cause," Hart said, smiling as he stepped over to the kitchen sink. He pulled a set of chopsticks from an old take-out container, then used them to pull the note from the fridge. He held it up, looking at the note under the kitchen's bright light. "What kind of marker do you think this is?"

"Some kind of Sharpie. They've all been that same black."

"Sharpies have a felt tip to them, right?"

"I think so."

Hart placed the note on the counter and stood there for a moment looking down at it. A career prosecutor, he'd probably spent hundreds of hours tooling around crime scenes. Maggie knew he'd want everything preserved and handled the right way.

"Looks fresh—" Hart paused, then ran a finger across one of the last letters on the note.

"Mike!" she exclaimed. "Come on, don't touch it."

"Strange." He stared at his finger. "This isn't a felt tip marker. That would've been dry by now." He smelled it. "Is that paint?"

Maggie was glad that Hart was the one to make the call. They'd discussed reporting the threats weeks ago, but she'd been opposed to the idea. *Help* had always made her uncomfortable, but now Maggie knew that was exactly what she needed.

"They should be about done in there," came a voice from the quiet. "Another fifteen minutes, maybe."

She turned and saw that it was the old deputy, he stood just inside the doorway to her office.

"Thanks, Tracker."

"Yes, ma'am." He nodded. "I didn't mean to disturb you, though. We'll be inside if you need us."

Maggie watched him turn and head back inside. The BCSO investigators could take as long as they needed to finish taking photographs of the kitchen, bagging the evidence, and checking around the office. She planned to stay outside and hoped the night air would make her feel better, safer.

I was in there the whole time, Maggie thought. *Just talking with Hart while that creep walked in and out of the building, undetected.*

Gross.

53

DAY FOUR

The judge walked in the door to the judicial suite at eight-fifteen. He stopped at the smell of coffee. It surprised him, as did the fact that the lights were already on in the small waiting area. He stood there in the doorway. The smell of a fresh pot wafted from down the hall. He started toward the opposite corner of the room, listening as he neared the turn into the hallway. He heard the familiar sounds of voices who hosted a local breakfast show, chattering on from a small radio that often played during the mornings.

"Hello, John." Sheila appeared from around the corner. "Hope you are well this morning."

It'd be an understatement to say that the judge was surprised to see her. It only took a moment, though, for him to start wondering whether she was only there to pack her things.

"Sheila." It was all he said at first. He cleared his throat, still dry from a night alone. "You're here."

"I work here." She smiled. "At least, last time I checked."

He wanted to hug her.

"Coffee's fresh," she said. "I also put a biscuit on your desk, if you're hungry."

He started to open his mouth.

"And I know you are, John." She sounded calm. "Sorry, that is."

"Yes, I'm very—"

"But just so we're clear," she said, her hand up, stopping him. "What you did the other day, what you said—it's not okay."

He nodded. "I didn't think before—"

"You most certainly didn't." She stepped closer, took his hands in hers. He wasn't sure he could take what he saw in those eyes looking back at him. "But this isn't your answer, John."

"I still think things could be different this time..."

"No." She squeezed his hands twice, then let them go. "There won't be another time for us. That moment is gone, John, and you can't go back. I want you to move on."

He took in the words with a deep breath. Sheila sounded genuine, decided. It was just as she'd seemed the other day, walking into his chambers to discuss his retirement from the bench, and letting him know that she was beginning to make her own plans to leave his office after the trial. *Perfect timing!* he'd thought. *Separated from Donna, their relationship would get the time that it really needed. And once the divorce was finalized, they could build a better life together.* But—no. Their conversation that day was one that'd quickly turned once Sheila explained her reasons for leaving. *There was someone new in her life. She wanted to travel, live more.* Tempers. Insults. Regrets. Then he'd gotten to his feet, towered over her, made his case. *No, John. All you're doing is lying to yourself.* Sheila backing away. *You won't be any different. You'll be alone, directionless, bitter.* Then, it was the back of her hand, he'd felt it before finishing his retort: *Slut.*

Balk finally spoke. "Don't you think you'll miss it here?" But what he meant was, don't you think you'll miss *me.*

"I have more to my life than what's inside these walls. You know that, right?"

He nodded. "Can you at least tell me who he is?"

"It doesn't matter." Not upset. Confident. Very unlike the other women Balk usually had flings with. Not that that's what this was. To him. "You don't have the right to be possessive of me, or anyone else. I have my own life, John."

"I know." He nodded. "I'm sorry."

Balk started down the hall that led to his chambers.

54

DAY FOUR

9:45 a.m

The judge stood at the side door to the courtroom, waiting for the deputies inside to finish organizing the gallery.

He looked to the old deputy. "What's the problem?"

They were the first words he'd spoken to the man all morning. The first words—period—that he'd said since his last apology to Sheila. He'd taken a much-needed cup of coffee with him into his chambers and hunkered down for the hour-plus, trying to get his mind in order. Sheila hadn't bothered him. None of the lawyers had called to say they needed anything. It'd been quiet. *Until now.*

"It's that article, Judge." He looked away. "It's not been received all that well."

Balk thought about the words *that article,* and wondered what it was he'd missed in the morning's news rush. Since moving up to the lake, the judge hadn't set up any services beyond the electricity and water that were already running to the house. He read. Listened to the radio. Looked at the lake. And drank. Mostly that.

"What article?"

"I skimmed that garbage, then the whole paper went right into the trash."

"Is it about the trial?" Balk asked. If it was about one of the deserters from their jury pool, they must've found a local mouthpiece. "About the jury?"

"No, sir." He shook his head. "It's about you."

A knock started on the door to his chambers. Balk sat at his desk, the morning newspaper spread before him. On the front page, there was a photograph of him. Above it, the headline read: *Retire? Why it's time to give it all up.*

He heard the knock again before the door opened.

"John?"

Just inside the doorway, Sheila stood there with a look that told him she wasn't too keen on walking much farther into the room. She'd backhanded him only five feet from where she stood now.

"What is it?" he asked.

"Deputy Buck is still in the waiting room. He'd like to know what he should tell the others in the courtroom."

"Bring him down here to see me, please."

The old deputy stood just in front of the desk. The door to the judge's chambers was closed.

"Thank you for getting the paper."

"Of course, Judge."

"Like you said, this is garbage."

"Yes, sir."

The judge considered the man for another moment. "Please, take a seat."

"I'm just fine standing, Judge."

Balk was about to insist, but then he noticed the old deputy glance toward the large window. The man took a few steps in its direction.

"What is it?" Balk asked.

"Looks like we might have a little gathering starting out there," he said, stepping closer to the window. His gaze moved back to the judge. "Sir, I'll need to radio down and let—"

"No." Balk stood from his chair and held up a hand. "Before you do that—"

The Walkie lowered.

"I'd like you to handle something."

55

DAY FOUR

10:00 a.m

"Do you want this closed?"

The judge nodded. The old deputy pulled the door shut, leaving Balk alone with the man who now sat across from his desk.

"Have you read this?" Balk asked, slapping his copy of the newspaper down. This sent several sheets of paper flying from the mahogany desk, the only barrier between the judge and accused.

Bill lifted his eyes, as if to see what *this* was. He leaned forward and picked the newspaper up from the wood surface. "It's a good picture, young man."

"Don't bullshit with me right now. Have you read it?"

Bill nodded. "I had it with my breakfast."

"Did you know—" Balk started.

"Before you get to running wild with accusations, John," he paused, then placed the paper back on the judge's desk. "I want to assure you that I had nothing to do with that."

The judge stared at him a long moment. He believed him.

"I was surprised, of course." Bill eventually added. "I thought to myself, either John went out and got him some balls, or he fucked up and talked too much." He smiled. "From the look on your face, I can tell it was *número dos*," he held up two fingers.

Balk let out a sigh. "It affects you too."

"Somewhat," he replied. "But bad press is kind of like that holiday weight my wife used to put on. Those extra five-to-ten hung around for a little while, but in another six weeks it was gone and forgotten."

"Don't talk about her."

"Stop with that."

"With what?" Balk shot back.

"I'm not getting into this, John." He started to stand. "Once was enough."

"Sit down!"

The senator ignored him, then turned for the door. The judge cursed under his breath. He glanced down as he felt for the handle on the heavy drawer to his left. He pulled it from his desk, pausing only for a moment before lifting his gaze. Balk trained it on the man's back and threw the drawer shut. *Slam!*

"*Sit down*, Bill." Balk kept his voice even. "I won't ask again."

The senator stopped. He rubbed his forehead, collecting himself it seemed, before eventually turning back to face the judge. They first made eye contact, but then the judge watched the senator lower his eyes to the *S&W*.

"John?"

"Lock the door." Balk motioned to it with the muzzle. "Now, Bill."

A minute passed.

Click.

The senator reread the article, one foot resting on the knee of his opposite leg. He held the paper low, as instructed to, so that the judge could still see his face and hands.

"These are mostly direct quotes from you, John." Bill chuckled as he continued to read. "You told these things to this reporter?" He stopped, looking for the name. "Moss. There it is, Ben Moss."

Balk felt his mood continuing to sour as he listened to the senator question the article. The front-page story blended the lakeside interview that he'd given to the reporter, with some investigative work that had apparently taken place after their sit-down together. It seemed Moss had taken records from several land conveyances, those between E.B. Acker and Bill Collins, along with an old lawsuit that'd been filed for E.B., then realized he had himself quite the story. The article highlighted the fact—several times—that all three of the suspicious deeds were file-stamped after E.B.'s suicide, and that all of the legal work involved was handled by only one attorney—John J. Balk, Esq. The reporter rushed a few details on the lawsuit itself, but his article nailed the important fact—the lawsuit against Bill Collins wasn't dismissed until after E.B. passed away.

"I didn't tell him most of this." Balk took the newspaper from the senator as it was handed back over the desk. "He never once asked about my work for E.B."

"But?"

"But nothing, Bill." Balk looked away. "The kid's not stupid. He's pretty sharp, actually. Good sense."

"Well, you're stupid."

Balk turned back to him. "Remind yourself that I'm holding a gun on you."

The senator waved a hand.

"I'm not?" Balk huffed.

"This is predictable." Bill paused. "Actually, no. It's *you*, John. *You're* predictable."

"Okay." Balk watched his face. "How about you go ahead and predict the likelihood of me shooting you."

"I certainly hope you won't," he said, appearing disinterested.

"You don't think I will?" Balk leaned forward.

Bill held his gaze for a moment, then looked away.

"Come on, Bill. Don't go quiet on me now."

Balk waited, still watching the senator. When the man finally responded, his eyes stayed with the large window in the room.

"I'm not yet sure," Bill said. "I know you don't want to kill me. But what I'm not sure about is if you think people expect you to."

Balk looked down at the revolver in his right hand, a Smith & Wesson he'd bought more than ten years back. He'd fired the forty-four maybe three times in that span of time. Twice at snakes that came up onto the porch at the lake. Once at the shooting range the week after he'd bought it. He'd never left the lake with it. Then, a few weeks ago, he'd just started putting it in the truck every morning. There'd been no forethought, no malice. He'd never even stopped to ask himself the question, *why*?

Balk took a breath in.

"This is what you're going to do."

56

DAY FOUR

11:00 a.m

The spectators in the gallery continued to grow even more restless. From her table, Maggie worked on her notes for the upcoming witnesses, but it was hard not to listen in on the discussions taking place behind her. A particularly loud group of men in the gallery had begun circulating the idea that they should all go down to the judicial suite and demand that the judge come out of hiding. It didn't take long for those few voices to metastasize, though, and soon the energy in the room began to strike a different chord, one not all that different from the day of the arraignment.

"This place is starting to feel like a powder keg," Hart said, leaning close to her ear. "I say we step out."

Maggie nodded to him. It was getting hard to think inside the courtroom, much less hold any kind of conversation. At least a third of the spectators chanted: *We want Balk! We want Balk!* Their feet followed along, stamping the hardwood and bumping at the old benches. It felt tribal, and it gave her an uneasy feeling about the direction the day might be heading.

"You good with this?" Hart asked her, nearly shouting. He pointed to what was left on the table, a few binders and a laptop. The bulk of their trial material was in the roller box he had ready to go with him.

"Yeah."

"I'm heading out," he said. "I'll let them know we'll be in the Suite."

As Maggie packed the laptop into her bag, she glanced over at the empty defense table. They'd exited an hour earlier, due to possible security concerns for the senator. She figured they'd really just wanted to find a quiet place to confer, recharge. Maggie wished she'd done the same. The day wasn't even half gone and she already felt the fatigue settling in. She needed to be calling witnesses, putting on her case. Not waiting amongst the mob while the judge wasted time.

"Let's push them out!"

Maggie heard this and turned to scoop up her three remaining binders. The call was one meant to start clearing the room. A young courtroom deputy passed by her table, making his way for the center aisle. He spoke to her as he went by.

"It's getting spicy in here!"

"It's about time you cleared this place out." Maggie smiled. "Have fun."

"And you be careful," he called back. "Things might get squirrely out in the halls."

He kept moving and she did the same.

Maggie pushed through the side door, out into the second-floor hallway that was open to the general public. She stopped as she didn't hear the door close behind her, a courtroom security policy. When she turned to check, the old deputy had it propped open.

He spoke from the doorway. "Good on you for following my little protocol."

"Of course." Maggie readjusted the binders in her hands. "It keeps us all safe."

He nodded. "That's what I'm here for."

The mass of voices continued at the far end of the hallway. It sounded as if the deputies were still clearing spectators from the gallery inside the courtroom. Even from where she stood, Maggie could hear the voices complaining as they made their way toward the building's exits.

"Is everything going to be okay in there?" she asked. "It got a little rowdy for a moment."

"We'll take care of it."

She heard what sounded like his phone ringing, then saw him place one to his ear. She was about to turn and head on toward the DA's suite when he waved to her. "I'll gather them up, sir," Maggie heard him say.

"Are we being summoned?" she asked.

"The man behind the curtain wants an audience."

She laughed. "I'll set my things down and get my sidekick."

He waited for her in the hall.

Maggie followed Tracker to the judicial suite. When they stepped into the waiting area, she was surprised to find Sheila seated at her desk.

"Are we waiting on Mr. Hart?" Sheila asked.

"I've already texted him. I'm sure he'll see it soon and hustle over."

"Good." Sheila smiled. "I just sent Mr. Hackett back."

"When?" Maggie asked, frustrated.

The secretary glanced at the old deputy, then came back to Maggie. "A few minutes ago, if that."

Maggie left them there without another word, ignoring their whispers while she made her way down the hall. When she arrived at the door for the judge's chambers, she stepped close and listened for a moment. No voices. She rapped on the door—*tap! tap!* Nothing. Louder this time —*knock! knock!*

She knew it. *More ex parte discussions.* Her hand formed a fist to hammer away on the door this time.

"Is he not answering?"

She lowered the fist, turning to the image of the old deputy ambling her way.

"I've knocked." A shrug. "I just didn't want to go barging right in."

She moved to the side when he arrived at the door. He knocked, plenty loud, then immediately went for the handle.

"Huh?" He stopped. "It's locked."

He seemed to wait a second, then looked over at Maggie.

"Do you have a key?" she asked.

He nodded. Keys jingled from somewhere around his utility belt.

"Actually, let's get Sheila to just call him."

"It's fine." Tracker was casual as always. "That Yankee lawyer probably bumped the lock on accident."

"Maybe so. I just don't want to invade their privacy."

"Ah, I do it to folks all the time." He fiddled with a large key ring. "And it's a lot easier when you have one of these." He held up a shiny key, winked. "Let's see if this one's it."

Maggie sensed something wasn't right, but the *ping! ping!* of her cell phone interrupted any serious thought on the feeling. Right as she pulled the iPhone from her pocket to check her messages, the door unlocked.

Click.

Maggie read from the screen.

Hart: *WTF. A status conference? Now? Tell JB we waited an hour for him. Be there soon.*

She typed her reply. *You tell him when you get here. Stepping in now.*

She looked up. Tracker still stood there beside her, the open door in front of them.

"After you."

As she stepped into the room, she checked to make sure her phone was set to silent. The screen lit up once more as another text from Hart arrived.

Hart: *Okay. Still in clerk's office. Tracker asked me to run down here for him.*

The door closed.

It'd taken a moment for Hart's message to register. But when it did, Maggie was already looking at the two men seated on opposite sides of the mahogany desk. Collins and Balk. No one else.

"Where's Hackett?"

It was the first thing that came to mind.

"He's not coming."

The reply came from behind her, where the door locked.

Click.

Maggie was quick. She pulled the phone from her pocket, hit the passcode, and the screen opened right back up to her conversation with Hart. She started to type, but a hand soon came crashing in from behind her. It ripped the phone from her grasp before she could fire off a few letters. She turned and glared at her attacker. The old deputy smirked as he grabbed her arm. He came in close with a whisper—*Gotcha*—then shoved her toward the desk.

"Don't touch me!" Maggie yelled, shaking from the sudden jolt of fear and adrenaline. Her heart pounded in her chest, jacked. She brought air in, deep through her nose, trying to calm her senses. She lifted a finger and pointed at the old deputy. "That's ever, you hear me?"

He only smiled as he looked to the phone in his hand. *Her phone.* His other hand went to his holster. *His gun.*

"Have a seat, Maggie." It was the senator who spoke. He looked over at her, still seated in one of the chairs near the desk. He smiled. "I'd stand to shake your hand, but that might make it hard for me to explain things."

Maggie considered the senator for another moment, his words. Her gaze shifted to the judge, who looked awful. *Worse than ever.* She watched his eyes. They looked to her first, and then she saw them move slowly to the old deputy behind her.

"Put that away," Balk growled.

"You first, John." But it was the senator who spoke. "How's that sound?"

"But—"

"But nothing, old friend."

Maggie knew it wouldn't do her any good yet to ask the question. She needed to listen first, then figure out what to do. She looked over at the old deputy once more. He still had his sidearm in one hand and her phone in the other. He kept one eye on the judge as he scrolled through her phone. She wondered if he'd already arrived at the last text from Hart, the photo with it. *He'll recognize everything in it.* Hart took the photo while standing over the head of courthouse security's desk. *His desk.* And the old deputy had left it all right there in plain view. Three black markers, larger than a normal Sharpie.

Hart: *At Tracker's desk. They're called quick-coat paint markers. Call me.*

57

DAY FOUR

2:30 p.m

There had to be over a hundred faces packed along the south end of the square. Inside the judge's chambers, Maggie stood at a large window. She looked out on the people below, recognizing plenty of the faces scattered throughout the crowd. Several in the media. Some friends. Clients. And most of the BCSO deputies. It was a bizarre scene. Not just because she could see them, but also because they could see her.

The phone rang on the judge's desk. No one touched it, as had become their routine. They'd let it ring and ring and ring—until it stopped.

It did. Then the next phase of their routine started.

"Step back from the window."

It was the voice of the old deputy.

"We're going to have to talk to someone." Maggie said this calmly as she stepped back from the window. "I can see about five different agencies out there. Pick any one of them."

No reply.

Maggie turned to where Tracker stood. He was messaging people from her phone—the last phase of their routine. This was what happened every ten minutes. Phone. Maggie. Creep. It went round and round and no one knew when it would stop.

No one.

"Why don't you just sit, Maggie?" Balk spoke from his chair behind the desk. "Good Lord, it's been just two hours of you standing there. Are you not tired?"

"Do you have a plan?" she asked, ignoring his questions, his *concern*.

No answer.

"Did you *ever* have a plan?" Maggie stared at him. "Come on, talk to me!"

Still nothing.

"There was no plan, Maggie." It was the smug, patient voice of the senator. "No, he's not like you and me because—"

"We're not the same."

"But we're not like John," he quickly replied. "We don't wait for tomorrow, nor live in the past."

She was the one not to respond this time, shaking her head as she stepped back to the window. Looking down on the square, Maggie saw that signs were being hoisted up by those along the barricades now.

Pray for Maggie. Save our senator! Please Judge, Don't.

It was the judge who'd made the move, but it was the senator who'd been ready for it. He had his plan, his people, his game. And she needed hers.

There were two guns in the room.

"I have a plan for you to consider," Balk finally said, keeping *his* trained on the senator. "Come at least stand by the desk to hear it."

Maggie rubbed her forehead, too tired to think.

"Did you hear me, Maggie?"

"Does your plan involve you shooting anyone?"

"No," he said, after a moment.

"Does it involve me shooting you?" Tracker asked. He stood several paces behind the senator, *his* trained on the judge. "That'd be one way to solve all of this."

"Are you sure, *creep*?" Maggie took a few steps from her place at the window, inching a little closer to the desk, and the phone that was on it. She felt an idea coming on. "You nasty, dirty, cowardly little—"

"You'll get yours if you don't keep that mouth—" Tracker didn't finish his threat.

"No, she won't." Bill was turned all the way around in his chair, pointing at the man. "Now, shut up, and let the professionals talk."

She edged closer.

"But you told me I could—"

"Shut up." Bill wasn't on his feet and hadn't been for hours. His presence still towered. "And I don't care what I told you then, because this is what I'm telling you now. You don't touch her."

Tracker didn't respond.

Maggie stepped to one side of the desk. She could see the revolver now lay on the surface, close to Balk's hand. Maggie didn't dislike guns, but she'd also never liked them. It'd been that way since she'd come to know them. You didn't stay around criminal defense work for long and not learn something about firearms. Nor did you find yourself married to a sheriff and not at least learn how to handle one on the range. In fact, between her work in the courtroom, and her personal life, Maggie probably knew more than most about handguns. And this was more than enough for her to be dangerous on cross-examination, and maybe even the real thing. Still, she'd never liked them.

"Hear me out." Balk's words seemed to be directed at Collins, not Maggie. "We tell them that I've suffered a mental break of some kind, and—"

"No." Bill sounded bored.

"Let me finish—"

"No." He wasn't interested in negotiating. "There's only one option. I've told you what it is."

Balk stayed quiet.

"You don't have any other options, John. You decide."

Maggie could tell from the judge's expression that he was at least thinking about it. The senator's proposal was the only one that'd been made available. And that was how it worked when one found themself in this kind of position. Delaying a decision didn't change the fact that one needed to be made. It only changed who it was that eventually made it. Because as time passed, a person's options narrowed, and narrowed, and narrowed, until there was only one option left for them—the one made *for* them.

Maggie turned to look at the senator. She took another step closer. The phone was only feet away.

"Okay, Senator, let me get this straight."

The senator carefully repositioned himself in the chair. She wanted so badly for him to do something ill-advised. It'd be easier for her then to make a move.

"I'm listening," he said, a knowing expression on his face.

"Your proposal, Senator—" Maggie eased over one more step. "It would have the judge pick up the phone on this desk, and call whoever he wants to call. And if that person answers, he'll then tell them: *I want to surrender a hostage.*"

Bill smiled. "You're correct, Maggie."

"Then, when the judge is asked who it is he wants to release, he'll tell them: *Bill Collins.*"

"Right."

Maggie turned to the judge. The weight looked to be more and more unbearable for him with each passing minute.

"Then, Judge, once Bill is outside with the rest of the crowd, you'll tell anyone who asks that you're willing to negotiate *my* release—but that you'll only do so with the senator."

Balk sighed. "And no one else."

"Right." Maggie patted the desk. No one moved. "And if you were to try anything other than negotiate *with the senator*, then that creep over there will shoot you, me, or possibly both of us."

Balk nodded. "But you're forgetting something."

"Ah, yes," Maggie turned back to the senator. "If the judge does this for you, then you will make your *best* efforts to not have him prosecuted—"

"Or killed," Balk added. "Don't want to forget that."

"Right, thank you, Judge."

"And don't forget the dismissal," Balk said. "That dismissal is apparently very important for the senator to—"

"That's right," Maggie said, nodding emphatically. "I would then have to sign a dismissal in the case and make a public statement to that effect."

A moment passed.

"Anything else?" she asked, stalling.

The senator was staring at her when the phone started ringing.

Ring, ring, ring...

His eyes stayed with her.

...ring, ring, ring.

Until it stopped.

Bill finally responded. "You're correct on the proposal, Maggie."

Another ten minutes, she thought. *That's nothing.*

"It won't work, though." She pointed at the two men. "But you two are who need to figure that out. Not me."

Balk started to speak. "It might if—"

"What else does the reporter know?" Bill asked. "Ben Moss, that is."

Maggie glanced over at the judge.

"No, Maggie, I meant that question for you."

"Okay," she said. "I'd say he knows plenty."

"Plenty about what?" he asked.

"Wouldn't you like to know." Maggie smiled. "I'm sure you won't have to wait long, though. He'll have another article for you soon."

He only nodded at this. "Have you given him any recordings for this article?"

Maggie paused. "No."

"You're sure?" he asked.

"I'm sure."

"What about the Ackers?"

Maggie only had one recording with Bill Collins's voice on it. She'd kept it tucked away for safekeeping, part of a file she'd built out once for Lee Acker, a client who'd left this earth too soon.

"You worried about a little negative press, Senator?" Maggie gave him a look.

"I'm not worried about negative attention."

"Oh, I've certainly gathered that about you by now."

He smiled. "Bad attention. Good attention. It's all attention."

"As long as you control where it comes from, right?"

A nod.

"Like with Park?"

The senator didn't respond.

"Not that she'd say a word," Maggie added.

"But it's really about control." Balk's voice sounded a little stronger than before. "That's where it all begins and ends."

"I don't control Ms. Park when—"

"You control that man over there, right?" the judge asked.

The senator didn't respond.

"You found a way to get to Sheila, right?"

Bill smirked. "She certainly got to you, John."

"Because you told her to, right?" Balk demanded. He leaned forward with the revolver out in front of him and started to stand. "Admit it."

"Sit down!" Tracker yelled from his post.

"Answer me, Bill!"

The senator stood once the judge was on his feet. They were yelling, shouting at one another when the phone started again.

Ring, ring, ring.

Maggie stepped the quickest.

"This is Maggie Reynolds!" she yelled, pressing the phone hard to her mouth and ear. "Collins is holding me and Judge Balk hostage with—"

The noise came from behind her—*BANG! BANG! BANG!* The deafening back-to-back-to-back blasts filled every inch of the room. Maggie spun to one side, held on tight to the phone. Its cord wrapped around her like a safety rope, yet she still fell to the ground.

She heard screaming. Someone. Somewhere. It could've been her. No, one of them was her. But there was another, too.

"Everybody down!" the voice yelled from nearby. Maggie lay on one side, head throbbing, eyes toward the door. She saw the men in bullet-proof vests move in. Dark suits under the Kevlar.

"You! Hands in the air!" came another. She recognized him, one of the federal agents. "Both of them!"

She saw that creep, Tracker, leaned on the wall, clutching his chest. "I can't—" but the bloody outline on the old deputy was beginning to spread. Down, lower and lower, filling in his thick stomach. He cursed as more men came through the door, coughing blackish goop on himself as one of the agents took the sidearm from his hand. The gun disappeared into the man's jacket.

Another voice moaned from just around the desk. "Aghhh!"

Maggie started to crawl toward it, but the cord from the desk phone tugged at her. She still had the receiver pressed to her ear and soon heard a voice. It was shaking on the other end. Maybe hers was, too.

"Aghhh," came another moan, followed by a deep breath. She knew it was the judge who needed help, but the woman on the phone held Maggie with her. "John, John, are you there?" crying, pleading, waiting on the line. "It's me, baby. Can you hear me? I know you're there!"

"Who—" Maggie started, barely managing to speak. Her head pounded.

"I'm his wife, dammit! I want to talk to him. There's time, sweetie. There's still—"

Maggie felt the throbbing in her head stop, then slowly let the phone fall from her ear.

58

DAY FOUR

6:30 p.m

Maggie sat on a bench looking on at the Blake County Courthouse. The February air made it hard to shake the numbness from her body, but she still wasn't ready to leave the square. The blanket around her shoulders anchored her to the spot, a quilt that smelled of Tim and that red dog of his. She pulled it tight around her, allowing it to warm her—calm her—as she started to walk back through the darkness.

BANG!

She remembered the blow to her body, a gut-punch that knocked the wind out of her. But it'd not come from a gun blast. No, it'd been a hand—Balk's hand—one that'd shoved her hard to the ground, spinning her away from the danger.

BANG!

She remembered the sound of his voice. It'd been the judge's last order, issued in a deep, guttural groan. *Down!*

BANG!

She reached up with a hand to rub her forehead, remembering the pain. It'd started quickly, right after her head caught the edge of the mahogany desk. *Smack!*

And he'd been only feet away. Coughing. Wheezing. Mumbling. She'd tried to help, tried to tell him that his wife was on the phone. But instead, they'd waited—together—for the one-who-wore-the-robe's time to end.

Then, it all went black.

But Maggie remembered there being a conversation in that darkness. Not with the judge, though. It'd been with her clients—the Ackers.

This might take a while.

Maggie watched her breath hit the cold, night air. She sat with the words, weighing their truth on the courthouse square. "No, this will take a while," she murmured.

Then it takes a while.

That's what Cliff Acker had said to her. Cliff was confident, certain about things that nobody had the right to be certain about. Different than his brother. Lee Acker didn't talk like that. Never had. Not to her, at least.

But only if you do it alone, Maggie.

That'd been Charlotte Acker. She was the one who wore her vision proudly and didn't hide it from others. Different from Cliff. Different than Lee, her daddy, in that regard. The Acker boys never talked like they considered much beyond today. They either did or they didn't. Not her, though. For Charlotte, there was only will.

Is there another way?

That'd been Grace Acker's question for Maggie. Which made sense because Grace understood the way things worked. Much more so than her husband, Lee, ever had. It was Lee who liked to sometimes sit, figure things. Not Grace. No, that was wasted time. She evaluated. Not speculated. Then traded always on what she understood.

Should I keep doing this?

That'd been what she really wanted to know, trapped there in the darkness with them.

Maggie asked the question again. "Should I keep doing this?"

She felt a hand on her shoulder.

"What's that you're mumbling about?"

Maggie turned at the familiar voice and found Tim standing behind the bench. His face reassured her that she wasn't still somewhere in that dark place.

"Hey," she said. "It's nothing."

"Hey yourself," he replied, then came around to sit next to her. "You sure it's nothing?"

Maggie considered the question.

He sighed as he threw an arm around her. "Come on, talk to me, Mags."

"I'm done, Tim." She leaned into him. "At least, I think so."

"Okay." He didn't say anything more.

"I need to be moving on," she added. "I have other things that can be accomplished besides working for—"

He stopped her. "You know what I think?"

"I think you're going to tell me."

"I think you're cold." He paused. "And hungry. And tired. And—"

"And done." She smiled. "With the Ackers, at least."

"I figured."

They sat there for a long moment together, watching the court building's lights as they turned off, one-by-one.

"You think I'm done with them?" she finally asked.

"Nope."

Maggie waited for him to say more. As she did, she stared at the last light left on inside the courthouse. It was the one that illuminated the large window from inside the judge's chambers.

"Try being done with it all for today, Maggie."

"That's not going to fix—"

"Just today," he said. "You can worry about tomorrow—"

"Tomorrow."

Tim nodded at this. Nothing more.

"I could've had him, Tim." Maggie had to say it out loud one more time. She wanted to believe it just one more time. "I would've won. I know it."

"I know, Maggie." He pulled her in closer. "And I have no doubt that you will."

Maggie sighed. "But not today."

He didn't respond. They sat there together, the darkened courthouse in front of them. Maggie finally felt the numbness leaving her in that comfortable, easy silence.

She sat up straight. "Tim?"

"Yeah?"

"Let's go home."

EPILOGUE

Washington, DC
Georgetown

He gave the man his name.

"Ben Moss."

It only took a moment. A glance at the clipboard and the man found it somewhere on the list.

"Welcome, Mr. Moss. Right this way."

Ben followed the man down a hallway. When they reached the door at the end, he asked for Ben to wait outside. He did.

There were other people in the hallway. He wasn't sure what you might call the place, but it wasn't public. It probably wasn't even here if anyone asked. But select people knew about it. People who paid him no mind as they walked by, arm-in-arm to wherever it was these things were done.

"He's ready for you, Mr. Moss."

Ben hadn't heard the door open. It was nearly on his elbow, yet it opened. It was the perfect door for a place that could only be found by the most private, respectable sort. He stepped back and glanced once more down the hall. There were more doors like this one. All discreet, provocative little pockets designed for those who sought a space to unburden themselves for a short time. A place where they could flip the dynamics of power, if only to remember why it was that they'd wanted it in the first place.

The reporter stepped through the door.

"Welcome, Ben. Have a seat over there."

Ben shook his hand. It seemed no one could deny his affable nature, his charisma. That was the gift.

"Thank you for seeing me, Senator."

"I rarely get to host another from Blake County, not here."

Ben wasn't sure if he meant in Washington, or here.

"Is this your first time?"

"It is."

"I thought I'd ask." The senator grinned as he said this. "How about in Georgetown?"

"No, sir."

He lifted a hand. "Then I insist."

Ben looked around the room. They were alone, it seemed. But the room, along with the senator, gave him the impression that the people who handled things here weren't far away.

"Would you be willing to talk about my article, Senator?"

He paused. "Yes, Ben, however—"

The reporter sensed a condition. He guessed it'd have something to do with the senator's choice in meeting space.

"I'd like you to pitch the article to an editor friend of mine." The senator leaned back in his seat. "She's with the *Times.*"

Ben felt the uptick in his pulse. "The Grey Lady?"

The man nodded.

"Anything else?"

"And I want you to leave my wife out of it. That is, my late wife."

Ben wasn't sure what she might have to do with it. He only knew that the offer being dangled before him was one with plenty of unknowns.

"Did John Balk know her well?"

"We all knew each other well, Ben. You know this being from where we are. That's how it is back home, even if you leave."

Ben nodded. "I won't mention her."

"And the meeting?"

Ben didn't hesitate. "I'll take it, Senator."

"Good." He looked pleased at this. "Now, your article, is it still about John? About why he didn't need to die?"

"Yes."

"Is that your thesis?"

"I wouldn't call it that, Senator. It's more of an assertion."

The senator nodded, waited.

Ben pushed on. "And I know the woman who prosecuted the case, Maggie, would feel the same."

"What do you think about her?" he asked.

"I don't think she planned to convict you of anything, Senator."

A woman interrupted them when she walked into the room. She wore mostly leather, what Ben expected.

Ben waited another moment, then asked, "Do *you* think that was Maggie's goal?"

"I have my theory."

"As do I, Senator."

"I'll hear yours."

Ben looked at him for a long moment, trying to determine the man's angle.

"I think she decided to prosecute your case just to show that she could, Senator. I'm not sure the trial was going to ever be about anything else. Not for her, at least."

"Which is to say what, Mr. Moss?"

"That she would have won if the judge hadn't unraveled. You wouldn't have stopped her from proving what she'd wanted to prove to people. Not even by way of an acquittal."

He seemed to consider this.

"And you believe John Balk couldn't see this?"

Ben shook his head. "I think the opposite, Senator. I believe he did. And I'm willing to bet you did, too."

"Then you didn't know him."

"I'm not sure you did either, then."

The senator smiled. “He liked you. Even the day you torpedoed him, he didn’t seem all that angry. Not with you.”

Another woman came into the room. Ben watched her leave.

“You told me you had your own thoughts on what the goal was—”

“For Maggie,” the senator finished the sentence. “Well, I certainly don’t view her as selfless as you might.”

“I view her as human, Senator.”

He smiled again.

“She’s inevitable, Ben. That’s what she is.”

“How so?” the reporter asked.

“Time moves on, and she moves with it, always changing.” He waved another woman over. “That’s what makes her very different than the featured man in your article. John Balk chose the past.”

“But that’s only how you viewed him, sir. You think that mattered?”

“It doesn’t. Only his own view of himself is what mattered.”

Ben nodded. “In the end.”

A Voice of Reason

In the quiet of the mountains, a sidelined attorney stumbles upon a case that could be her salvation...or downfall.

Amidst the fallout of a career-threatening scandal, lawyer Maggie Reynolds finds herself serving a six-month suspension. In search of some peace, she retreats to a secluded mountain cabin nestled deep in Georgia, a sanctuary offered by a reclusive friend connected to the Ackers family.

Clive Mortlake, the property owner and a man of keen intellect, seeks Maggie's legal expertise in return for her stay. He presents her with a case that's as personal as it is perplexing: the inexplicable disappearance of his son, Art Mortlake. A senior at Duke University, Art's sudden vanishing act after an evening at a local bar left no clues, no communications, and a cold trail. The official investigation has dwindled, and a haunting suspicion of murder looms over the unanswered questions.

Contrary to the grim theories, Clive is adamant that his son is alive, and ensnared by vindictive corporate rivals from his past. This conviction is bolstered when an enigmatic message surfaces, suggesting that Art might indeed be alive.

For Maggie, this case, laden with mystery and risk, could either mark a triumphant return to law or spell the end of her legal journey, challenging her resolve and her ability to untangle truth from fiction in a world where everyone has something to hide.

ABOUT THE AUTHOR

Joe Cargile is an American novelist, lawyer, and displaced Southerner. The pages from his books are filled with settings that have been influenced by his love for travel, sports, and the ever-evolving South. With stories inspired by his work in the courtroom—an arena he believes plays host to fearsome competitors, and often some of our world's most interesting characters—he holds deep admiration for those tireless advocates who set the standard for the trial lawyer. He lives and works in London, England, with his wife and three daughters.

Sign up for Joe Cargile's newsletter at
severnriverbooks.com